SUICIDE BLONDES

A NASHVILLE SUSPENSE NOVEL

T. BLAKE BRADDY

JINX PROTOCOL

For Beau, for giving me a reason to dream big.

READ LIKE A 'QUEEN'

OTHER BOOKS BY THE AUTHOR

The Rolson McKane Series
Crystal Queen
Boogie House
The Devil Came Calling
Dirt Merchant

Learn More

1

I'm pretending to work when my mom calls. I don't even bother to look at my phone, because I *know* it's her. There's something otherworldly or precognitive about a daughter's relationship with her mother—she can just *feel* a phone call coming on. Something in the rhythm of it, the ebbs and flows, that tells you without telling you. And no matter how far away you move, a mother can always detect when you don't want to talk.

That's when she strikes.

Plus, because of everything that...happened way back when, people don't much want to talk to me. I get an occasional call from your garden variety true crime crank, posing as a *journalist,* when in reality he—it's always a he—is really looking for an *edgy* story for his blog. Other than that, I might as well be invisible.

Or dead.

The phone buzzes again, rattling on my desk. Reminding me of its existence. Begging for attention. Pleading for me to tend to it.

I don't fall for the bait that easily.

I'm nobody's candidate for World's Best Daughter, but I would challenge *anyone* to endure my mother's endless ruminations on her mortality. She's been "dying" for the last twenty years, give or take.

It's never once been true—not a single time—but she is convinced it's the big one at least twice a year. Whenever brain cancer or lupus or Parkinson's drags one of her bridge club buddies down to the dear hereafter, I have to hear about it. Since I'm an only child—dad's been gone since my freshman year—I am the point of contact for her histrionics.

And yet she's still here. Sounds callous. I get it. But you can bury your mother only so many times before the idea of her death becomes a little...stale.

The phone rattles, beckoning me once more.

Last chance, it seems to be saying.

I'm not going to pick it up, I tell myself.

But then I sigh.

Like always, something in me breaks, and I can't quite let the call go to voicemail. I slide my thumb across the screen's display, anticipating her litany of grievances, pretending to be shocked about the color of her neck mole or the longevity or persistence of her headaches. Maybe she's sleeping too much, or not enough, or the hallucinations mean she's in the last stages of some neurological disease.

"Mom, this isn't a good time," I say, staring at the nearly blank document on my computer screen. "I'm really busy—"

Only, it isn't her on the other end.

For a moment, I wonder if someone's stolen her identity. But then, why would they be calling *me*?

I check the display again.

It's her phone. Her number. But the voice on the other end is a young-sounding nurse at the hospital where my mother practically has her own ward. As the woman speaks—telling me this isn't normal protocol but that my mother had begged her—the subsequent words pass through my ears and into my brain, but the shock won't let them sink in.

All of a sudden, my whole body is trembling.

You can never guess when it is *the* call, and no matter how many times you play it out in your head, it's impossible to prepare yourself for the real thing.

And this is the real thing.

This is *the* call. The thing you prepare yourself for when you occasionally look up from your computer screen or your phone and think, At some point, I will cease to be me, and the ground will open up wide and swallow me whole.

By the time I replace my phone to its current position on my desk, my eyes are brimming over and I'm having trouble catching my breath. As if the roof of the office has just been ripped off, and the loss of cabin pressure is sucking the breath right out of me.

The nurse had used a whole lot of lingo, but the gist of it was, Your mother doesn't have long to live. If you want to say goodbye, get home right this instant.

So, naturally, I go out for a smoke. I need something to get my hands to stop shaking, or at least get my mind off how they won't stop shaking.

I get up and amble past all the cubicles at the start-up where I work in a non-creative position writing code. I suspect this place is a money pit, a simple but effective way for tech billionaires to launder money, but I never name it aloud, mostly because I don't think I can find another job where people will literally leave me alone for twelve hours a day, sixteen during crunch periods.

I stop at my supervisor's desk, dreading the conversation I'm about to have.

Ian, the human equivalent of a man bun, smiles benignly as I tell him about *my needs*. Being a *people first* organization, how I function is a top priority for the project managers, and the touchy-feeliness of it all sometimes makes me want to gag.

It's the sort of place that strives not to look or feel like work. There are scooters in the office. Ping pong tables in the break room. Some people sit on bean bag chairs. They'd prefer you use the term *inspired employment* or something equally as euphemistic.

When I'm done half-explaining myself, I just come out with it.

"I need a cigarette," I say, my voice quavering, and he frowns disapprovingly.

I'm not surprised by the reaction. It's almost comforting, given the bit of news which has just ripped the veneer of comfort from my life.

Still, I can't help but be annoyed.

Among the granola-loving crowd at Morning Manatee—ugh, I know—smoking plays in the same ballpark as burning crosses or eating corn-fed beef. The lifers here are way into smoothies and pilates, a juice cleanse or a morning run, while I'm more of a bourbon-and-Ambien kind of gal. I don't fit in, not in the least, but I'm quiet and somewhat productive, so I'm allowed to exist within their organic cult.

But the smoking. It seriously bums Ian out.

He leans contemplatively back in his chair.

"I hear you," he says. When combined with the beatific smile, it's his introduction to a long-winded rant about the environment.

Instead, his face contorts into a look of concern.

My second surprise of the day.

"It's your mother," he says, sage-like.

I bunch up all my emotions into a tight knot and respond, "She's not doing well."

It's all I can manage without tearing up, and that seems like enough for him. He nods, showing me the top knot on the back of his skull, like a tumor made of hair.

"And I assume you'll need some time off."

"Listen," I say, not quite ready to broach the topic, "I know it's getting crazy here, pre-launch and everything—"

"Say no more," he says, hold one of his long-fingered hands up to silence me. He cannot be aware of how passive-aggressive that gesture is.

"It probably shouldn't take more than a week or so," I say. "Maybe two at the most. It just depends on—"

I can't finish the sentence.

He watches me idly, holding up a box of tissues I refuse, before continuing.

"I know," he says. "These things, they are never expected. I am totally in tune with that. I get it. I am *with* you. Take as much time as *you* need. Not the time we *allow*."

There is an awkward silence, wherein I ramble through a paragraph strewn with gratitude. Like a résumé littered with buzzwords.

He lets me finish and then steeples his fingers in front of his face.

"Not to pry," he says, "but it's coming up on the twenty-year anniversary, isn't it?"

I nod. It's my hope that he doesn't dredge up the past, but I'm willing to cop to anything to get downstairs for my cigarette.

I *need* one.

"This place," he says, "works very much like a family. You've got a lot going on up top, so you can take that time to clear your mind. We'll need you in full form when you get back, so it's actually good this is happening right now. I mean—"

He catches himself, mid-*faux pas*, and blushes.

I wave it off.

WITH A CIGARETTE PERCHED between my lips, the world makes a lot more sense. I stare emptily at the Seattle skyline. I wonder what it looks like from the top of the Space Needle, how it would feel to base jump off of it. Or just not open a parachute and see the ground come rushing up at me from below.

Anything to keep me from thinking of my mother, but of course that doesn't work. I'll be going back home for the foreseeable future.

Nashville.

The word sticks in my brain like popcorn seeds to teeth, and I mull over Music City and all my own personal associations with it as I finish off a second cigarette. My head spins from the nicotine, and relish the high.

Growing up, Nashville was a blinking, shuffling, denim nightmare, a place to grow up and move away from. But even on the other side of the country—as far away from Nashville as possible, without jumping into the ocean—I can't escape it.

The city haunts me, though I am its most prominent monster.

Someone talking angrily on her cell phone seems to recognize me, and her eyes go dull as she passes by. She looks like she wants to say something.

She ends up twisting her mouth into a frown and rolling her eyes.

My past owns me like an old debt I cannot escape.

I'd nearly forgotten about the network TV from a few weeks back. These things pop up occasionally, stoke the flames of everyone's anger, and then eventually calm down. I've learned how to keep my head down and avoid public confrontations.

These things can end up on the internet, after all.

It's like an omen, this woman's reaction. Foreshadowing. Even without the blonde hair, with shades on, I am recognizable as one of the quote-unquote Suicide Blondes. It speaks to just how angry the story makes everyone.

Understandably.

I've tried for twenty years to escape the title, the reputation, the truth. Nashville isn't just my home; it's where I helped kill someone.

LATER, I'm standing over an empty suitcase in my smallish, underfurnished apartment, waiting for the clothes, shoes, and make-up to dive in so I can attempt to be on time for my flight, when my phone chirps, a bird with no nest.

I check the phone's display, see the familiar blue-and-white icon which means *someone* has posted *something*.

It doesn't take much to distract me.

This moment breaks the fever of pretending to pack.

Instantly, I'm entranced, and the distraction feels like two mid-afternoon cigarettes.

If the brain had salivary glands, then that sound—any digital sound, really—would have the brain drooling. It's the clarion call of our generation. The Pied Piper of post-9/11 America.

But it's not all candy.

At least a million people per year crash their cars because of cell phones. Because the urge to be involved in someone else's world—or to create your own—is too great to ignore.

This is my generation's great struggle. Darwin's plan for Millenials.

And I am not immune to it.

I check my phone and see: Someone I know has updated her status.

Not just anybody.

Madeline St. Clair.

The Queen of Green Hills.

The Bitch of Belle Meade.

One need only peer at her profile to see she doesn't live like the rest of us. Oh, she eats and shits and probably still has her period—I assume—but she doesn't exist in any world but her own, and *she* decides whom she let across the velvet rope of her friendship.

Even if it's had its own sort of miraculous revival, Nashville hasn't changed *that* much, especially when it comes to the Belle Meade crowd, the upper crust of southern gentility. The people may change, but the last names never do, and the St. Clairs have been in Nashville since before the first bricks of Fort Negley were set.

It's absolutely annoying.

I read the status, and my stomach does a backflip.

> Looking forward to the twenty-year reunion with all my girls! it says, and I can't help but scream FUCK! into the pillow next to my computer.

It's *that* time of year. It's *that* year.

Twenty years, coming up.

Couldn't my mother die some other point in my life? *Any* other point in my life?

The comments are all what you'd expect, obsequious servants to heir St. Clair—she never took her husband's last name, because why would she—trying desperately to win her favor.

It's been this way her whole life. Madeline's only existed in a world where people agree to each and every request because they're afraid of what will happen to them if they don't. She is like a mercurial, inbred king of some foreign country, with an executioner on hand for all of her public pronouncements.

I will avoid the blade. My FaceBook persona is one I've crafted out of whole cloth, in part because I like the anonymity, but mostly for the simple reason that no one would knowingly befriend someone they considered a murderer.

Well, I mean, unless I had something like the St. Clair fortune backing me. Then, silly obstacles like bullying someone into committing suicide would be a footnote in her life.

Which it is.

No one seems to mind who she is and what she's done. Madeline St. Clair has never suffered a moment's worth of setbacks for her role in Everett Coughlin's death. She's the socialite of all socialites.

She has as much blood on her hands as I do. Or Gillian. Or Audrey.

Everybody knows. Nobody cares.

Nobody, it seems, except me.

I've spent the whole of my adult life in hiding, like a refugee from my homeland. I haven't exactly been dreaming of going back to Nashville, but it would be nice to be able to walk down the street without people staring.

Because of the way I've been portrayed over the years—the mastermind of an adolescent plot to destroy another kid's life—I live my life like a Yeti Charles Manson. Widely reviled, rarely seen.

I'm not a *victim* or a *survivor* or anything. I don't believe I've been given a raw deal. I was totally complicit in the whole debacle. I deserve the title *Suicide Blonde*.

But I'm not the only one.

And there's no way to tell my side of the story.

There is no *my side of the story*. Not really.

I don't do interviews. There's no need to. The public has made up its collective mind, and I am the Jim Jones of this whole People's Temple. I've always felt like trying to make some grand gesture about, well, spreading the blame out would only make me look bitter.

Not that it's untrue.

I *am* bitter.

Depressed, even. I spend entire nights with the sides of my pillow pressed against my ears, staring at the ceiling, trying to make sense of my life.

But none of it makes sense. I can't escape any of it.

If I were a murderer—a killer—then it would be easy to put the instrument of my evil away. The gun I'd used to fire on my victim. The knife I'd used to stab them.

I can't. How do you deprive yourself of a computer? Of social media? Of your phone?

Each day I wake up, I am reminded of what I did. And I should be. What I did was horrible. And yet, I wish each and every night for some kind of absolution.

Twenty years on, and I'm still wishing for it.

There's a part of me that thinks maybe I could bounce back, if only I could get the right break. I don't even know what that means.

I just know, I hate Madeline St. Clair. I hate her for who she is and what she represents. I'm not the only one. I am intimately aware of the jealousy that surrounds her like a cloud—an intoxicating perfume of envy—but my reasons are wholly my own.

These are the things I think of when I stalk Madeline online.

I've spent the last twenty years hiding from myself, from *them*, from *it*.

But that time is over.

Now, I'm heading back to Nashville.

Here we go.

THE FIRST THING I notice after de-planing at BNA is just how corporate Nashville has become. There's always been a price tag dangling from the city, but the booming economy has turned Music City into a Metropolitan dollar sign.

You can buy red, white, and blue shirts emblazoned with the unofficial motto, *I Believe in Nashville*, or hats festooned with the airport's logo, if that's your sort of thing. *Aw shucks* propaganda.

Even the city skyline has become a commercial venture. Flabby tourists buying Johnny Cash coffee mugs and guitar pick baseball caps. Oh, and *hockey jerseys*. Hockey. In Nashville. For God's sake. Almost overnight, it's as if Dwight Yoakam had transformed into Chris Hemsworth.

It's not bad. It's just...different. I haven't been home in years—though I am loathe to call this place home—and I don't know, but Nashville never seemed all that...cool. Tourist trap? Yes. Southern Mecca to country music? Absolutely. Legitimate destination for Brooklyn hipsters fleeing Williamsburg? No freaking way.

But no matter how hip it has become—or how many bachelor parties grace the streets of Broadway—there is one thing that is incontrovertibly the same as before. The same as it always was, ever since I was a little girl.

Nashville. Is. Hot.

Temperature hot. Like, the combination of heat and moisture in the air. It's not swamps-of-New-Orleans hot, but it definitely gives you a good sheen if you spend more than a few minutes out-of-doors.

I tromp through the carpeted, airy terminal in a Seahawks hat, sunglasses, nondescript t-shirt, and jeans. It's my purpose in life to blend in, and I'm usually pretty successful at it. I dread being noticed. I'm not *famous*, but people know me, so I have to be on guard in public places.

It's like I can see their eyes on me, the people who seem to know me. They stare until their face *pop*s with recognition. Sometimes, they move their lips, whispering *monster* under their breath, but mostly they just stare *fuck you*s into me from a distance.

Only, the girl at the Starbucks does a double-take when I step to the counter for my usual latte. It's readily apparent *why* as soon as I order my latte.

The recent TV special. It aired a few weeks ago, and so the public interest is peaking right now for the Witches of West End, the Haints of Hillsboro Pike. Whatever. Pick a road or a neighborhood from Nashville, and attach a really cruel adjective to it, and you've got me pegged.

She nods as I talk, but you can just tell when someone is just going through the motions. I pretend not to notice, but I know what she's thinking, even as she takes my card and swipes it through her machine.

She's thinking, How do you live with yourself? What is wrong with you? Do you ever wish you were dead, instead of *him*?

The answer to that last question is *yes*—all the time—but that's beside the point.

Ugh. I can't wait to fall back into obscurity, go and get my coffee in peace. But, for the time being, I'm a pseudo-celebrity. Like Twitter famous, but way fucking worse.

I was big news.

At one point, I was *the* symbol of internet violence, the way Eric Harris and Dylan Klebold were 90s poster boys for school shootings. I was the first in a long series of tragic situations involving low self-esteem and high internet usage.

I'll go back to being nobody again, but for not, I'm a sickening curiosity.

And that's precisely how she's looking at me, though there is certainly a star-struck quality to her ogling. I guess even *People* is putting true crime on the cover these days.

She gives me that look, that I-want-to-say-something-but-I'm-not-quite-sure look, and then I get the inevitable rhetorical question. "You're *her*, right?" she says.

She doesn't actually want to know. She already does. She's just confirming her suspicions, and I'm left to play the opposite side of this little badminton game.

She's a stupid college student, or maybe she's still in high school, so I don't tell her to go fuck herself, though I get close.

"I'm nobody important."

"No," she says, sliding the receipt across to be signed, "you're her. The girl from the TV documentary. You're the girl who—"

She stops herself.

Bullied a kid into killing himself.

That's what she wants to say. That's what's in the back of her mind and on the tip of her tongue. Somehow, I keep myself in check, and I sign my receipt without much of a response.

"I'm not that person," I say, and I jet out of there.

I get weird looks from the people behind me, but I'm outside the shop and hurrying toward my destination before their eyes really settle on me. Not that it matters. I am who they say I am.

I am Mary Ellen Hanneford, the original Suicide Blonde.

2

THEN

Mary Ellen Hanneford has come into her own. She spent the summer before junior year at Dallas-Dudley Academy getting herself right, eating nothing but salads and running three miles every single day, winding through the labyrinthine neighborhoods on the outskirts of Nashville proper.

And now she's ready.

She's got a new 'do—with highlights—and a whole new wardrobe, courtesy of a mother-funded shopping spree at the Green Hills Mall. Also, she's grown an inch-and-a-half and has lost the remaining baby fat around her middle.

This is the year she wants to distinguish herself, to make an impact. She's tired of living in the shadows of her school, barely going along to get along, and so she's decided to give it her all. If she can't turn it around this year—actually become someone she would be proud of—then maybe there *is* no turning it around.

Luckily, the hard work pays off at the year's outset. One day, as she's grabbing her bowl of yogurt—with banana and granola, of course—the most popular of the popular girls eyes her, as though seeing her for the first time, and then waves her over.

This is it, she thinks. This is the way things are supposed to go.

She feels the weeks and months of discipline rising slowly to the surface and spreading out in the air all around her, creating a new reality just for Mary Ellen.

It's Gillian Meitner and Audrey Winstead, two kids largely considered royalty in the halls of Dallas-Dudley Academy. They stir a whole lot of emotions in the student population, but mostly it's fervent jealousy. If other kids are pretty, they're beautiful. If most of the girls are wealthy, they are old money. If everyone else is cool, they're ice cold. They are popular and snarky and envied, but they are also vicious and mean, so standing near them is like falling into a tiger cage at the zoo.

Oh, and there's Madeline St. Clair, the end-all, be-all of the upper echelon at school. She exists on a different plane of existence than the rest of humanity, even the underlings who snarl and growl at the hem of her gown. She is long-legged, tall, and wispy, as if composed of air and body parts cut from magazine centerfolds.

"Why don't you come sit with us?" Gillian Meitner asks, glancing timidly at the long-legged blonde at the head of their table.

Mary Ellen knows who she is, just as she should know who Mary Ellen is. Just last year, this very same group of girls spread rumors about a very private, very embarrassing phone conversation she'd had with a boy from Briley Academy. How Madeline St. Clair found out, it was anybody's guess, but Mary Ellen got called DSL (for *dick-sucking lips*) for a month before it finally let up.

So, yeah, this should be an awkward situation.

But there is no guarantee Madeline St. Clair knows her. Mary Ellen is not worth knowing, in the sense that Mary Ellen is neither a rival nor a supplicant to her, and she sure as hell is not looking to be in their crosshairs any more than she has been.

However, she is drawn to them the way gazelles happen upon water near crocodiles in the African Savanna.

"So, are you going to sit down, or what?"

It's then Mary Ellen realizes she's been standing there awkwardly for nearly ten seconds. Just kind of holding her tray and grinning.

"Sure," she says, lowering herself to a seat as her real friends at another table stare on silent horror. They all know Mary Ellen is making a mistake—even Mary Ellen—but she knows she can't help but make it.

And the truth of why presents itself almost immediately.

"But, there's a catch," Madeline adds.

She glances conspiratorially at the other members of her coven. Her eyes twinkle. "You have to tell us something about your friends over there, the frumpy ones with the bad skin."

Madeline giggles, and the rest of them react, but Mary Ellen is still in too much shock to do much at all.

"I mean," Mary Ellen begins. She clears her throat, stalling for time. "Brenda plays field hockey, and she's more into The Backstreet Boys than N Sync—"

"Girl, you know that's not what we're looking for," Audrey says, her nostrils flaring so slightly it almost gives her nose a new look. One that her parents did not pay for.

Mary Ellen glances over at them, her real friends, who seem unaware of what's about to happen. They've been with her for *years* now, supporting her. Helping her. Encouraging her.

She considers all of the embarrassing secrets, one by one, wondering what she could get away with without actually destroying friendships.

Madeline and the rest of them look on in a kind of fascinated anticipation. Mary Ellen is no dummy. Cruelty is their currency, and so this represents her way in. These kids operate on secret information, and they need a constant supply to stay on top of the food chain.

But, in the end, Mary Ellen shakes her head and turns away. "I can't," she says. "They're my friends. I couldn't do that to them."

For a moment, she considers running back to her table. Back to the comforting presence of her own friends. And she doesn't know this, but if Mary Ellen had walked over to her old table, where her friends are discussing the latest episode of *Dawson's Creek* with bated breath, her life would have turned out much differently.

But the star of this universe leans forward and asserts her authority.

"Oh yeah?" Madeline St. Clair says. "*They're* your friends?"

"That's right," she replies uncertainly.

She suddenly doesn't know. *Are* they her friends? What doesn't she know?

"Who do you think told us your deepest, darkest secrets, the ones that got passed around the school like cheap weed? *Those* friends. Yeah, but go on back to them, if you love them so much."

"That's not true," she barks, almost out of instinct.

Mary Ellen means to take a step. If only she can get her feet moving, she believes she can break free of the force field holding her here, among these vipers.

She has the chance to use her newfound swan status to assert independence, but inside she is still the little girl—an ugly duckling —and the death of her father still bleeds fresh on her mind. Thinking of him, of her Daddy-O, still cuts like a sharpened blade through her guts, and so she finds that wounded place in her, and she treats it.

By sliding closer to *them*.

It's like pouring rubbing alcohol on it, but the burn feels so good.

With the eyes of her only friends burning holes into the back of her North Face jacket, Mary Ellen leans forward and begins spilling all their worst secrets.

Soon, she will be an unwitting accomplice in their worst schemes, but for now she's just glad to be anything at all.

NOW

MOTHER IS PRESSED into her hospital bed like a chocolate from a Whitman's Sampler. Like the bed's been made *just* for her. I can't help but stare. In the luminous hospital room, it's impossible not to inspect her. Even from behind sunglasses, my eyes linger on her painfully thin arms, the veins protruding like crisscrossing roads in a poorly planned city.

This is her masterpiece. Her *Guernica*. She is finally sick in a way she's always imagined, and even with her eyes closed, it's obvious she's not ready for it. She has the look of someone whose whole body is made of pins and needles, as if unclenching her body and relaxing would cause her to bleed.

Maybe it would. Maybe she is bound to have some kind of horrible, otherworldly experience, to burst open and spew gouts of blood like the elevators from *The Shining*.

Not that she deserves it.

She was a good mother, up until the point she wasn't. Once the paranoia set in, she became this...figure in my life. Not a parent. Not a friend. Not even a nuisance. An oddity, perhaps. She's always existed in the periphery of my life, veering in and out of focus as her many neuroses slowly subdued her. At one point, I thought seriously about hiring a priest to do an exorcism. Truly. I thought she was possessed, and I figured it wouldn't hurt to give God a chance. I'm not Catholic, and I never went for it, but there always seemed to be more to her condition than simple hypochondriasis. (I learned the proper term a long time ago.)

Out of a kind of instinct, my eyes dart toward the chair in the corner, where no one sits. Where my father would have been, had he not dropped dead of a heart attack when I was a freshman at Dallas Dudley Academy. His death was just enough of a shock to drive a wedge between us, but not enough to permanently ruin the family. I came home in college and endured holidays in a kind of dulled silence, but over time the trips became rarer and rarer. Now, I don't really visit at all. I just have to survive the four-alarm fire phone calls from my mother and then slink off to my own life, pretending she's not actually mentally ill.

You can almost draw a straight line between my father's death and my mother's current...situation. I almost hate my mother more for what she has done to my memories of my father than I do her obsession with death. I could handle squeezing her breasts for lumps or listening to her long-winded recitations of symptoms for Hodgkin Lymphoma as if they were a poem she had been forced to memorize in school.

It was the way she sullied my relationship with my father that I'll never forgive her for. His death became her death, in a way, and then it became a self-involved mission. No matter how long I played her medical Sancho Panza, it was never enough.

One day, I just...stopped caring. It was as if the freon in the A/C vent had just...leaked out. The cerebral cortex or whatever physiological doo-dad that doled out empathy still pumped air. It just turned out to be hot and stifling and poisoned.

"Hi, mom," I say, taking a seat on the edge of a chair next to the bed. I don't want to touch more than necessary. The sickness seems to float all around me like pollen.

She doesn't answer. She's fast asleep, her eyes fluttering from behind the lids, but there's no real *there* there.

I sit for a long time before the tedium becomes predictably boring. Since she's asleep, and there's no one around, I catch her up on my life.

"I'm working at a startup," I say. She responds with a single bark of a snore. An electric drill ramping up. "I'm not dating anyone, and I don't have any friends. I've been working really hard, though, and I wish I could grow up and get out of this...funk. But I can't."

Funk. It's such a strange word. Like *soul*, but not. My funk feels, if I'm being honest, like riding in a plane flying on autopilot slowly descending toward a mountain. No one's even in the cockpit, and it's not like they'd stop the crash, even if they could.

There is comfort in being mildly suicidal, knowing that at any point in time you can take up your cause and end it.

It's not like other people couldn't; they just haven't yet.

I'm don't actively think about killing myself. Just keeping my options open. This is where my mother and I are both achingly similar and completely different. She's always wanted a way out but was afraid to take it. I, on the other hand, know where the exit is. I just haven't found a reason to turn on the blinker and get off the interstate quite yet.

I'm in the middle of telling her about my loneliness when the words catch in my throat. I've been hanging onto something, but I don't think it's grief. It's like something's lodged inside my esophagus and won't come out.

A nurse wanders in and sees the tears, and there is a kind of sympathy on her face.

Little does *she* know.

Eventually, the lump passes, the nurse leaves, and I'm able to continue. "I know I've been a shitty daughter," I say, "and I wish I could change...everything."

As if my own self-reflection is a tonic for her, she opens her eyes, fluttering the lids like a silent movie starlet. An aging Mary Pickford. An unwell Clara Bow.

She seems to digest what I've said.

"Oh, darling," she says. "So good to see you."

"I know," I say. I prepare myself. "Me too."

"I hate it's come to this," she says cryptically.

It takes me a moment to realize what she means. It's a dig. The subtext is, *I hate that it's taken me dying to get you to come see me.*

I try my best not to react, but I have been told I have a severe case of Resting Bitch Face. It's a weakness; Mom sees that she's gotten through the armor, and so, for the time being, she's mollified.

It's time for her to revel in her grief.

"It's the worst they've ever seen," she says, measuring my face to see how *I* react. I try—I really do—but I can't muster up the kind of fawning terror she expects.

But I go through the motions.

I clench her hand, squeeze it appropriate, and look into her eyes. "Well, I'm here now," I say, even if I would rather be anywhere else.

The nurse checks her vitals, writes some numbers on a sheet on her clipboard, speaks briefly about what is going to happen in the next few hours, and then she goes away again.

My mother watches the woman waddle all the way out of the door, and then, eventually, her eyes return to me.

She sees me, really sees me, and then something curious happens: her eyes go blank. She doesn't know who I am. There is a spark of recognition in there, but some synapse or other thing has misfired, and it takes her a long, drawn-out moment for that thing to pass. It's like she's just realized I'm in the room.

I suppose I could help, could prompt her, but I don't. I don't have it in me, not yet.

Then, as if a switch has been flipped, memory floods back to her, and I take off the sunglasses.

Time to be seen.

"Oh, Mary Ellen, how *good* it is to see you," she says, her mouth struggling around the words like she's chewing awkwardly-shaped food. "I didn't expect for you to come."

I hold the phone up like a subpoena.

"You called me," I say. "Remember?"

She regards my device suspiciously. "Ah, yes. My, days feel like *weeks* at this point."

One hand rubs mindlessly at the IV in her wrist. She says, "They've got me on so many drugs, and plus I bumped my head this time..."

She trails off, as if expecting me to finish her thought, but I don't. I feel sick. I feel completely helpless and unnerved. Like most people of my generation, I was not raised with the poise to deal with loss. I was given a trophy for everything. Also, ever since Dad, I've always been repulsed by hospitals.

Death's waiting rooms.

"Well, what are you going to do with yourself while I, erm, recuperate?"

Mouthing out the word as though it's an impossibility for her. I'm still not entirely convinced this is the big one. Part of me wonders if it isn't some grand hallucination meant to punish me.

"There's a reunion...thing, um, happening with all the girls from DDA."

"Huh."

Immediately, I fall into the old call-and-response, a child desperately trying to seem competent at the feet of a judging parent.

"But I probably won't go," I say.

A long silence settles between us, the quiet mediating this situation like a non-judgmental psychologist, and for a moment I think she's gone away again.

But she sighs, a gesture I'm well aware of. And I can almost guess at her next words.

"Goodness, what a development," she says. She scratches at the IV again. "Haven't you suffered enough at the hands of those evil harpies? Me, here dying, and you go off to fill your social calendar. What world do we live in?"

"I never said I was going for sure," I reply, "but there are people I'd like to see beyond *them*, Mom."

A total lie. Were I to go, it would be for the purpose of ogling these people, to silently judge them from a distance and then go back home and maybe masturbate to the thought of their misery.

Not something I'll tell my mother, obviously.

"I know you hold in your heart a delicate spot for the people who wronged you. But I was there. I knew them. I've known girls like them all my life, and they never change. No matter how much you want them to be different, they won't be. Underneath the shimmery crust, they're all black with rot. You just remember that."

In these moments, I have a vague sense that my mom is going to lean over and tell me she hates me, that she despises for following Madeline St. Clair to the ends of the Earth.

Instead, her mouth twists around, and she smiles. "Either way," she says, "I'm glad to see you. It's been such a long time."

I balk at the opportunity to volley the sentiment back to her. The words get stuck, but thankfully, a doctor interrupts and asks to see me in the hospital's wide corridors.

THE OPINION of the medical wonks at Vanderbilt is that mom is beyond help. In fact, it's so bad, I kind of blackout halfway through the doctor's chat and nod as I wait for someone—anyone—to offer me a Kleenex. My whole face is wet, and I can almost *feel* the mascara on my cheeks. The doctor glances down every so often but continues with his escorted tour into my own personal Hell.

At least he doesn't sugarcoat anything, I guess.

"She has severe mobility issues, and she apparently struggles to remember to take her myriad medications. I also understand she has been in less than optimal shape for some time."

I shrug. "At least that's what she thinks."

"Unfortunately, this is a long-term problem that cannot be solved with short-term solutions."

He goes on, and though there's some medical-ese, it all washes over me like a religious conversion.

The doctor even goes through the options for care. The most obvious, it seems, is to shovel her off to one of the many assisted living communities springing up around the city, like multi-floor cattle pens for the elderly.

"Unless, of course," he adds, "you are willing to take on the role of caretaker."

I shrug, telling him I'd need to think about it. The truth is, I have no interest. I'm no caretaker. I can barely take care of myself. I'm a hot mess. I don't eat. I drink too much. I've had one-night stands with disinterested men and women but have never been involved in a *single* long-term relationship.

Sometimes, I think I'm just slowly disintegrating, like aspirin under the tongue, and I don't mind it. I think it's probably the best thing for me.

Sad.

Whatever.

3

NOW

After an awkward hospital goodbye, I cruise in my rental car to my temporary residence, a boxy-looking Airbnb off 51st in The Nations, where all the streets are named after states. There's an Indiana and a Georgia and even a Tennessee, which I've always found odd.

The house is clean but empty, like it's being shown for a sale, so I can't quite get comfortable, at first. I snag a beer from the fridge—so far as I know, it's all there for me—and then I snag another. Before I know, it's dark, and I find myself graying out on the upstairs porch with my phone in my hand.

I don't use my real name or a real picture on my accounts—that would be social media suicide—and so I'm able to comfortably exist without harassment. I made the mistake of using the name Mary Ellen Hanneford on MySpace, and it took me *years* to get rid of my account. I was getting a dozen harassing messages per week, each and everyone telling me some variant of how I should kill myself and go to Hell.

After that, I thought, fuck the terms of service.

I've got a real problem. When my thumb touches the little blue icon that brings up my obsessively personal app, I begin to tremble. I feel a warmth rise in my jeans, and all the blood rushes to my face. It's a high that shortens my breath and lengthens my orgasms. Anonymously peeking into the lives of people, even people I never really cared about, is erotically amusing to me. I don't know why. Perhaps it's the way things went down senior year, or maybe I was always programmed to get off on obscurity and namelessness, but I spend more time flipping intently through the photos of my class-mates than I do working. I bring home takeout Chinese or just a fifth of vodka, and I begin my nightly rounds, like a security guard for a business that hasn't hired one.

I attended a somewhat prestigious all-girls high school because of my dad's job—he sold life insurance—and so for a brief period of time I was in a small sorority, of sorts, even if they no longer claim me. Over the years, my name has been scrubbed from the official records of Dallas-Dudley Academy.

It's like I've been excommunicated.

Either way, after a few glasses of Tito's, I land on a post by a familiar face in the DDA Official Group. Even though I'm a lurker—obviously—I have it set so I receive notifications anytime someone posts an event to the social calendar.

I need to see the notification.

I just do.

This is my version of hypochondriasis.

I click through to the invite, consisting of a picture taken at the ten-year reunion—to which I wasn't invited—and I feel that old, familiar feeling return.

If only they knew they had incidentally invited me—or, rather, "Margaret Sherwood," an actual alum who isn't even on social media —they'd have shit a brick.

Come one, come all! The invitation says. Alumnae mixer for any DDA graduates, circa 1995-2000.

A photo appears below the invite. It's the official DDA page's admin, a former classmate of mine.

Audrey Winstead, once the lapdog of the Queen Bitch of Belle Meade, now runs her own equity firm or advertising firm or something. It's a way of massaging funds away from the *nouveau riche* under the auspices of "networking." She provides them with a service of some kind, and they provide her with boatloads of cash.

Audrey is pretty, a blonde. Like me. Like all of us. Or like all of us *used* to be. She has sloughed off the role of obsequious sidekick, but the look in her eyes on the DDA page tells everyone who used to know her that she is now her own person.

Audrey, with her botoxed eyebrows and photoshopped profile pic, has everyone fooled, that she was once a monster and is now a normal citizen, just going to work and paying her taxes, but I remember the other her, the high school her, the Audrey who once wondered aloud if she could convince Everett Coughlin to wrap his lips around a shotgun. The rest of us laughing, getting in on the action, trying to outdo one another. *I can get him to leap off the Batman building. I can hand him a rope and have him dangle from the sign at Ernest Tubbs' Record Store.*

And so on. It was all a game: a simple, sick, twisted, solitary game, played by girls who had no idea how much power they had. It ended with a kid dying face-down in his parents' garage.

That is who Audrey is to me.

I'm not going to go, I tell myself, but the inkling to do it, the urge to see everyone's reactions, is undeniable. It'd almost be worth it just to throw their smug, self-congratulatory bullshit back in their faces.

Look at how sophisticated we are.

Oh, to be the cockroach in their midst.

This is my fantasy.

It's never coming to fruition, of course. To be there, to go into that room of well-dressed vipers, would make me physically ill. It's just something I have to contemplate, to envision, like my mother with her cancers and neurological diseases.

But just as I'm about to close the app, a message appears. Not a notification, but a message, sent very obviously to me and me only.

I don't get messages, because I am an island. I am a digital Keyser Söze. I do not comment on statuses, nor do I react or share them. My online life is as empty and meaningless as my real one, and I like it that way.

I have to. It keeps me safe.

I maneuver the mouse over the red dot filled with the number 1 that indicates someone has typed out some form of communication to me.

Silly, I tell myself, even as my heart thuds rhythmically against my chest.

It's an honest-to-goodness message from someone I went to school with. Gillian Meitner, one of my high school...accomplices, just like myself, has sent me a direct message.

Hey, there, Mary Ellen.

The greeting causes my breath to catch in my throat. The fact that she's picked me out of the thousands upon thousands of friends of hers as THE Mary Ellen is something of a miracle. My shock is only outpaced by my curiosity.

> Been a long time, right? Don't worry. I'm not going to blow your cover. I've been looking for you online for some time now, and something about the name and avatar on your profile has always bugged me. Today, I decided it was because the person you claim to be is, in fact, *you*. How do I know this? Secrets, Hanneford. We all have to keep secrets.

> Anywho, I decided to take a chance. There's this...thing tonight at a place called Dorsia, over off of 12th. I don't know what's happened to you. At some point, I heard you lived in Portland or somewhere, but if you're in town, you should definitely stop by. It'd be good to see you.

At first, I ignore the message, but Gillian persists. She's always been persuasive.

> I know what you're thinking, but it won't be that way. The people there will be one hundred percent CHILL. If you're worried about...you know...don't be.

When people tell me not to worry, it's a sign I should run in the opposite direction. But I don't. Instead, I stare at the screen, feeling the tingle of an old desire. It goes against my personal edict to be invisible, but that's probably what is enticing about it.

But eventually the more cautious—and, one might say, more *intelligent*—side wins out, and I follow through with the message I had been crafting in the back of my mind.

No thanks, I respond in the messaging app, and just like that, I've walled off another part of my life, like closing the door to a room where someone special died.

Only, then something happens, and later I will spend a lot of time wondering what in the hell I ever answered my phone for, but the phone rings, and I answer it. The excuse I will use with myself later has to do with the hospital. I'm worried about my mother, so any call can be *the* call, and I don't recognize the number, and yadda yadda yadda, but the truth is probably somewhere askance of that.

"Hello?"

My voice feels thick in my throat.

The one on the other end isn't, though. It's light and airy. "Is this Mary Ellen?"

I hope like hell it's a nurse telling me to haul ass back to the hospital to sign some insurance forms or give a fucking pint of blood.

But it's not.

It's a reporter from a local station, vying for the chance to interview me.

This lady has no clue. I don't do interviews.

By the time I catch up with the elevator pitch, she's already halfway through her second paragraph. It isn't until I hear *his* name that I perk up and pay attention.

"...or some kind of interview to coincide with the recent cable special."

My knee-jerk reaction to these sort of sit-down interview requests is to say no or to give them runaround and then disappear, so that's precisely what I do here.

Except, it doesn't quite work. I'm a little rusty and don't stick the landing.

Instead of saying *never in a million fucking years*, instead I blurt out, "I haven't scheduled any interviews since the documentary came out."

My response leaves an opening for the fame-hungry reporter to give me the business.

"Why don't you sit down with me and set the record straight? Believe it or not, people want to hear your side of the story."

"I don't want to do that," I manage to say.

Her response is cool and rehearsed. "You can do what you want, but I think the people are ready to know the truth about the death of Everett Coughlin."

It feels like a small knife being inserted under my rib cage.

"I'm sorry?"

My brain is a bit sluggish, and I have trouble coming up with the necessary words to get her off the phone. I veer insanely close to the phrase *Go fuck yourself, lady* but manage to hold off.

Instead, the woman's off to the races again.

"In recent years, questions have been brought up about what really happened and how much involvement you even had in—"

"I am *Bloody Mary Ellen*," I respond with vitriol, "and I did every-thing the cops alleged I did. Everything else is just tabloid magazine gossip."

I have a response cocked and ready for such situations—I've been dealing with this for two decades—but she cuts me off before I can even get to it.

"I have it on good authority that you took a substantial settlement from the other families—undisclosed and all that—and did the time to protect your friends. Is that true?"

"Not in the least," I respond.

Maybe a little, I think.

"If you're worried about the publicity this will cause," she says, "then you can speak to me on background. Just give me a quote for attribution, and then everything else—"

"No." I've made a pact with myself. *The past stays in the past.* Digging anything up will cause everything to come up, and I do not want that.

"Listen," she says in a conspiring tone, "I know it has to sting that all of those country club *bitches* have used you as a whipping post for the last two decades—"

"Who *are* you?" I ask. In the past twenty years, I've seen my fair share of attention-starved cable TV hosts, but this one is on a different level.

She has a short bark in place of a laugh, and I'm trying to imagine what she looks like. A sharp-nosed, bright-eyed wannabe starlet with cold ambition in place of genuine feeling and good humor.

She's a lot like me, I guess.

Save for the ambition.

"I'm the woman who can tell your story so you're no longer the tragic scapegoat." She pauses for dramatic effect. "So, what do you say?"

I give her an equally long pause. "I say you can sit on your microphone sideways. Now, leave me the fuck alone and give me my privacy."

"But—"

Before she can try to steamroll me, I hang up and block the number. She'll have to get a new phone before she can call me again.

I stare at the screen for an inordinately long time, feeling the weight of the device in my hands. There is much more than gravity pulling down on it, and I try to recognize it every time I use one of these things.

And the weight drags me down into it.

I re-open the app and find Gillian's message. The message comes in fits and starts, but eventually, I get it all on the screen.

> Okay. I guess I can make an appearance.

There is an immediate reaction.

> I knew you'd answer! Okay, so I can't promise some people won't

turn and look, but it's been twenty years, M.E. I'd like to bury the hatchet, put water under the bridge. All that. Plus, I can give you indelible gossip about the rest of the girls from our graduating class.

And just like that, everything in my entire life is knocked sideways.

4

THEN

Gillian Meitner's dad is a tech nerd, and so when he brings home a state-of-the-art desktop computer outfitted with Windows 98—which no one realizes is a big deal—his attempt to connect with his daughter on a social level is met with cries of derision.

"Dad, you really need to get your D&D group back together, because we are *not* going to use this stupid thing. It's just going to sit and collect dust."

Because these girls know who they are, or at least who they aren't.

They are more *Clueless* than *Hackers*. More *Dazed and Confused* than *The Net*.

Even *You've Got Mail* appears to be something out of a Philip K. Dick novel when compared to the current iterations of their lives. They are social, and it isn't until the prospect of chatting online with strangers and enemies becomes a possibility that any single one of them takes it seriously.

They aren't sisters, really, but they are close enough they might as well be. When they aren't at one another's houses, they are on the phone, tying up the main line and ignoring call waiting.

Because they can.

At first, the computer *does* collect dust. They are more interested in the other gift Gillian receives, a handheld video camera that allows them to film their shenanigans in full over the Christmas holidays. They take it with them when they get trashed on Zima and smoke teeny tiny joints out at Sevier Park. They aim the lens at one another and then zoom in as the victim hides her face in shame.

But then that, too, loses its luster. Eventually, Audrey and Madeline sneak off with it to plan revenge on their asshole parents.

Which gives rise to the summer of the desktop computer.

Slowly, the internet rises up from the lagoon of technological newness, and Gillian and her friends become acquainted with the idea of using something other than a phone to communicate.

"It's like something out of a spy movie," Madeline says when she first encounters a chat room. It couldn't be simpler—scrolling white text on a black background—but to them, it is a marvel. Seeing people from around...wherever they are from engaging in conversation is tantamount to landing on Mars.

The fact that they are the first people from their friend group to explore the dark corners of the World Wide Web contributes to the mystique of it all. They feel privileged—which they are—and this curiosity soon becomes a mainstay of their friendship. It's like the cyborg sidekick that improves their lives through the wonders of technology.

The reversal from geeky to *chic* occurs almost overnight. Soon, they reach the point that they're bored with flirting over chat. It's always the same cycle: eager boys go from asking about their favorite TV shows to begging for pretend handjobs within the span of a few minutes. Even *mention* the fact that you're a girl, and the hounds come a-running.

One night, when they're scrolling mindlessly through the chat,

90210 reruns on in the background, Madeline pops out of her digital malaise with a start.

"I've got an idea," she says.

The girls all pile in beside her, excitedly waiting on edge for her brilliant plan. Mary Ellen follows suit, though on the inside she is wary.

Madeline St. Clair does *not* have ideas. She doesn't just *come up* with plans. She is a plotter. She thinks about what is going to happen —or, rather, what she is going to *make* happen—from the moment she wakes up.

So whatever she is about to say, it is not the result of neurons firing randomly inside her head. She uses this pretext because she knows it will be easier for the girls to swallow, if they assume it's just a wild fancy.

They know, too. It's not like they're dumb. They might pretend every once in a while, but they're not stupid. They are as hip to Madeline's wiles as Mary Ellen, they just aim to please so as not to upset the apple cart.

You do *not* want to upset Madeline.

There's a reason they call her *Mads* behind her back.

Never to her face. Uh-unh. Never. But they know. It's an unspoken covenant among them that she is the queen, and they are her loyal subjects. There is a clear hierarchy, and they must play their roles at all times.

Mary Ellen had heard stories of the last girl who had been in her place—Sarah Margaret Clifton—so she knew not to cross Madeline.

Apparently, in ninth grade, Mads had been friends with a girl who went to an elite Catholic school in the area. The two of them had been inseparable, save for the normal school hours. Just peas in a pod and all that. They ran their respective schools like wardens, and in some ways, Madeline had met her match.

But when she found out that Sarah Margaret had rubbed Philip De Santis's hard-on over his jeans at the movies, she—well, she disappeared.

This part, Gillian and Audrey told her in hushed tones well out of

Madeline's earshot. It wasn't like Madeline to back down from a fight, especially where her *territory* was concerned, so they kind of freaked out, thinking maybe she had committed suicide or something over it.

But that's not Madeline's style.

Instead, when she finally emerges from the depths of her cavernous room, like a funerary Barbie playset, Madeline is stone-faced and minimally expressive. A princess who has been deposed and vows to regain the throne. It's a determined look, but there's an edge to it. Like she's cried her tears and refuses to admit defeat.

She remains distant and quiet as the other girls trip over one another to prostrate themselves before the altar of *her*. When Madeline has heard enough, one corner of her mouth turns up, and she puts on a smile that is not quite even a smile.

"I have an idea," she says, and even though none of them says it, they cannot bear the sound of Madeline's voice when it reaches this register.

In retrospect, it appears that this plan could have been burbling up near the surface for some time, and Sarah Margaret Clifton just happened to pull the short straw.

Once they were done with her, she spent a month in a psychiatric ward for a suicide attempt brought on by severe post-traumatic stress.

Mary Ellen remembers the sorts of things that got passed around. That she was a slut, that she had slept with the entire starting basketball team. Your standard fare for the high school enemy.

But the worst of them shocked even the most cynical gossipmonger.

It involved a video camera and one of Sarah Margaret's prized show dogs.

Of course, it was insane—of course—and no one should have believed it—again, it was absolutely bonkers—but it made the rounds, due in no small part to the efforts of Madeline and her underlings.

As with all gossip, it should have died quickly and allowed the poor girl at its center to go about her business.

It didn't go away.

The rumor persisted into sophomore year. Stretched for months and months and months, tormenting her in part because of its peculiarity but mostly because of the alleged existence of the tape.

At the heart of the rumor was the tape. She had supposedly filmed this inexplicable act of sexual congress, and so—naturally—people attempted to find it. People either claimed to have seen it or claimed to know someone who had seen it. Because of that, the rumor dragged on and on and on, almost to Halloween.

When the cops visited her parents and asked about the video, thinking maybe they were dealing with a case of child pornography, that was the breaking point. Turns out, someone's mother had contacted the Metro Police, and the resulting fight between her parents ended up causing them to separate for a time. They thought they had failed one another, had somehow failed their marriage vows and had even failed their God.

And then there was poor Sarah Margaret.

The salacious details and white whale of a video drove her to ground, like a plane with one engine down and the other flagging badly. She ended up taking a whole bottle of her mother's Xanax in a single gulp. Her mom found her frothing at the mouth when she returned from an early dinner with friends and rushed her to the hospital just in time to save her.

She survived, but she was never quite the same after that.

All because of a failed bit of heavy petting in a dark movie theater.

When she begins hanging out with them, Mary Ellen considers the case of Sarah Margaret Clifton a red flag, but for the most part, she ignores it. There is no real evidence they started the rumor, and even if they did, it was the public-at-large who had spread it around, like feces on a bathroom wall.

Besides, Mary Ellen considers herself beyond reproach, in this respect, because she would *never* betray her friends.

Well, she thinks. Not these *new* friends, anyway.

And so, on this night, when Madeline smirks and tells them, "This internet thing, it seems like we can have *a lot* of fun with it," it's the first time she feels that strange feeling in her gut, the one that will grow and grow until it feels like it is lodged in the back of her throat.

When they hear the details, Mary Ellen will remember looking over her shoulder at the bedroom door and wondering just how difficult it would be to get up and walk out.

But she doesn't, so she will never actually know.

NOW

It's obvious what I'm getting myself into as soon as I step through the door.

This isn't a mixer or a reunion; it's a networking event. Everyone is drinking and laughing, but it is just as evident they are itching to hand out business cards and pitch old acquaintances about their new restaurant, boutique, or real estate deal. People are so enamored with their own elevator pitches, I make it halfway to the bar before someone recognizes me. She turns to gab with her friends, to alert them about the psychopath in their midst. To stare and laugh.

I can't help but roll my eyes, and for a precious moment, I'm tempted to spin on one heel and dart back outside, but a mere glance of myself in a wall-sized mirror makes me stop. My whole body looks apt to cave in, as if trying to turn itself inside out. I am physically smaller, in this moment, than my normal self.

I clench my teeth.

Somehow, my feet take me further inside.

One drink. I promise myself one drink. Then I will get the fuck out of there.

The bar is cool, at least. A small, renovated factory building that gives Dorsia a legit speakeasy vibe. There's not even a sign outside, so you have to find it on your own.

Secrets have become a fetish, it appears.

Gillian Meitner doesn't miss a single thing. She and her Selina Kyle spectacles are busy surveying the room when our eyes meet.

She makes a confident beeline for me. Her bowstring lips are turned up at one corner. It's the most evident show of emotion she can muster. Laconic doesn't even begin to describe her.

"Mary Ellen Hanneford?" She lilts my name like it's a question, but she's as sure of it as she is that E=MC^2 or that the first numbers in Pi are 3.14. Gillian doesn't do questions. She does answers.

In high school—before everything happened—she spent her spare time on homework or extra credit projects to ensure her role as valedictorian. That the title eventually eluded her is a testament to how fucked up our junior year was. She ended up at a state college well beneath her abilities, but the bitterness doesn't look like it's gotten the better of her.

She hugs me. It's an awkward gesture, clearly not one of her strengths. It feels like a robot trying to figure out human gestures.

But she doesn't sweat it. She's already a step ahead.

"You're in Seattle," she says, "not Portland. That was my first mistake, wasn't it?"

Not a question. Not even that conversational. Just a fact she feels needs to be out in the ether. This is her MO, and she hasn't given that up. She could very well run through a list of my recent accomplishments, and though she doesn't, I can see her resisting the urge to show off.

"I work in coding," I say. "You ended up doing something with numbers, didn't you?"

She's somewhat shorter than the rest of our crew, but she makes up for it in the looks department. Hair longer than it used to be but flipped out at the edges, sort of like a blonde Liz Lemon with a healthy dose of self-confidence. She's bespectacled and sharp-featured but also really well put-together. She's also no longer blonde. Her hair is a deep chestnut, highlighting her eyes.

I can see the vagueness of my answer annoys her. She admires precision, even when she is the subject. She abhors the big picture. Everything, for her, is a moment-by-moment struggle for the truth.

"I'm a certified public accountant," she says.

It's hard not to roll my eyes. Classic Gillian. She can't even shorten it to the initialism everybody knows.

I suddenly want to be very far away. It was a mistake (a) to come here and (b) let myself be seen with one of my former *accomplices*, so I begin eyeing the exit. I figure if I convince her I need to run to the restroom, I can make it up the stairs and outside before she's aware of my absence. Then it's a matter of changing my FaceBook profile before she gets online again.

I'm on the verge of making my excuse known. But then the girl with the golden brain does something unexpected. She sips her drink, leans in, and says, "I fucking hate my job."

She smiles, her cheeks reddening, and suddenly, the night seems a little more bearable.

"I'VE BEEN to a couple of these mixers, and trust me: everybody *hates* everybody else," Gillian says later, once we have plowed through a few drinks. She's expertly sipping her second or third or fourth Manhattan, while I've relegated myself to rosé.

She and I are perched on stools next to high back chairs in the far corner of this industrial speakeasy, and she's spilling the goods on the girls from our graduating class. Even though she went away for school, Gillian moved back shortly after graduation and is well-read enough on Nashville gossip to make me wonder if she's a government agent.

"Lora Spielman got pregnant from a one-night stand in Puerto Rico, and her dad disowned her," she tells me. "He's running for Senate next year, and he thinks it will hurt his relationship with *The Base*."

I don't remember much about Lora, other than she always looked like she was trying to dislodge a stick from her ass.

"She was always so stuck-up," I manage, and Gillian nods. She *is* drunk, and it is that fact I like the most. It slows her brain down, which makes me comfortable, and since Gillian is unloading both barrels on our old classmates, I don't have to say much.

Thank God.

Talking shit about other people is like chewing glass. Whenever I feel the urge to say something negative about an acquaintance, my mouth cramps up, and it feels like I am going to spit blood. I've actually caught myself literally chewing on my tongue to stay quiet, and I think it was spending my senior year in a juvenile facility cured me.

But that was then. This is now. It's easy to stay quiet when you're a stranger among strangers, but this is *Gillian*. She's one of the *girls*. She knows me well, and there are...expectations, I suppose, that accompany this kind of discussion.

My stomach tightens up as I wait for it, wait for the moment to arrive. It circles the drain for at least an hour, and then it just happens. By then, I've prepared myself.

An uncomfortable silence pops up, and then it lingers there like a third member of our conversation.

Finally, Gillian swirls her drink and asks, "Do *you* ever talk to any of the girls?"

I shake my head furtively.

I feel like I'm being primed for something.

"I don't," I say. "You're the only one who's ever even contacted me."

"So you don't have any idea how we all turned out," Gillian says.

Again, a shake of the head.

It's both true and not true. I've not kept up with them in person, but I sure as hell stalked them when I joined Facebook. They friended "me" without much fanfare, and so I've managed to stay in the shadows of their lives, silently watching them from a comfortable distance online.

That's over now, I think.

"That's fascinating," she says. "I've spent my whole adult life thinking everybody knows too much about everybody else in this town."

"Long time since DDA," I reply.

"The DDA d-d-days," she says, using an old joke of ours, and the laugh she produces is infectious. It almost erases the sadness which has crept into her eyes.

When I was a student at Dallas-Dudley Academy, I was the very picture of an all-girls private school kid. It was a type, and I played the role perfectly, even if I was a complete fraud. I never belonged, not for a moment, but by the time I was "asked" to leave, I had almost convinced everyone I belonged there.

Almost.

After taking a slow drink from my rosé, I ask the obvious question, the one that's been floating above me like a thought bubble all night. "Where is Madeline? I'd have expected her and Audrey to be running the show by now."

The statement is slushy with sarcasm, but Gillian walks right past it. Maybe she knows, somehow, that I am aware of their falling out.

"Madeline said she would be here," she says, taking a sip from her own drink. "Though she's not having the best go of it these days."

"Looks like none of us are," I say without thinking.

That statement pulls my eyes from Natalie Schaefer, who never quite became the hot shit she always thought she was. Everything she does screams *trying too hard*. Poor thing. She never quite recovered from the time she went down on Logan Niedermeyer in the locker room after a lacrosse game.

Looking around, it's a shame we're all not happier. Most people here, they're successful. Mostly rich, too. But it's a sad fucking consolation for happiness.

I think it, but I don't say it.

That's the major difference between the old me and the "new, improved" version of myself. When these awful intrusive thoughts occur to me now, I just push them down and pretend they're not there, like hallucinations in the corner of a room.

But now my mind is working on Madeline St. Clair, and I can't quite keep silent about her. The decades have brought me much bitterness, and Gillian is precisely the person to

"What could possibly be wrong with *Madeline's* life?" I say, feeling a little jolt of venom at the idea that Madeline St. Clair might not be the Queen of Nashville.

Gillian glances around conspicuously, and she mouths the words *her marriage* to me from across the table. As if people at this event are on the lookout for gossip about Madeline.

I dig through mental photo albums until I pull up an acceptable image of Madeline's husband, a private wealth analyst named Colton Ambrose. I'm pretty sure he's a III or a IV, or at the very least a Jr., and I'm suddenly, deliciously happy. I feel the old joy come back, the edge from relishing in other people's pain.

I catch myself smiling, and Gillian gives me a knee-jerk frown. She still must hold some tenuous allegiance she doesn't want to jinx.

"You didn't hear it from me," she says.

I lock my lips and throw the imaginary key over the bar.

"What happened?" I lean in and ask, but about that time, Sophie Matthews saunters up and jumps right into our conversation. She doesn't seem to remember me, and I turn away to avoid speaking.

Several minutes elapse before Sophie finally stumbles back to the bar for another drink. It isn't until she wanders away that I notice the square of toilet paper stuck to the bottom of her wedge.

"So?"

"*Infidelity,*" she says, with a little more intrigue and exuberance than necessary. "Colton is splitting time between Nashville and D.C., and word is, he got caught up getting the Lewinsky treatment from a staffer for the Speaker of the House."

"Bullshit."

"It's what Audrey said happened."

"Now I know you're lying."

Back in school, Audrey Winstead—the least of the Suicide Blondes—was so loyal to Madeline, she would habitually refrain from revealing *anything* about her, lest she violate her role as the Queen B's lapdog.

Gillian holds up three fingers in a Scout's Honor salute. "Things have changed between those two," she says. "Among all of us, I guess."

"No shit," I say without thinking.

Us. Such a strange word, and though she means well, Gillian doesn't understand. *I* was the one they plastered all over the newspapers. *I* was the one who ended up in a courtroom. *I* was the pariah labeled as a murderer and a witch and a devil worshipper and whatever else. *Not* them.

To soften my last comment, I add, "Not for nothing, but there hasn't been an *us* for twenty years."

At this, Gillian checks the bottom of her drink with a wry glance. She's only just realized now that she and I, though old friends, are not what we used to be, and I'm not suddenly *on her side* now, just because she reached out to me.

"I know," she responds. "Listen, I—"

"Don't mention it," I say. "Really, don't. I'm not trying to hold a grudge. It's just...*hard* sometimes. You can't just wipe away twenty years."

As she struggles for a response, I glance in Audrey's direction. Sure enough, she's holding court for some dignitaries of the Nashville social world, whose last names even I remember from way back in the day. These are people with wide networks and deep pockets, and Audrey isn't so much sucking up to them as swallowing every bit of them down.

She's finally figured out who she is, it seems.

"The big shock is, Audrey and Madeline don't speak anymore," Gillian says.

"They were so close."

"Since Mads isn't Queen Bitch anymore, Audrey is doesn't have to be her puppet."

I nod. "She doesn't have that 'whipped dog' look about her. She looks, I don't know, peaceful or something. Maybe she's better off without Madeline."

"Maybe we're all better off without Madeline," she adds.

That sends us both to staring into our drinks, but eventually that contemplative note passes, and we're back to our gossip.

"She's hit every shitty branch on the way down. You've been in the

Pacific Northwest, so you aren't privy to the Gone Girling of Madeline St. Clair. You follow her on Facebook?"

It catches me sideways, and I nod before I know exactly what I'm admitting to.

"She went from the biggest, baddest chick in our friend group—one-in-a-million—to a walking cliché."

Gillian says. "You know, you...you had to, you know, *deal* with everything that happened, but I've wondered more than once if the shoe had been on the other foot, would it have even *affected* Madeline?"

"What do you mean?"

"I'm sorry," she says. "I think the liquor is starting to go to my head. Let me clarify: Would you say your life remained basically the same after...everything came out?"

It's an obvious question, bordering on stupid, but I want to see where it goes. I shake my head. "It's like the Robert Frost poem, except the road I traveled is covered in broken glass and lit cigarettes."

"Precisely," she says, as if explaining calculus to me. "I mean, you didn't become a serial killer or a carny or anything, but I'd be willing to bet there is a considerable difference between who you became and who you *could have* become. Am I wrong?"

It has crossed my mind. I think about all of the joyless one-night stands and evenings spent alone on my couch, spooning freezer-burnt Ben & Jerry's into my mouth.

"I wasn't always going to be the person I've become," I say.

"Damn right," she responds. "And yet, even with the stain of being, I don't know, an *unindicted co-conspirator*, Madeline went on to marry a rich local yuppie from a respectable family. It's like she's allergic to adversity."

"*Was*. Sounds like it's not true anymore."

"The point I'm making," she says, "is that she could have easily absorbed the blame in...*his* death without having the overall arc of her life be diverted. Her family's money would have shielded her from, well, what happened to you."

"And now, even though she's slipping, she's all we're talking about."

"Well, she is going to keep hurtling through space—and by space, I mean Nashville—until she gets carted off to an old folks home—"

"Or an insane asylum—"

"—and that is just not going to change."

She smiles. "Unless you were to kill her. Haha."

And there it is. The first sour note of the night.

"That's not funny, Gil," I say, though I don't know why I'm saying it. Maybe the years have made me cautious. Maybe I'm gun shy about murder jokes. Or maybe there's a part of me that thinks it would be really easy to slide back into old habits, and I have to draw a very distinct line.

"I know, I'm sorry," she says in a single breath. "I'm drunk and tired and I wanted to know what's happened to you after all these years. I'm sorry. Really."

Gil isn't the joking kind.

But I let it go. I don't have the cache to start poking around just yet.

Then her face brightens as she walks right past her own comment, and she says, "What *did* happen to you, M.E.?"

M.E. is the nickname I answered to when we were teenagers. Just hearing it causes the release of a certain kind of adrenaline. She's working me, and I have to admit: It's kind of working.

I shrug. "I went to juvie. Spent some time on a bunk with my hands under my head. And then I graduated."

"Then you disappeared."

"After I graduated from the weird school I attended, I drifted around. Went by a different name. Worked for a few charities, thinking that sort of thing would...absolve me. After I became disillusioned with that, I just kind of floated along as if I expected something big and unwieldy to come and swallow me up."

"And the drifting, that was a way to rinse the mold off?"

"Basically."

"Did it work?"

"Not really."

"Well," she says, "if it helps, I spend one night a week gazing at my ceiling, because I can't stop thinking about the things I typed in that chat room."

Just then, a hand appears on Gillian's shoulder. We both turn to see Audrey Winstead standing there, her perfect hair and gleaming teeth shining through an obvious champagne buzz.

"How come nobody told *me* about getting the band back together?"

Audrey Winstead is the very picture of put-together. Designer clothes. Artificially-aligned teeth. Perfect blowout. Highlights. Everything.

When she graces us with her presence, the conversation veers wildly in the direction of *her*. How well she is doing. How much money she made in "the market" last year. How many celebrities and country singers she's rubbed elbows with.

"Honestly, I don't mean to brag," she says, finishing up her résumé, "but I've helped make the strip on 12 South what it is today."

Everything that comes out Audrey's mouth has an air of bullshit to it. So much so, you have to turn away to prevent getting a whiff of the stuff. It's a schtick, and if she knows how fake it sounds, she can't seem to help herself. She oozes the *quid pro quo* of sleazy southern politics.

She's the exact *opposite* of Madeline, who never bragged because she already had everything she needed. She was motivated by pure spite and the need to manipulate. Everything else was just so much empty air.

"Well," Gillian says, "We've been talking about you-know-who, and here you come over. I figured you would have some...*interesting* words to contribute on the topic."

A strained blink from Audrey. "Let's just say that karma is in full effect."

She's drunk. It's obvious the networking portion of this event is over for her, so she can move on to guzzling elaborate, pricy cocktails without fear of losing any personal business.

"You know, it's like that night," Audrey continues, slurring her words ever so slightly. "I mean, Gillian you weren't there, but—"

"Shut up, Audrey," Gillian says.

I'm confused. Or maybe Audrey's confused, so I offer up, "But she *was* there. Gillian and you and Madeline and I. We were *all* there."

It's framed like a question, but I'm not quite sure why there should be any confusion at all. On the night of Everett Coughlin's death, we all had a role to play. Madeline was the mastermind, Audrey was the sycophant, Gillian was the computer's owner, as well as the one who did the bulk of the typing.

And I, as it turns out, I was just the scapegoat, brought in to play a very limited but impactful role.

When I glance from Audrey to Gillian, the latter is giving her a death stare to end all death stares. It is the nuclear holocaust of death stares. It would render a Russian city useless for centuries, and I don't quite understand it.

But Audrey appears to be off on her own tangent, massaging a different wound.

"Madeline has always been like a bookie," Audrey continues, "keeping a secret little notebook—figuratively speaking—of all the wrongs she's perpetrated to give herself power in this town. And now —now—it's finally all coming down. I, for one, welcome a change. In fact, you know what would put the final nail in Madeline St. Clair's coffin?"

"Audrey," Gillian says. "Don't."

"If you went on TV and just told the truth. Just clear your name. None of us will come out looking good, but you will definitely be able to change the narrative about that night. About all of it."

"I don't think—"

"I'm serious, Mary Ellen," she says, ignoring Gillian. We've even been contacted by the networks to do sit-down interviews to put the whole thing to rest, but they only seem to want to do it under the condition that you be there, too. You're the John Lennon of this whole scenario. We don't matter. You do. Nobody wants to see Ringo hop onstage and play the old hits, and that's coming from me, the media whore of the group."

She smiles sardonically, a sharp edge of hurt in her voice. Her eyes move to Gillian, who sits stone-faced amidst her sudden pronouncement.

"I mean, it's not like it would hurt us," Audrey continues, finishing up her argument. "We've already been made out to be monsters. We could finally put this to rest. Just get it all behind us, don't you think?"

"I don't know," I respond. The truth is, I don't *want* to talk about it. I feel as though the more it's out in the world, the more power it has.

"Well, you should think about it," Audrey replies, "because we'd all like to speak our truth before somebody else gets to do it for us. You know, when we're dead."

And then, just as she had wandered into our conversation, she curtsies and turns back the way she came, waving to a few key members of some entourage in the corner.

"She's more like Madeline St. Clair than she will ever know," Gillian says, shaking her head as she watches Audrey disappear into the crowd.

5

THEN

They are at a house party when they first see Everett Coughlin.

"How about him?"

Madeline sits in one of the overstuffed chairs in the living room, her legs cocked over the arm as she glares at a particular someone in the room. Her skirt almost—but not quite—reveals what she calls her "goodies" as she bounces her legs up and down. An interested party—and there are several here tonight—could probably get a compelling glance, were he so inclined.

But Madeline is not trolling for men at this sad excuse for a party. She's interested in something else entirely, the result of a game they've been playing, one which has grown increasingly bold—and one might say, sadistic—as the year has worn on. They've become bored with starting rumors and blackmailing classmates. The stakes must be upped to account for their burgeoning bloodlust.

The person in question, a guy in glasses and a cardigan, looks like the lead singer of Weezer, only slightly more socially awkward than his MTV counterpart. He's smirking to himself, but it's all a show. He stands stoop-shouldered in the corner of the living room, a red Solo cup pressed to his chest like a priceless amulet or personal totem.

He doesn't have anybody.

He *isn't* anybody.

He is what they want him to be.

And they want him to be a victim.

"Oh, he's *perfect*," Audrey says, glancing first at the guy and then back at Madeline for approval. Her eyes betray a sense of enthusiasm. Only Madeline, the ring leader, is able to maintain her dispassion. She has the languid, insouciant manner of a bored monarch, able to order a parade or an execution with the same characteristic detachment.

Gillian nods in agreement, though less emphatically. Only Mary Ellen falters at the suggestion. She tucks her fabulous dirty blonde hair behind one ear and tries to find something to hate about this kid.

But she can't.

He looks totally harmless, the very definition of a dweeb.

It's obvious he's come to the party with someone else, or else he heard about it and is crashing it because he thinks he'll make him some friends.

He's no mark, though. It would be punching down to take him on as a project.

And maybe that's why she—she, being Madeline—wants to wreck him. Because his only fault is his weakness.

However, Mary Ellen can't see herself ruining his life.

And at this moment, he sees her. He's scanning the room, looking for any excuse not to seem completely and utterly alone, when his eyes meet hers.

He smiles. He thinks she's into him. Or that she *could* be into him.

Madeline nudges her from her place in the seat. "Looks like somebody's got a crush," she says.

This is how it begins.

NOW

LATER, the sound of fist on door knocks me from a troubled sleep. At first, I think it's coming from inside my own head, or is the result of a dream folding over onto reality. There's an accompanying wail that sends my hand reaching for the pint-sized aluminum bat under the bed. The owners included it—*gratis*—just in case something happened at the house.

My mother used to tell me about haints walking the perimeter of graveyards at midnight, with their blood-curdling screams, and for a moment, this is what I imagine.

As the cobwebs get washed away and then bathed in darkness—the darkness of the room, of reality—I put everything into perspective. There's a woman raising hell outside, and it very well could be the owner's ex-girlfriend or something. So, even though I carry the bat in one hand, I no longer fear for my life. That said, it doesn't prevent me from doing a crook-kneed waddle toward the sound.

Finally, I reach the door. I do the thing where I kind of press myself against the wall so the person on the other side can't see me.

I get spotted almost immediately.

The face in the window is stark and wide-eyed, but I recognize the person under the fright wig and makeup at first glance.

It's Madeline St. Clair.

Or whatever she has become.

When I unlatch the front door, she barges in as if on roller skates, the vodka creating a heavy wake behind her.

"How did you—"

"Just pour me a drink, old friend," she says, veering heavily for the couch in the living room. She moves like someone who's just done a series of spins in the front yard and needs a place to sit down, hard.

Luckily, there's plenty of furniture to catch her fall.

She dumps herself shoulder-first onto the sofa as I mix her a vodka-soda from the ingredients in the kitchen. I hadn't planned on using the owners' stuff, but I suppose this is a dire situation.

I return with the drink and look her over.

If I'm being honest, right now she is Cruella De Vil with a Nordstrom's charge card. Her hair is pointed in several directions, her face twisted into a drunken leer. She doesn't look real. She looks like a method actor in a really challenging role.

But then she glances up at me, unabashed. She's Madeline St. Clair, for fuck's sake, and she doesn't have to be embarrassed by anything she does.

"I heard you were back in town," she slurs. "How the hell are you?"

I'm zen as fuck right now. I'm Buddha after a bong rip. I'm a bag full of Xanax. Since I'd already seized my anxiety by the throat with Gillian and Audrey earlier tonight, I feel fine.

"Well on the way to a hangover," I tell her, and she smiles.

She closes her eyes and lays one forearm over her head dramatically. Same old Madeline. "You and me both. But I meant, you know, in general. How are you doing, *in general*?"

The words come out in a listless drawl, her mouth working around the syllables. She's sloshed beyond sloshed. This is an entirely new version of her, way different from the artfully buzzed high school rebel with a penchant for letting randos slip their hands up her shirt at parties.

Ignoring her baiting question—she's already looking for some kind of leverage against me—I say, "I saw Gillian and Audrey tonight."

The lower half of her face, the part not covered by her arm, twists into a half-frown. The botox prevents any real expression. She says, "Don't listen to a word either of those bitches has to say. They'd just as soon slit your throat as talk to you, and I haven't heard a good word from them in *years*."

"They seemed to say the same thing about you."

"Exactly what I'd expect the traitors to say. You go and get one DUI, and look where your friends go. *Poof!* Up in smoke. Good riddance, I guess. Shit."

"They seemed concerned about you," I say.

It's a lie, but it's a start.

"Oh, the hell with them," she says. "They were never the interesting ones, and we both know it. Girl, you and *I* made all the headlines, and they were the background ornaments."

She manages to pry her arm from her face and sit up. She's flush and slack-eyed, on the verge of passing out.

"You want me to call you an Uber?"

She gulps at the vodka soda and then replaces the glass on an out-of-date magazine.

"Fuck no. The night is just getting started. How long's it been since I seen you?"

"Long time," I reply.

But I know the truth. It's been twenty years, almost exactly. I can still see her sitting in that formal way with her parents, putting up the angelic child front, pretending she's been pulled astray by the poor girl from the other side of Nashville. She probably doesn't remember it, but I'll never forget.

"Still, maybe it's a good time to call it a night," I reply. "I don't know if you've heard, but my mom is sick and—"

"Aw, fuck that. Let's have a drink. You can forget all about that depressing shit. I've *missed* you. I really, truly have."

She doesn't mean it—insincerity is as much a part of her DNA as blonde hair and stock options—but the compliment sends my heart to fluttering. She really knows how to work a room, and I find myself teetering between anger and admiration.

And even though she looks like hell, I can't quite take my eyes off her. She's manic and fidgety, knocking over everything she touches, but still in possession of the kind of magical aura people are born with but cannot craft. It's what separates her from common folks.

"My life is pretty unremarkable," I say, "but I've heard you are going through quite an exciting time."

Her head is listing forward. "I'd say. Fucking DUI. My husband is a lying, cheating scumbag. And I've got more money problems than Paul Manafort. It's like a triumvirate of fuck-ups."

My head is cracking open, and I just don't have time for the games. "Did you come here to complain about your life, because we can—"

She looks up at me, almost confused. Her eyes are pleading. "I can trust you, right?"

"You did once," I say. "You can do it again, I guess. What's the worst that could happen?"

"You could ruin your life and spend the rest trying to make up for it, only to fuck it up much worse."

"It's not that bad."

"Things are bad all over," she murmurs, her voice a mushy exaggeration of the one I remember from high school. "I've got reason to be fucked-up and depressed, you know?"

Sitting next to her, her beauty slips through the sadness, like smoke under a door jamb. Her face is drawn and tight, and not from the botox. I'm convinced she couldn't smile if she tried.

"I don't remember you like this," I say, and even though it feels preposterous, I place one hand on her upper back and rub. Wax on. Wax off.

She doesn't seem to notice at first, but then she places her head on my shoulder.

"I miss you," she says, hiccuping. "You weren't a bad friend, you know?"

Even though this whole experience is surreal, I try to find the authenticity in it, the reality. The words that come out of my mouth do not feel like my own.

"What happened was bad," I say. "I don't think I ever recovered from it."

She places her clasped hands between her knees. She's shivering, even though she doesn't feel the least bit cold. "Yeah, me either. It was such an awful thing, wasn't it?"

I bite my lip. So far as I know, Madeline has never, not once, admitted responsibility for a single mistake in her life. The urge to tell her exactly that and get it over with, get it out so I can move on with my life, is so strong it makes my stomach burn, but then time gets away from me and I can't find the words to say.

Her hair is redolent of vodka and cigarettes, but she still feels soft and clean, the way babies are preternaturally soft. Underneath the facade of adulthood, I can still smell *her*. A flash of junior year, all four of us piled into Gillian's bed, drunk on 99 Bananas and giggling over a pop song about Barbie dolls.

My pulse quickens.

She clasps my hand with her own, her thin fingers intertwined with mine, and the old emotional scab is torn away. The blood flows freely from a place deep within, and my whole body tingles with the force of it.

I wonder if there is some new and underhanded way she can twist the knife in me, but there is something new about this experience. This person next to me, untouchable for so long, is now mortal. The Golden God has been ripped from her throne and dragged through the streets with her nakedness on display.

But there are places in my mind where the past is still a fresh wound.

She spread a rumor about Gary Pinkerton, a jar of peanut butter, and his yellow lab, on the off-chance that he had intentionally ignored her for the spring fling. She told everyone at school about the herpes Lacey Portnoy ended up *not* having. Lacey had to drop out of DDA after that, and eventually her parents sent her away to boarding school to quell the rumors about their daughter's voracious and risky sexual appetites.

And the low point: she was the first one of us to casually mention to Everett Coughlin, "Maybe you would be happier if you just killed yourself."

My mind picks up a series of memories, flashes of memories, like the claw vending machines that pick up cheap stuffed toys: fingers on a keyboard. The neon palette of a late-90s chat room. The feathered, crinkly texture of the ceiling above Gillian's bed. The words *suicide* and *better off dead*.

Even the *thought* of those typed statements makes the blood rush to my face, the sweat pop on my skin like morning dew, and I, the scapegoat, can't imagine what Madeline St. Clair must feel.

And right now, she feels sorry for *herself*.

"I never forgave you for leaving," she says into my shoulder, her voice thick from the tears. "I just feel like it was the ultimate betrayal, you turning your back."

"You didn't say a word to me once I was arrested."

"That was all a public show. Because of the lawyers. It had to look like we were no longer friends. You know that was the game."

As if that is a completely understandable statement.

Is to her, I guess.

I pull away from her and seat myself in an adjacent chair. "It wasn't a *game*, Mads. It was my *life*, and I paid a price. A *real* price for what we did. And it changed me."

"That's not what I meant," she says.

"What do you mean?"

She grimaces like she's trying to hold something in. Or hold something down. "I expected us to go back to normal once you came back. But you never came back."

"So *I* violated our bond. That what you're saying?"

The way she nods makes it clear she doesn't see anything wrong with that belief. How *could* anything be the Mad Queen's fault?

She's not looking at me when she speaks next. "You said we were forever. We were *all* forever. And now we're not. Now, we're nothing."

Leaning forward from her perch on the seat, she seems to peer at the spot on the carpet between her feet, and two tears, like solitary raindrops, create the tiniest *thud*.

"I'm sorry," she says, at last. It comes out hurried and high and choked, but she gets it across, and part of me relaxes. "I'm sorry I fucked everything up. It will never make up for lost time, and it will never change the fact I was such a raging bitch, but I'm sorry. I'm sorry, and I'm learning. My life is in ruins, and I need someone to talk to."

She's crying now. This is not a few tears. This is not someone being "emotional." She's breaking down, and I can't say it doesn't give me a slight thrill to see her cry. If she only knew how many tears I'd shed over my role in Everett Coughlin's death.

I need to keep a healthy distance. She's the scorpion and I'm the frog, so to speak.

"Please," she says, pleading. "Please don't turn your back on me. I'm begging. Please."

"I won't," I say. Anything to get her to stop drunkenly sobbing.

"I don't know how to be a nobody," she says. "People have turned on me, and I feel completely anonymous. It feels like I'm *dying*. How do you handle it?"

"It's just who I am," I say. "I prefer it to the alternative."

"I don't have anybody else right now, M.E. Don't abandon me, too. Please. Please. Just be my friend. Or at least pretend. I just need someone to acknowledge I'm here, or I'm afraid I'll disappear."

"Okay," I reply, more out of a fear of what she might say next than an actual acceptance of her offer. "Fine. We're friends. I'm your friend, Mads."

We sit there—completely silent—for what feels like an eternity but is probably more like a few minutes. The whole time, there is this inexplicable hum in the room, and it doesn't seem to come from anywhere, but I just know it is the unspoken thing between us that buzzes around our heads like old mosquitoes.

"M.E?"

"Yes?"

Then there is another long pause.

"What is it, Madeline?" I ask, at last.

"Nothing. Never mind."

"You can't do that. You have to tell me."

We are still sitting there, bunched up on the couch, and the hum I seem to hear slowly builds to a crescendo, but like most things in life, this secret energy goes nowhere, and soon it goes out completely.

"Maybe I will," she says. "But not yet."

"Then why—"

"Can I go to the bathroom real quick before I jet? I know I look a mess."

"Sure."

SOMETIMES I WONDER what it would be like to leap off a tall building, not for the death-and-dying, suicide-y aspect of it, but because it would be exhilarating to experience that first moment. The air whooshing past you. The sight of the ground coming up to meet you. The knowledge that, in a few moments, the whole world will be black and unknowable.

This is how being friends with Madeline St. Clair makes you feel.

6

THEN

> **Y**ou should just kill yourself.

Madeline floats the idea like somebody trying to convince a friend to change their hair color. *You should go brunette. You should try out for cheerleading. You should ask Dave to the winter formal.*

Except it's *you should end your own life.*

There is a long and nerve-wracking pause on the other end of the internet. Madeline, Audrey, Gillian, and Mary Ellen stare in a kind of desperate interest at the blinking cursor in the *Café Chat* where they've been meeting Everett Coughlin for weeks.

Mary Ellen is in the middle of all this, but she is uncomfortable. Her teeth feel too big in her mouth from all the fake smiling. Like she's wearing a pair of those Halloween fright teeth, the ones that make you look like an old hillbilly.

It's not just her mouth. Her whole *body* feels out of whack, like she's a Frankenstein's monster of complete and utter teenage awkwardness.

She thought this would be fun. She knew there would be some meanness, but ever since joining the group, her enthusiasm has flagged. At first, she enjoyed being angry for no good reason, to feel looked up to and envied, but that sensation quickly passed, if it ever even existed in the first place.

Now, it has been replaced by a tense, muscle-tensing anxiety. Anxiety about what will happen next, what plan they will drum up to entertain themselves.

She still enjoys the benefits of it all, but the dangers outweigh any fun she's had over the last few months.

Ironically, she spends a great deal of her time wondering how her old friends are doing. She fantasizes about watching MTV and eating popcorn while playing disgusting games of *Would You Rather*.

She thought she would enjoy the danger of being with these girls. They are known around the school as the defiant, rebellious members of DDA, the ones always out drinking and smoking. Cheating on tests and hooking up with boys.

Only, none of them seems to enjoy it.

For example, when they drink—and they *do* drink, a lot—they go about it with zeal and purpose, but no fun. There is no risk. There is no challenge. Audrey's mother doesn't really care at all what Audrey does, so long as she doesn't get pregnant or embarrass the family. In fact, they can drink in front of her parents, so long as they don't make it seem like they're getting hammered. It's the antithesis of what Mary Ellen always thought it would mean to drink while underage.

Same with smoking (or smoking weed). They do it as if it's some status symbol, like, *I bet the squares at our school wouldn't do* this! But they don't get baked and talk about the universe, or giggle helplessly at cartoons on TV. They just kind of sit around and talk blandly about how much the other kids at school fucking hate them.

If there is one thing Mary Ellen's learned from being in the cool group—she had begun to wonder if that was even true—then it is that Madeline and the others spend a whole hell of a lot more time wondering what other people think of them than considering what they actually want to do.

It's the working paradox of their whole existence. *What thing can we do to completely piss off everyone in the world?*

No, only the pursuit of evil seems to inflame them, and they take no joy in that, either. As they torment Everett Coughlin, they take on these...nasty faces. They look like cult members waiting for their turn with the Kool-Aid. Audrey has gone full Manson Girl, and Gillian isn't far behind. Only Madeline seems sane, by comparison, but then again she's the one hurtling toward this infinitely depressing future, pulling them all along with her.

Mary Ellen desperately wants to exit the program, but she is in this as much as the rest of them, and so she feels significant pressure to see it through to the end.

Her stomach hurts. It constantly hurts. She thinks she has an ulcer or stomach cancer or IBS or something, and there are times she hopes it kills her, just like the heart attack that killed her father. It would put an end to her fear, her terror that they might at any moment go too far.

But since it's just happened—suggesting suicide to someone counts as going too far—she supposes she should feel somewhat relieved.

It cannot get any worse, can it?

Only, the miserable irony of the whole thing is, she's never been more popular.

Boys from their brother school ask her out all the time. Not that she can go out with them. Madeline's obsession with destroying Everett Coughlin's life takes precedence over everything, even Mary Ellen's own personal life.

All their lives. They've had to forgo their own lives for the sake of *Herr St. Clair*, and it does not do anything but make them miserable.

And she's had enough of it.

There is a fear, of course. She is afraid of what Madeline would do if she abandoned ship just before the Mockingbird Ball, *the* most exclusive social event in all of Nashville.

But there is a part of her—the part that always got somewhat teary during the ABC After School Specials—that tells her she should defy her overlord just to see what would happen.

Finally, Mary Ellen stands up. "I can't be part of this," she says, her voice quivering. "It's one thing to do, I don't know, whatever we were doing. But this is a step too far, and I think—"

"Sit the fuck down," Madeline says.

She is staring. Her eyes—full of black hatred—stop Mary Ellen's words in her throat.

There is a moment in which Mary Ellen thinks she will do the right thing, the thing that is just out of reach. She envisions herself yanking the computer cables from the wall, unplugging everything and tossing the monitor out the window.

But she doesn't.

She does the thing she always knew she would do.

She sits back down, folding her hands over one another as she tries to avoid her friends' pitying glances. Gillian and Audrey are in full-on Heaven's Gate mode, and they watch this exchange like apes hoping to avoid a challenge from the Alpha.

When the awkwardness seems to have evaporated somewhat, Madeline smirks as if nothing happens and then continues barreling toward the inevitable conclusion of all this.

"Let's begin the end game," Madeline says, rolling her eyes and sighing. "I'm getting bored with this...project."

Everett Coughlin is a dog too loyal to know he should turn tail and split, and, like a cruel master, Madeline St. Clair is going to punish him for his devotion.

The way she punishes *all* of them.

Eventually, the tinny speaker attached to Gillian's computer *dings*, officially breaking the tension in the room. Madeline's gaze softens, and her attention returns to the screen.

Everett's response is terse and clear.

> That's not funny.

"Oh, yes it is," Audrey replies, giggling, glancing at Madeline for approval. She smiles and nods, ready for the next phase.

> I think I better go.

Yes! Mary Ellen thinks. Turn off your goddamned computer and run as far away from there as humanly possible. Even if she herself is too weak to turn her back, perhaps he can. All he has to do is exit the conversation and never return.

She leans over Mary Ellen's shoulder and takes over typing duties, not just because it signifies her role as the leader, but it places her in direct contact with Mary Ellen, who just has to sit there and take it.

> I'm really concerned about you.

This is how Madeline responds. This is how she leads him along. Afterward, she steps away, staring at the computer screen, a painter admiring the last few strokes of a masterpiece. Then, she stands up and tells Gillian to compose her messages for her. When she speaks, Gil types.

Gillian always seems so logical, but she is as under the spell as Audrey.

She would stab a pregnant actress.

She would carve a swastika into her forehead.

She would step out of a crowd and fire at the president.

Gillian's fingers move on the keys, and the words appear on-screen.

> You have been really unhappy, haven't you?

They wait. There is only the waiting, because they are all too afraid to speak without Madeline's approval.

A series of messages appear in quick succession.

> Yes.

> I don't know why I feel this way, but I do.

> The thing you said,

> Sometimes I think about it.

> Like, seriously think about it.

"Oh, we know you think about it," Audrey says from behind them. She sounds like a malfunctioning bird. A cockatoo with Tourette's.

Madeline directs Gillian to type.

> If only your dad really cared to get to know you, maybe it wouldn't be this way.

A long pause. Mary Ellen feigns disinterest, but her eyes remain glued to the screen. She may not like the direction of this conversation, but she has to see where it goes.

> It's all just your garden variety, private school white boy stuff. He works too much. He ignores me. He believes I'm weak and won't let me see a therapist. He thinks depression is a choice.

> Sometimes there's only one way to break through the noise.

> I can't talk to him about it anymore.

> Then fuck talking. SHOW him.

> How?

It is abundantly clear to Mary Ellen at this moment that he is fishing. Everett Coughlin is looking for an out. He doesn't want it to end this way.

But it will.

And though she hesitates for just a moment, eventually Madeline gets down to it.

> You know how. We've discussed it.

> I'm not doing that. No way. I'm not. It's just. I'm not.

> Suit yourself. If you want to be miserable forever...

> I don't. I DON'T! But I don't know if I can do that. It's like they say: a permanent solution to a temporary problem.

> But you've said yourself in the past: your father never learns. He never WILL learn. He only knows control. Only knows how to keep people in line. He demands LOYALTY.

> Right. But is...that...the solution?

> This is coming from a person who cares for you THE MOST. Why continue to suffer, if the people who SAY they love you do not intervene?

> Maybe. I mean, I have...everything I need in the garage.

And then Madeline plays her trump card.

> Ev, I think I love you.

Three of the four wait in exultant, delirious silence. Only Mary Ellen seems unhappy to be there, and she must hide her discontent if she doesn't want to end up on the other end of one of Madeline St. Clair's pernicious attacks.

> I've been waiting for you to say that. I love you, too.

They scream banshee wails of approval, like the climax of some furious dance.

> Then you know what you have to do. It's time.

The wait this time is breathless and extended. No one looks around or makes a sound. It is as though they've just read aloud an incantation and need to see if it's worked.

> I trust you. If you think I should...

> I do. I really do. I really really do.

> Ok

Just like that, it is done.

7

NOW

Bobbi Jo's Barbecue and Chicken Shack is precisely what it sounds like, only it's not dirty and dingy and full of shadows. It's meant to look like a hole-in-the-wall, but the truth is, Audrey—as the financial backer—has pumped hundreds of thousands of dollars into the establishment to make it *seem* cheap.

Still, there's local beer on tap, and the chicken smells divine.

I get the tenders—medium—and park behind my sunglasses to keep the sunlight out.

The hangover hurts worse than the time we mixed vodka with white grape juice after seeing *There's Something About Mary* at the Green Hills Mall. I can feel the little men chiseling away at my sinus cavities, and even though the beer is good, it can't keep the tired, drained, absolutely undead feeling from creeping up and dragging me down into the depths.

Audrey has invited me out to apologize for the night before. It's her way of mending fences, but part of it is, she just wants me to see how successful she is.

Whatever. I'm beyond caring. I just need something in my stomach.

As we wait for the food, I try to make small talk, but it's like starting a fire with wet wood so eventually, I just go for the real thing.

"Madeline came to see me last night," I say.

"And how *is* the Bitch of Belle Meade doing these days?"

It's like code for them. See, Audrey, she wants me to know that she doesn't want to talk about Madeline. But what she doesn't realize is that I don't *have* to play by their rules anymore. As much as they'd like to paint me as the girl from high school who played the role of John Proctor, dying for my principles, it's not like that.

"She was drunk and crying, like someone had just broken her heart."

And, just like that, I can play both sides.

Audrey smiles, in part because she knows there's blood in the water, and though I should feel guilty about it—Madeline is in a vulnerable place—I don't feel anything. Nothing at all. My whole life has been chasing down or running away from feelings.

Right now, I am living novocaine.

Audrey's eyes light up, and suddenly there is life to the conversation. Madeline St. Clair's downfall has always been an interesting point of contention in our friend group. We all knew she would be a superstar, even back in high school, so a secret game we played had to do with guessing when she would flame out.

Nobody expected her to live this long.

But it's like marine biologists say: *Sharks don't evolve because they don't have to.*

So I just keep talking. I reveal every detail, and when I'm done, Audrey's chin is almost touching the straw of her Diet Coke.

"She did that? She cried? Like, on your shoulder and everything?"

My beer is starting to reach room temp, so I gulp the rest and replace the pint glass on the table between us.

"It seemed like she had something she wanted to say. Like she had something she meant to get off her chest."

"To apologize, maybe?"

"She did that," I say. "A big, wet, blubbering apology. So it had to be something else."

"Any ideas?"

"I don't know. I've been thinking about it all morning. Madeline is not one to unburden her soul."

"She'd need one first."

"Harsh," I reply. "But fair. If history's any indicator—"

"She's straight up playing you."

"Could be."

"Don't let her fool you, M.E.," she says. "She hasn't changed, M.E. Trust me. She's the same old mean bitch she was in high school."

Audrey raises a hand to the barkeep, and he brings over a second beer for me.

I take a sip and then lean back in my chair. "Maybe so," I say. "I just don't think so. I think maybe whatever she's going through, it's leaving a mark on her."

With a flick of the wrist, Audrey dismisses the whole thing. "Bullshit," she says. "The woman wouldn't know humility if it turned her around and fucked her from behind."

"Christ, Audrey."

She smirks. "She's just angry she met her match."

"Colton Ambrose is the real deal," she says. "Whatever Mads thought she was—the Queen of Nashville—Colton actually is. His family basically owned Nashville before the Civil War. Some of the stuff that's named after the Brileys and whatnot—yeah, that actually used to be named after the Ambroses."

The food arrives, and I'm forced to contemplate this new information as each of us arranges and organizes our plate.

I vaguely remember this guy, Colton. He went to school out-of-state, so we only heard about him second-hand. He was friends with Jefferson Bisby and Lyle Renault, and they told us a crazy story about Colton slamming his dad's Porsche into the side of a White Castle wherever he went to school. One kid died, we heard, and Colton had to go to rehab. He was into Oxy before it was mainstream around the trust fund division of Nashville.

The other strange thing about him—this I found out through Google-stalking him when they first got married—is that he'd also been friends with Everett Coughlin.

How small the world grows when you are from Nashville.

"You know, she never truly wanted to accomplish anything on her own," Audrey drones on, after sipping from her Diet Coke. "She just wanted an M-R-S degree so she could stay home and spend her rich hubby's money."

She wraps her mouth around an awkward bite of potato salad, and I think about that. Madeline never seemed to care about *things*. She only ever gave a shit about *people*, and it was mostly out of a desire to destroy them.

"I mean," Audrey continues, as she tangles with another bite of her side item, "I went to college for business, and then I came back— yes, to make money—but also to give *back* to the community. This is my *home*, and I don't intend to just feed on the city."

She plucks at another hunk of potato.

"But Madeline," she continues, "she has done nothing but *use* Nashville."

"Like what?"

"Huh?"

"What has she *done*? Be specific."

"Colton sleeps around, or so I've been told. But at least he has the decency to do it when he goes out of town on business. She fucks people he *knows*, her friends' husbands. She's subhuman. I wouldn't wish her on my worst enemies."

Madeline never had friends. She had acquaintances.

We were her only friends, and Audrey knows that.

"Anyway," she continues, "I hear Colton's hired a private investigator to keep tabs on her."

"Oh." It's my turn to be obtuse. I don't know what to say, and I can tell by the way Audrey is staring at me from behind her sunglasses she knows something's up.

Still, she goes back to her plate, dipping fries into a glob of ketchup. "He's got millions upon millions of dollars," she says. "If she can successfully prove there is a repeated pattern of infidelity, he can royally fuck her in the divorce, which I hear is more painful than that *other* place men like to get women."

"You don't think Madeline would allow such a thing to happen, do you?" I ask.

Imagining her pulling some kind of Hitchcockian switcheroo to peg Colton. Maybe she has recordings of him. Maybe she paid someone to sleep with him. It isn't beneath her, and it isn't that far-fetched, honestly. Big plans are for big people, and Madeline is the biggest around.

I have dirt on her. Everyone she knows has dirt on her, but nothing seems to stick. She gave a handy to Blaine DeSotel in the theater at Hundred Oaks. She convinced Ryan Adwell to cut Sissy Weaver's hair after prom. She mailed nude photos of Lynne Stockton to that poor girl's parents while they were on vacation in Tahiti.

The original revenge porn.

And one rainy night in the spring of our junior year, she first typed the sentence, *Maybe you should just kill yourself, then.*

"Don't know," Audrey replies, after a long pause. Perhaps she is also thinking of all the wrongs people have suffered under the tyrannical rule of Madeline St. Clair.

"This time, though, I think it's different."

You can see it in Audrey's eyes, the desire to see Madeline publicly humiliated. It's just too close for her to say it aloud, as if speaking the words might somehow rig it against her.

The sad thing is, Audrey doesn't know who *she* is, which is why Madeline was always the alpha, and Audrey was just her lap dog. Mads always rode Audrey hard, treating her like an animal to be trained. Even though Audrey conveyed a sense that she was Type-A, she always ended up groveling the hardest at Madeline's feet.

She is successful now, but she is weak, and the more I stare at her, the more obvious and definitive her weakness becomes.

"So," Audrey says, at last, "enough gossip. What about you?"

I roll the napkin splayed across my lap into a tight scroll and tug at each end.

I realize I don't have anything in common with the woman across from me.

I did once. We used to drink beer and smoke cigarettes in Sevier Park, back when we felt like danger couldn't touch us. We shot pistols with some skeevy-looking guys in East Nashville. We skipped school to go see movies, and we got into cars with boys we had just met.

And now, we are complete strangers.

"Your mother, is she doing all right? I know that's why you came home, but..."

She trails off. Doesn't quite know how to ask.

"She's not dying," I say matter-of-factly, even if that's not the truth. "She fell. She's going to get better. She just can't take care of herself anymore."

"Oh," she responds. She pokes at the last of her fries. I'm pretty sure it's dead, but she keeps forking it.

Once the food is done, so is the conversation. It seems to dry up, and even Audrey can't quite put lipstick on this pig.

But then something happens.

She gets around to the thing she really wants to ask. "Mary Ellen, have you...been receiving weird messages?"

I peer at her from behind my shades. "What do you mean?"

"Like, text messages. Ever since the *TV* special, someone's been harassing me. It's not like in the past, when people annoyed me. This feels...more sinister."

There's this one thing stuck in my brain like a rock in the sole of an old pair of Adidas, but I can't bring myself to speak it aloud. My eyes never quite leave her face, even as I risk silence.

Is this a test?

"I...don't think so," I reply.

It's not true—I'm always receiving messages—but I need to hedge, just to see what she has to say about it.

It feels good to be in control.

"I mean, they're not credible, I guess. Someone just straight-up threatening to murder me out of nowhere, but I suppose that's what you get when you have a stalker."

I can't help but laugh. "You don't have a stalker," I say.

Audrey was always a little dramatic.

Silly girl.

Then, she's up and grasping her fry basket with one manicured hand. There is no eye contact, and her glasses seem darker than before as she flicks the whole plastic container into the trash and saunters out into the heat of the midday sun, trailing all that refinement with her.

I catch up to her by the treeline behind the chicken joint, where she's actively looking for her keys in her oversized purse.

The strong me is momentarily replaced by the girl I was back in high school, the one who would have done anything for *their* approval. Even Audrey, whom we all derided in private.

I can almost feel the chicken coming back up as I let my emotions take hold.

Audrey looks around conspicuously and pulls a half-used pack of Parliaments from her purse, offering me one in the process. At first, I demur, but then I acquiesce and we're both smoking in silence when I let her in on one of my secrets.

"I had a legit stalker," I say, staring into the trees as if looking for something or someone to appear there. A bird coos and then takes flight, and I watch it disappear. "He got...aggressive, and I ended up calling the cops. It got ugly."

"Oh," she replies.

"But I didn't mean to laugh."

"Is that an apology?" she asks.

"It's the best I can do."

"Well—I guess I can accept that, for now."

"The real question is," I say, changing the subject, "is, who has been contacting *you*?"

"It's a random number," she says, beginning to dig in her purse. "I haven't blocked it because I didn't want to—"

"Wait a second," I reply. "You still have the messages?"

"Well, *yeah*."

She retrieves her device and hands it over.

You can't describe someone's phone as a rat's nest, but Audrey's is as close as one can get. It's a collection of broken text threads and mass messages with people whose numbers she doesn't know, or barely knows. She cares about the breadth of her influence but not the depth. Most people are entered into her contacts by first and last name and also by company name.

Once she actually finds the messages—a process she undertakes by pointing over my shoulder at the phone—she says, in a quavering voice, "That's them."

One need only take a cursory glance at the messages to see that they were penned—or thumbed—by a maniac. Punctuation and spelling worse than the president's, and there is a random quality to the capitalization that gives me pause.

There's also the lack of violent threats in the messages that always seemed to accompany to ones I received. Whereas this person says something like You better watch You're (sic) step Bitch, mine would say something like, When I find you, I'll gut you like a fish. Leave your stomach lying next to you, like a designer handbag.

That sort of thing.

It sounds like somebody might be trying to intimidate Audrey, but that could be anything. To hear her talk, she's a titan of the business world, so there's a possibility someone is trying to keep her from investing in this business or raise money for that one.

Still, by the time I'm done reading the threats, my hands are shaking. I try not to let Audrey see, but they are practically thrumming, like hummingbird wings.

"It's, um, it's not him," I say through a voice that barely sounds like my own. "It's not the guy I knew."

"How do you know?"

"I know," I reply.

Because my stalker was literate, I guess.

"But what do you think?"

"It looks like a freak, but I can't say anything beyond that. Are you taking precautions?"

"What, like checking under my bed, shit like that?"

"I'm serious," I say, thinking of the perpetual sense of doom I felt about my own situation. "Something bad can happen, and I—"

"Oh, I know," she replies. "I live in a good neighborhood—"

—As if that matters—

"—And besides, if he decides to track me down, then I can have my own #MeToo moment, am I right? Not that we didn't all have to, you know, *endure* back in the day. Do you remember Flynn Sutter?"

I can feel the bile rise to the back of my throat, and not just because of Audrey's ambivalence toward sexual assault. Flynn Sutter was the very definition of a *difficult man*. We all had run-ins with him at parties in high school, and some of us didn't make it to the other side. He was a wolf in the path on the way to grandma's house, and you didn't dare take a drink from him or wander off to pass out in someone's bed at a house party. He preyed willingly on the girls who ran in our circles, and even three serious and credible accusations against him in college did not prevent him from marrying into an absolutely, deliciously wealthy family and getting a job shorting bonds or some other financial nonsense.

"Of course I do," I manage to choke, my own memories of him intruding on the moment.

His hand sliding up my shirt. The drink he kept pushing on me. The soreness the next day, causing me to walk bowlegged back to Madeline's car.

Her smirk as she picked me up.

"Anyway, maybe the stalker is someone we tormented back in high school," she says.

"Maybe."

I don't want to consider such an idea.

"Still," I say, "you should call the cops. This isn't something to play around with."

Although, of course, I can clearly see her eyes, and so I know she won't call the cops. There is another way she is like the old Audrey.

She *likes* this.

"I'm serious," I tell her when she doesn't really respond. She's got that look.

"I know, I know."

But she doesn't. So I roll my eyes and turn to go.

The heat from the sun bakes the back of my head as I walk without really feeling it toward my rental. There's a scratch just above the door handle, where someone—

"Oh, and Mary Ellen?"

I spin to see a shadow of the person who has become "Audrey."

"Don't tell *her* about the things I said today. I don't think she'd understand."

I give her a jubilant thumbs up and then shrink away to my car, where I feel somewhat dirtier than when I'd arrived, and not just because of the decadent local chicken.

8

My stalker had a name.

Still does, so far as I know, but to my knowledge, he is locked away in a deep, dark cell somewhere in the wilds of Washington.

Timothy Allred.

There was nothing sexy or mysterious about the whole experience, no matter what Audrey chooses to believe about the cheap thrillers they air on LifeTime. The whole episode was terrifying and violating.

I still wake up some nights, covered in sweat.

It began innocently enough, with him pretending to be a blogger in need of a good yarn for a series he was doing on modern miscarriages of justice.

My case, he said, happened to fit the bill, and I suppose he caught me in a vulnerable state, because I dove right in, sending him reams and reams of information about the case.

It progressed—email by email—to the point that he and I shared some personal things about ourselves. He, too, was going through a hard time, or so he said. His girlfriend had recently dumped him for a drummer in some heavy metal band, and besides, he was interested in me outside of our current...circumstances.

It should have been a red flag—*actually, it was* a red flag—but then again my entire concept of what was a normal, healthy relationship was so warped I expected a little weirdness.

But it went beyond even *my* concept of the bizarre very quickly.

He'd send these midnight emails with questions ranging from the mundane—*what is a bigger regret, befriending Madeline St. Clair or not calling the police that night*—to the downright sinister—*have you ever fantasized about being on top of Everett Coughlin's corpse?*

By the time I realized I was in something very bad and very dangerous, it had escalated beyond my control, and so I thought I would just try to land the plane before it crashed.

I was unsuccessful at that.

At a certain point, Timothy...changed. He'd always been a little strange, but he went from idiosyncratic to scary within a few weeks' time. He knew where I was, what I'd had for dinner, and what time I got home.

It should have been easy to file a report, but this was before #MeToo, and besides, I was basically *persona non grata* with anyone in an official position. I always felt more pressure to stay quiet, in part because of who I was, but I also knew the moment I made a claim, my texts and emails would be seized, and the resulting narrative would turn me into a different kind of monster.

The irony, for most people, would be too delicious to ignore.

Suicide Blonde claims man is harassing her online. Tough shit, world replies.

So I just tried to let it go. I ignored his texts, the pictures taken from outside my place. I left at odd hours and kept a different schedule to avoid being easily tracked.

That only exacerbated the problem.

He became *convinced* I had murdered Everett Coughlin. For many, it was an issue of semantics, but Timothy Allred believed—legitimately believed—I'd held him down and choked the life from him.

It wasn't much of a jump—for him—to conclude that, because

Madeline St. Clair's family was involved, the autopsy report did not get completed. They tossed a few hundred thousand dollars the coroner's way to ensure he came to the conclusion that Everett Coughlin died by self-inflicted asphyxiation, or whatever kills people who fill their cars with exhaust fumes.

And this one delusion—that I had killed Everett Coughlin with my bare hands—is what finally sent him over the edge. He became (even more) erratic, posting his thoughts in blog entries that read like 4Chan conspiracies.

And then *it* happened.

I came home—to a place I've since abandoned for a high rise apartment—to find Timothy naked and bleeding on my living room floor. He'd broken in by getting a key from the security guard—I guess girls like me always have "boyfriends" who've lost the spare—and disassembled my laptop, placing each piece on the ground in my living room.

Meant to be some kind of metaphor, I guess.

Then, his *pièce de résistance.* He slit his wrists and disrobed, pulling a .38 revolver from his jacket pocket before taking up residence on my couch.

I found him lying face-down on my computer parts, a red puddle slowly expanding beneath him. He'd planned this little murder-suicide based on my normal departure time. Only, this night I'd decided to stop for a burrito on my way home.

Lucky me.

I called 911, and they managed to save his life. He was charged with a litany of offenses and taken to a mental hospital for testing. His stay was extended after he stabbed two guards and then tried to hang himself with his bed sheet.

I could go on, but the moral of the story is, he is bound to spend a very, *very* long time away from society, and there is something to be said for that.

Some nights, I still check over my shoulder for a bony, bespectacled figure to be following me, but there's never anyone there.

And therein lies the truth of life—you're more alone than you think you are.

And I guess I am okay with that. Most of my flaws have been dragged through the public square.

That's what separates me from *them*.

The other Suicide Blondes believe the same old lie, that no one can have any dirt on them because all of their dirt is public. They rant and gnash their teeth about their very public indiscretions, thinking those are as bad as it gets.

But it gets worse.

And I know, because I have access to their social media accounts.

All of them.

From Facebook to Twitter to Instagram, I can peek into the lives of Audrey, Gillian, and—oh yes—Madeline St. Clair.

That is *my* secret. What began as a simple exercise in ability—I did it because I could—quickly transformed into a quiet, burning obsession. I'm sure I could dig into a personality profile, maybe get psychoanalyzed, and trace it all back to junior year, but I have no interest in that. This thing I do works like a shot of adrenaline straight to the chest, and I could get off on it, were I so inclined.

There is just something so erotic about the secrecy of knowing the exact keystrokes Madeline St. Clair uses to log in to FaceBook. Or the secret questions Audrey uses to retrieve the password for her Instagram.

Madeline St. Clair has no idea how many times I check her profile on a daily basis. Has no inkling of how closely I pore over her direct messages, precisely when I should be working. How I try to glean her mental state at the time from the words and phrases she uses. She is clueless as to how many times I have photoshopped my own face over the multitudes of friends in the glamorous pics on her profile.

Ditto for Audrey and Gillian. The intensity of my admiration for Madeline's life outshines all other so-called "stalker" activities.

It's why hearing Audrey talk about her little text messages—none of which were sent by me—makes me so angry.

Because I know—for a fact—Audrey *doesn't* want a stalker. It's a horrifying, demeaning, life-altering situation.

Plus, I'm more of a stalker than that other person will *ever* be.

I DECIDE to go for an afternoon walk. It's a nice distraction from my own self-delusions and paranoia, not to mention the fact that I need to sweat out some alcohol. Besides, I can't bear to see my mother right now, and I need some alone time.

I'm not an athlete, and usually my only exercise comes in the form of leaving the office to go get a latte, but my whole body feels juiced with electricity—and anxiety—so I make a pilgrimage to Percy Warner Park, which lies on the outer edge of Belle Meade.

It provides me with some much-needed time to think. I've received a lot of information over the last two days, and I don't want to burn out and go to my dark place. I've experienced a few...setbacks over the years, each one preceded by one of those prying cable documentaries, which inevitably brings the crazies out of their nests.

The inclusion of the other girls heightens my sensitivity, and I can feel something ungodly brewing deep within my psyche. I can always call my psychiatrist, but I've resolved to believe this time it's different, this time I refuse to be weak.

Getting out of the car and hiking the gentle, sloped road at the path's outset, I feel some of that bad karma begin to slip away, get lost in the hum of the background noise. Not long after, I'm full-on in the woods, my feet pumping to the music in my headset, and I no longer have the taut cable of my anxieties cinching my stomach into knots.

And yet, I experience a distinct and unalterable loneliness out here.

Although, loneliness isn't the word.

Isolation. That's more like it.

The trails feel abandoned. Even though it's early on a weekday afternoon, Percy Warner is never this...abandoned. I've somehow managed to find myself alone among the leaves and the trees and rocks adorning the path, and it leaves me on edge.

I can't help but think about my conversation with Audrey. I wish I had access to her text threads, because then I could scan them for details, try to make sense of what she's going through. I'd also place money on the fact that Gillian is probably experiencing the same thing, too. These people, they tend to get fixated on a topic more than a single person.

I know I do.

And the shared look between Audrey and Gillian makes more sense now. I didn't get it at the time, but now it seems so clear. They've discussed their shared *stalker*, and they didn't want me to find out.

But why?

Either they're worried about me finding out—

Or they're just worried about me.

It feels good to think so, even if there is a sharp edge to the thought.

That doesn't solve the problem of who could be stalking them.

Not Timothy Allred, I have to tell myself. I imagine him in the darkest, most impenetrable cell in all of Washington state, and somehow it calms me, as if thinking it can somehow influence the result of his incarceration.

His misery is my own personal vision board, I suppose.

If not Timothy, then who?

A few names pop out of nowhere, and I consider their motivations. There's Madeline, of course. She is exactly the type of person to engage in this kind of espionage. Nothing would give her more perverse pleasure.

It would also explain why she came to see me before. A way of getting her hooks in me before pushing me off the nearest cliff. Or seeing where my loyalties are.

But that's not right. Something seems different this time. She seems...fragile in a new and authentic way.

The other option comes from within the St. Clair-Ambrose household. Judging by Madeline's personal DMs, Colton Ambrose is no stranger to underhanded tactics to get his way in business and personal matters. If his wife is to be believed, he has rat-fucked every single business person he has ever dealt with. If nothing else, it leads me to believe he is capable of some pretty extreme dealings, if motivated.

But why? Why would he threaten his wife's high school frenemy?

Maybe Madeline is blackmailing *him*, and this is his means for extricating himself from his wife's iron-fisted grip. It would make sense, I suppose, but I am not ready to go kicking in their door, guns-a-blazing, to accuse them of something that just occurred to me right now, as I make my way up a low-grade hill in the middle of Percy Warner.

At last, the fever of solitude breaks. I pass a middle-aged couple in Lululemon workout clothes, and they smile. I turn up one side of my mouth and look away. I'm wearing my Seahawks cap and sunglasses, but I feel vulnerable, so I pull the hat way down on my forehead and avoid eye contact.

Even with my earbuds in, I think I hear one of the women calling back to me. Maybe I dropped something as I passed them.

I glance behind me, and that's when I see someone.

Percy Warner is well-trod, as parks go, so it shouldn't freak me out, but it does. I get that feeling, an intuition, and the alarm bells start ringing like crazy.

I speed up, and though the person is far enough behind that I can't determine the gender, I feel the need to get the hell out of there before I can.

As a precaution, I drift off the paved path onto one of the many trails that weave along the park. It's counterintuitive, because who in the hell would choose to take a *more* isolated path, but it's the best way to confirm my paranoia. If the person behind me keeps walking straight, I'm crazy. If he or she turns to follow me—

I'm dead.

Once I've made some headway, picking up my speed, I feel comfortable glancing behind me. I listen to the *thwock-thwock-thwock* of my feet on the gravel and sand, but the nagging sensation of being watched fills me with newfound anxiety.

I tilt my head and glance behind me.

They've closed the gap.

I am really hitting my stride, and yet this person is *gaining* on me. It occurs to me I should break into a galloping run, screaming all the while, but my fear has bridled me to this power walk, and I'm afraid to do anything at all, let alone run away.

The irony of it isn't lost on me.

But still I persevere, managing to pick up some speed without making it too obvious that I notice. My whole body feels like it's going to go rubbery on me any moment, but I hold it together. The thought of someone reaching for me from behind, grabbing me by the arm, dragging me off into the wilderness, it sends acid through my veins.

My mind flashes—

(*blood, clattering keyboard letters*)

—and I am taken all the way back to my apartment in Seattle, where I had to literally scrub my stalker's blood from the hardwood floors.

And maybe he's back in my life. As crazy as it seems, maybe Timothy Allred has come to Nashville.

I try to shake it off, the completely ludicrous idea that my stalker is (1) out of prison and (2) somehow in Tennessee.

But I am not hallucinating the fact that I am tromping through the woods with someone on my tail.

As fucked up as my life has been, it's never felt that...dangerous. Even when I was in the midst of the Timothy Allred situation, I never thought it would end with anyone dying. In retrospect, that was a crazy belief, and yet it turned out to be true.

But this—this is different.

I wouldn't be surprised if someone ended up in the morgue. It would be a fitting epilogue to the story, and the news would absolutely eat our deaths up.

My heart throbs behind my eyeballs. I pump my feet harder, try to get away, try to get further down the trail, away from this person.

I want to puke, I'm so nervous.

There are plenty of places to dump a body, I figure, and one of us might end up in the bushes on the other side of the trail.

As I top a hill, a miracle occurs. A guy in shorts and a Nashville Rock N Roll Marathon shirt passes me, shuffling along at a measured gait. He's an older guy, a veteran runner, and he's coming right for me.

I've never been so happy to see a guy in short shorts in all my life.

This is my moment. I'm nothing if not momentarily courageous. I turn on one heel and follow the aging marathoner, picking up the speed to keep pace with him.

Down the hill and turning a sharp corner, I see the follower.

The stalker.

The...nothing at all.

It's not Timothy Allred.

Not Madeline St. Clair.

Not even a half-assed reporter.

For a moment, it looks like Madeline. Same skinny arms and high-end workout clothes. Giant, bug-eyed sunglasses. The whole get-up.

But it's not her.

When we finally pass one another, I see it's a random woman on the far end of middle-age. Gillian or Audrey in two decades, but not yet. She has shoulder-length blonde hair and—when she lifts the sunglasses—a pair of starkly blue eyes. When they settle on me, her smile is self-satisfied, almost withering.

I smile back.

She has no idea how close I was to bludgeoning her with a fist-sized stone.

In scurrying back to my car, parked down by The Stairs at the park's entrance, I can't help but single out a feeling drifting around in my head like harmful bacteria.

My intuition is confirmed when I open the door and peer up into the depths of the woods above me.

Someone is watching.

I *wasn't* alone in the woods. I just happened to get out-flanked.

And so it begins, I think.

9

The next time I see my mother, I'm surprised at her lucidity. There's no gobsmacked bewilderment on her face, and gone is her yellowish hue. She seems more herself, and though I still don't breathe normally—who *can*, in a hospital—I nevertheless manage to keep my pulse below heart attack range.

"Why, Mary Ellen! How long's it been since I've seen you?" she says, her eyes as bright as polished gems. She's sitting up in her hospital bed.

"It's been a minute, mom."

At this, her glowing face falters. "I've been somewhere else, haven't I?" she asks.

This is her preferred metaphor, as though she just got back from a milk run.

I comfort her. "That doesn't matter," I say. "The truth is, I'm here now, and you're here now, and we can enjoy this moment."

She doesn't need to know what she's missing. That hurt look in her eyes is enough to prevent me from correcting her. Instead, I sit and clasp her hand.

"I see the way you're looking at me, and I don't like it. It's not my intention to sit here and talk about my health. So, why don't you tell me all about your trip?"

She has me go through each and every detail, from the look and feel of the understated Seattle airport, to my impressions of how much Nashville's changed.

I go through it all again—even though she's heard it once before —because it feels good to talk to her, and my heart swells whenever we're not mired in the talk of her mortality.

"Sometimes, I don't even recognize this city," my mom says. "I feel like—who is it?—Rip Van Winkle, waking up after a long nap. By the time I get out of this place, I'm sure there will be a new, hip neighborhood rising from the ashes somewhere."

"Or a new burger joint," I add.

"Or coffee shop."

"Or hot chicken place."

"Or a barbecue shack."

I try to think of something else but come up short, and my mom laughs. I've been told I have her smile, and it's a compliment I'll accept.

She was once a beautiful, spirited person, the kind of woman you want to be around. The kind of woman who doesn't always get her way but does things her way.

Now, she has the haggard look of a bag lady trundling down the street behind a shopping cart full of cans.

It just goes to show there is no dignity in the process of dying. She's withering away before my eyes, and the years of cancer scares and tumor probes have left her a shell of her former self.

Before my mind drags me further into the quagmire of Mom's ailments, I change the subject.

Too bad for me, it's the one subject *she* doesn't want to hear about.

"I've seen Madeline and the rest of the girls since I got back."

My mom peers at me, her eyes going to slits. "Oh yeah? I hope it wasn't near a bus they could throw you under."

"Mom—"

"Those girls are no good, and I don't think I need to go on and on regarding how I feel about them."

"No, you don't."

"They are horrible human beings."

I sigh. "I know, mom."

"Raised by the devil himself."

"Okay."

"And I don't want you getting yourself involved with them again."

"I just said hello," I say.

It's a minor lie, but one I immediately regret.

"Mary Ellen, they used you up, and then they just left you to hang in the wind. Whenever I see mention of them, I get so angry, I want to spit."

"People change, Mom," I say, but I can't quite get any weight behind it.

"Only out of necessity," she replies. "Those...girls, they've never had to become better people because nobody's ever required it of them."

"Their lives aren't perfect."

"Remind me to book the world's smallest violin for their pity party."

She's not wrong, and I can't quite figure out why I feel the need to defend them. Complicated relationships bring up complicated feelings, I guess.

"Let's change the subject," she says, noticing my frustration. "How long are you planning on staying?"

Out of the frying pan and into the fire, I think.

"How about this: I don't know how long I'm staying, but I promise I won't leave before you get better."

"What a lucky mother I am," she says. "I can tell all the old biddies at dialysis that *my* daughter is willing to stick by me until I'm less likely to croak."

I bring her hand up and kiss her knuckles, smiling. "Oh, no need to brag on me."

She chuckles to herself. "I always said we could develop a fine

Laurel and Hardy routine, if only we could decide which of us is the fat one."

"Neither. We could be Laurel and Laurel, or Hardy and Hardy. I can't remember which one is which."

"Oliver Hardy was the big one. I shouldn't call him fat. Plus, he was born down in Georgia, so I guess we should claim him, being a good southern boy and all that."

"So we should be the Double Hardys?"

"Or something similar."

She shifts uncomfortably in her bed and winces.

"You okay?"

She smiles through the pain. "I'm fine, my girl. It just hurts to get old, and I think maybe all the years have waited until just now to stack up on me."

At one point, her mouth goes slack on one side, and she looks up at me. Behind her once-vibrant eyes, there is now only a look of confusion.

"Mary Ellen?" she asks.

"Yes, mom?"

"Are you okay? Is *everything* okay?"

She reaches for my hand, clasps it with hers, and her eyes are extremely insistent. I lower myself into the seat next to her hospital bed.

"Of course, I am, Mom. I'm doing all right. Just fine, fine, fine."

"If you get yourself into anything you can't get out of," she says, "I don't want you sticking around this town, just for me."

"What would I—"

"Those girls are trouble," she interrupts. "I know they are, but I also know they have a magnetic pull on you, one that even you don't realize. So, all I'm saying is, be careful."

"I will," I reply, hoping I sound convincing.

Truth be told, I already feel myself being dragged down into something dark and murky, something where the sun above is hardly visible.

"I love you."

"I love you, too," I tell her.

She smiles, and we sit quietly for minutes on end, basking in this moment in which no worry and no fear exists. Just a mother and her daughter. No one else.

Soon after, her mouth opens, and she loses clarity, so I call the nurses and take leave of the room until they've got her stabilized.

Outside, the doctors and nurses relate more bad news. It's worse than they thought. The prognosis is not good. Long-term care. Extended physical therapy.

Maybe a home.

It's too much.

Thankfully, over the years, I've developed a keen sense for zoning out when I feel sad or threatened, so I spend most of it nodding.

Mom's health care is good, so I don't have to worry about her or money...yet.

***

THE WHOLE OF Nashville is my oyster, but I find myself falling into old habits.

Audrey convinces me, through some not inconsiderable begging and pleading, to attend one of her "get-togethers."

I think she feels a little guilty about how the chicken shack conversation went and wants to make amends. She is perfectly amicable on the phone and steps right on past any comment that could be misconstrued as salty.

When I arrive, I have to psych myself up, physically forcing my hand to open the door so that the valet could park it in a neighboring driveway.

This is it, I think. This is how the downhill slide begins.

But by the time I find my way to the front door, I'm feeling much, much better. Or at least *less* bad. My stomach does its normal loop-the-loops, and then I'm inside.

Her house is situated on a hill overlooking the city, though at this point in the summer, the foliage obscures most of it, so the Nashville skyline looks more like fallen stars than a series of flashy, high-rise buildings.

I leave my coat with a hired doorman and walk tentatively into the main room.

This is not a game night, a get-together, or any other quaint euphemism.

It's a flat-out party. A celebration. Words almost fail to note the lavish nature of this rendezvous of the rich and famous in Nashville's social circle.

I make my way to a nearby table, just to catch my breath. I need a minute, and I might need it to stretch out to five or ten before I can make an actual appearance.

The spread is immaculate.

There are appetizers—catered by a celebrated local company—and a *ton* of wine. I pick through *hor d'oeuvres* and select a fancy, speckled piece of delicate meat and pair it with a particularly stinky cheese. It's all an act—a means for me to keep my head down and avoid eye contact—but for the time being it works.

Until, of course, a group of loud, brusque men elbow drunkenly in and start snapping up food as if it were just for them.

I bolt, hoping to God they don't recognize me.

When I finally make my way to the main room, I come to realize: there are enough people to sink the Titanic. Audrey swims through dozens upon dozens of well-dressed, well-coiffed hangers-on to meet me. She's all smiles and twinkles, and her dress a shiny match for her face.

"I hope you found the place okay," she says as she leans in for an uncharacteristic cheek kiss. This is who she is now. Or at least who she pretends to be. "Parking around here is a real bitch."

She smells like wine and sweet, sweet perfume. It almost reminds me of some earlier time in my life, but before I can clasp it with the tips of my fingers, it floats off into the air like smoke from a dying cigarette.

I want to tell her about my experience at Percy Warner, about the possibility that we are *all* being stalked, but she's got me by the wrist before I can get a word in. Audrey guides me through the crowd and has her man behind the bar pour me a glass of Malbec.

"Isn't this a fun time?" she asks, full of manufactured cheer.

Looking around, it's clear these are not my people. They might have been in another universe, had I been able to finish my time at DDA. Or gone on to a degree in finance or law or some other respectable profession. But as it stands, I am an interloper in this world, one whose reputation precedes her, and so I can't even fully immerse myself in the crowd as a stranger.

I settle into a spot where no one will spill their drink on me, and I try to look disinterested. It's a pale impossibility, because the party-goers seem to have a knack for making eye contact with me.

I feel their questions like poisoned air all around me.

How could you?

What was it like?

Do you regret it?

They pretend like I'm beneath them, but in truth they'd probably trade the pearls around their necks for an intense five-minute conversation with me.

Unlike Audrey, who glows like lamplight at dusk, these people smolder. Fires about to extinguish themselves. They wear dark clothes and discuss dull ideas. It's all houses, houses, houses and traffic, traffic, traffic. A few ebullient mothers on the outskirts discuss the rigors of breastfeeding, but otherwise, it's all pretty one note.

Nothing about it strikes me as interesting, so I look for an exit strategy. I've made my appearance. Audrey has effectively turned me into a coffee table book, a provocative piece of art. Something to discuss in hushed tones over by the wine bar.

I'm a living conversation starter.

It seems as though I've fulfilled my purpose, so I give Audrey the I'm-getting-out-of-here thumb from across the room, and she responds by hurrying over and begging me to stay.

"You can't leave *now*," she says. "Everybody wants to *meet* you."

I can't help but take a look around.

These people are living gutter balls, and it'd be kind of sad if I didn't already know them by face and reputation. I mean, through Audrey's social media accounts.

Greta is the closeted daughter of a local politician, which would be fine, save for the fact that she publicly calls gays "animals" to be consistent with her mother's political brand. She thinks no one notices the eyes she makes at Audrey.

But I do.

Bethany and her husband—over by the champagne punch—are swingers, and they have hooked up with at least three other couples here. Based on the conversations in Audrey's messenger app, they've propositioned her but have made no progress.

Rosemarie just got out of rehab and is downing drinks on the sly when she thinks no one is looking. She's a little hung up on Donovan, who just finished up his season on *The Bachelorette*, where he got drunk and mishandled a hot-tub hook-up, so he got sent home.

Schuyler is involved in shady business deals, and his wife Margot almost let a kid drown at her one-year-old's birthday party because she was doing coke in the bathroom with a local chef named Stefan.

Is this what Audrey thinks of me? That I'm yet another ornament on her human bric-a-brac shelf? Do I fill some void in her clique?

Okay, I tell her. I'll stay for a drink. I promise.

Yadda yadda yadda.

Once she is sufficiently mollified, Audrey wanders away, leaving me to fend for myself. I find myself watching Audrey's husband manage himself among the flocks and flocks of wine drinking clingers in his midst.

Jenkins Finnell is a nice enough guy. He smiles at all the right moments, makes a few well-placed jokes, but there is something innately sad about him. Whereas Audrey lives for this kind of function, her husband exists on the outskirts, visible but withdrawn. Like me. It's probably better that way. Audrey has blossomed into quite the attention-seeker, and it just wouldn't do for her to have to compete for the spotlight.

However, I find myself kind of enamored by this man, and so I pay way more attention to him for a time than I do the rest of the party.

He seems to be looking for something that isn't there, his eyes scanning the scene but never really settling on any one thing or person. It's easy to ignore, to shrug off, but I see it, having been that very person for the last twenty years myself.

When he takes his drink and spins away from the group, I follow him out to the balcony. He catches me in his periphery and turns to regard me.

It takes him a moment to figure out who I am, but when he does, his gaze softens.

"Mary Ellen Hanneford," he says, smiling gently. "I never thought I'd see you at one of these parties. What a hell of a thing for your nervous system."

He's reaching into his jacket pocket, and he retrieves a half-open pack of cigarettes. Being a Belle Meade gentleman, he offers me one before lighting a cig for himself.

"Is this not *your* scene?" I ask.

Peering through the trees, I see the twinkle of some financial building or another. It would be a beautiful sight, if it weren't ruined by this downer of a party.

"Yeah, well, most of these people assume I'd just prefer to discuss finance all night, or some other thing, but I'm just not—I don't know. Maybe I'd just rather not talk at all. How's that for good cheer?"

"I think it's perfectly fine," I say. Then something occurs to me. "Do you actually remember me? Like, I know that Audrey's probably mentioned me at some point, but didn't you go to school with—"

He nods, somewhat sadly, as he puffs on his cigarette. He looks away. "Yeah, I don't think we ever ran in the same circles, but I was friends with Everett in a kind of casual way. He was a good guy. Why?"

I try to shake my head noncommittally, as if it just occurred to me, but the truth is, it's all people seem to want to discuss. "I don't know. It seems to follow me like an evil spirit. Part of me just wants to know more about *him*."

"Everett."

"Right. Everett. I don't mean—"

"No, it's okay," he says. "I wasn't best friends with the guy or anything. It just seems, I don't know, *necessary* to regard him by his first name, lest it—"

"Fade away?"

"That's right," he says, and his smile is more melancholy than I'd like. "One thing people didn't say a lot back then—he was sad. A real sad guy. His parents, they pushed him to be something he wasn't."

"Which was."

"Popular."

"Say that again?"

"They wanted him to be popular," he says. "He was quiet and—what's it called—introverted. Quiet and depressed is not good, when you exist in a world of sharks."

"What's that supposed to mean?"

"Everybody had it out for that kid. He got it from both ends, at home and at school. It's like this: he tried to kill himself once. I mean, obviously, *before* the final time."

"I've never heard that."

"It's true. Doesn't make what eventually happen any less horrific —it actually kind of makes it worse—but Everett spent some time in a hospital to...heal from his injuries."

"Why does no one ever mention it?"

He shrugs. "Ask a closer friend. I do know he fell into these dark, cavernous depressions. It was one of the reasons he fell for that fucked-up scheme, I guess. No matter how many times he was burned by shitty people in life, he always wanted to believe in, I don't know, the goodness of humanity."

"Oh."

I don't have much to say, because what can you say to that?

"I don't mean to come off as harsh or bitter," he says. "Personally, I blame Madeline St. Clair for everything bad that happens."

"I haven't been home long enough to make up my mind about her."

It's the first time I've seen true emotion from him. "Nothing to make up. She's the closest thing to a demon as I've seen in my life."

I see an opening, and I take it, though I'm sure it will ruin this perfectly genteel conversation.

"Except for maybe the person sending Audrey threatening text messages."

The words are out before I can catch them, but by the time I say them. I'm glad they're there. Jenkins doesn't seem surprised, either. His face betrays nothing, even if I can sense this is the first time he's heard about it.

"I don't know what you're talking about," he says.

I'm a little shocked by this admission. "She hasn't told you about them?"

"She doesn't tell me anything," he says, as politely as he can, but it still comes off a little sharp. "I mean, nothing that she wants has anything to do with me. I guess the same is true with the things she fears."

"I'm sorry to hear that," I say, as sincerely as I can without sounding pitying.

"People drift apart," he replies. "I suppose the writing's been on the wall for some time, only Audrey hasn't looked up long enough to see it."

"But about the text messages—"

He holds up one hand. "If Audrey has something going on, it's probably of her own doing, or else she's playing it to the crowd to ensure she gets maximum attention for it."

I can't disagree with him, but something about his response rings hollow. "I guess you're right," I reply. "I haven't been home long enough to make up my mind about *her*, either."

"Aud's got a good heart—she just doesn't know when to let go of old grievances."

I let that sink in, and I take a step back to acknowledge the end of the conversation.

"Thanks for talking," I say, and he winks in return. "Want to head back in?"

He waves me off. "I think I'm going to catch up on my fresh air. Thanks, though."

***

I LEAVE the party a little early, much to the host's chagrin.

"But we never *see* one another," she slurs drunkenly, insisting that I stay for one more hour, but I can't quite pull the trigger. I'm afraid I'll say something bitchy, or—worse—she'll say something off-color and offensive.

It's obviously better off this way, and even Audrey will see that in the morning. When she's sober. For now, though, she's a little clingy and a lot weepy. I've got to cut the cord before it permanently attaches, and I have to spend endless hours listening to Audrey's boo-hoo stories, which are a living embodiment of the phrase *first world problems*.

On the way out, I run into Gillian, who stumbles in with a boyish early twentysomething in a leather jacket and super tight jeans. He looks like he's barely out of puberty, but he's handsome. Dark hair, dark eyes. Strong brow.

They both smell like weed.

I mean, it's obvious he's in a band. *He*—whoever *he* is—is always in a band. Gillian's dad works as a PR rep for a few big-name country acts, and so she attracts what we used to call Broadway Barnacles—no-name musicians using any means necessary to get a big break. This poor guy thinks he's being clever and manipulative, when he is clearly the one being used. His whole schtick is played out, and he doesn't have the slightest clue.

I can only smile as he introduces himself, Andrew *something*. He pretends not to care about me or who I am, but his voice breaks when he tells me he knows me.

"Where'd you find that one?" I ask, as soon as the dude is out of earshot. He's gone to get them both a drink.

"Belmont," she says, looking slightly guilty."He plays guitar at—"

And then she goes into the particulars of his gig. He's a musician, working a very famous honky tonk on Saturday evenings, but he has a demo he's shopping around.

"And I guess I'm the foot in the door," she says.

"I was wondering what that smell was," I reply, and Gillian actually laughs. A short, little bark, but still.

"That's the pot," she replies, "but *he* got it...so same thing, I guess?"

I lean in, searching conspiratorially for gossip.

"Whatever happened to whats-his-name?"

"We never talked"—she pauses—"you followed that on Face-Book, didn't you?"

I don't respond, but I can't control the slight upturn at the corners of my mouth.

"Stalker," she says, smiling, even if I can see the sadness beneath.

When the guitar guy returns, he's got a beer for himself and a drink for Gillian. He thinks he's cool, but as they saunter away, Gil turns and winks at me once before disappearing into the crowd.

I wish her the absolute best with this asshole.

I take a slow, cigarette-fueled ride back to my rental house, blasting some song from a guy named Jason about Elephants along the way. I've got the windows down, and the frigid breeze has me within spitting distance of sober by the time I wheel into the neighborhood.

I stop a few houses down from mine and kill the engine.

I have a bad feeling.

In my head, I can see—

(*the pistol*)

(*shocking nakedness*)

—*him*. I can see him, Timothy Allred blended conspicuously with the visage of Everett Coughlin. Somehow, they have become intertwined in my head.

The person just over my shoulder in the park.

Stumbling down the road on uneven legs, I stop at the mailbox and peer through some bushes into the house windows.

And then I see it.

The overhead light on in the living room.

My stomach does a series of violent toe touches inside my body.

I didn't leave it on. I'm OCD about turning every single light off and checking the oven twice before stepping outside.

But it is one hundred percent casting dull, yellow light through the house.

I gasp at what I see next.

A silhouette drifts across the living room, slinking into the back bedroom.

My bedroom. Or at least the one I've temporarily rented.

I take an instinctive step back, clutching at my mouth to keep the scream from working free of my throat.

Someone is in the house. Someone moving with a purpose. Someone waiting for me.

The stranger is moving quickly, bouncing from room-to-room as if searching for something in particular.

It occurs to me that this might not be the same person as the stalker from the park.

I step forward, kneeling behind the car in the driveway. I can see inside the house clearly now, and if I can just get close enough for a picture, I will be able to turn the photographic evidence in to the police.

I'm no private eye. There is no *way* I'm going to investigate *anything* on my own, let alone a situation in which someone is rummaging through my stuff.

It is the worst possible case of *déjà vu*, and I've got it *bad*. One person breaks into your house and starts rifling through your junk, it's a wash. *Two*? There's obviously something wrong with you.

I retrieve my phone from my back pocket and turn it on, pressing the screen against my chest to keep the glow from alerting the intruder.

The camera acts as an acceptable periscope so I can avoid raising my head into plain view. I reposition the phone once I see this person, and I'm just about to get a good look, when *it* happens.

The figure stops.

It's like something out of a horror movie. I should probably drop the phone, but I freeze up. I can't do anything.

The figure turns and looks in my direction. It's like they are looking directly at me, and my blood turns to freon. I snap a photo and pull my hand down. My heart is thudding out a symphony orchestra as I press myself against the car's rear bumper.

I wait there, eyes closed, and hope I don't hear the sound of the front door opening. I've got nowhere to go. All I can do is be still. Be still and wait.

I half expect this person to come rushing out of the house, to drag me screaming back inside and violate me in one way or another. Violence. Rape. Probably some combination of both.

For a minute, nothing happens. I breathe. I sweat. I stare down the driveway at the corner and wonder how long it would take me to get from one end to the other.

In the back of my mind, though, there's a *but*.

But what if he happens to see me?

But what if the cops can't identify him?

But what if this isn't the end of it?

When I finally peer around the side of the car, the shadow figure has disappeared. All I see is an empty, unassuming room. A bare light bulb above the piano. And then, without warning, the light flickers off, leaving the whole house in hushed, vertiginous darkness.

The kind of darkness where anything can happen.

Someone is gaslighting me.

I rise from a squatting position. I let my eyes adjust, enough to make out the raw edges of things around me, before I spin and dart for the rental car parked along the road.

My legs feel rubbery from the cigarettes and the wine. Tonight is not the night I will be run down and caught by a serial killer from central casting.

Keys in hand, I fumble for the fob and manage to hit the button just as I reach the driver's side door. A bubble of anger and frustration makes its way to the surface. I scream—once—loud enough to wake the neighbors.

A few miles down the road, I decide where I'm going and head there as quickly as I can, looking in the rear view mirror with such great frequency it makes me dizzy.

10

I leave the car running when I arrive at Madeline St. Clair's *residence*.

It's too grand to be called a house.

Staggering up to the front door, I plan an impassioned speech to give to Madeline. I don't quite know *why* I've come here, but it's the first place that occurred to me when I was in the car.

So here I am.

It's well after bedtime for most people, so I shouldn't be shocked if no one answers, but as I wait there, the interminable time between the doorbell ring and the door opening, I get overwhelmed by anxiety.

It becomes clear to me—I *must* speak with Madeline. It is not optional.

She needs to hear how she made me feel when she ducked out on me all those years ago. How she used me. How she used *everyone*. There is nothing new about this, and Madeline copped to it only a few nights ago, but suddenly it seems so important.

Maybe I need to say it, to verbalize my frustrations, to finally let go.

But my speech dissolves the moment the front door opens.

Colton Ambrose turns out to be a tall, imposing figure, and nothing about him is inviting. He has the cool stare of an owl checking its prey, and when his eyes settle on me, I feel the need to scream and run.

He stinks of scotch, and despite the late hour, he's still in a collared shirt and tie.

"I need to see Madeline," I plead.

It's obvious I sound drunk, but I'm already in this, so I can't just turn and go home. *He* is back home, or she. *Someone* has invaded my space, and one of my friends knows something. I figure that, since she came crying to me only nights before, Madeline must have an inside track on what's going on.

Plus, I hope she's willing to give in and tell me the secret she backed off of before.

Maybe it's the same thing. Perhaps she is being followed by some insane stalker.

But Colton Ambrose is having none of it.

"You're drunk—go home," he says.

He makes a gesture to close the door, but I stuff one wedge into the doorframe and stop that from happening.

"Please. It's important."

"What it *is*," he says, "is after midnight. Now, you can extricate yourself from my front door and go back to your car, you fucking *murderer*, or I can call the cops. It's really just that simple."

I weigh the options and decide to call his bluff.

"Where is she?" I demand. "Is she here? Why won't she come down to the door?"

"Because this," he says, waving one hand up and down, "is about *your* problems, not about hers. If she comes down here, you'll only drag her into...whatever is going on with you. I don't want that, she doesn't want that, and if I'm being honest, neither do you."

This is not going how I imagined it would go, and I'm desperately trying to think of things to say to keep the door open, but my mind lands on a single point, and because I cannot let it go, I just have to dive headlong into addressing it.

"She's not here, is she?"

His eyes remain fixed on me, but they've changed. Shifted, somehow. He's not the predator of before, though he wants me to think of him that way.

"She's upstairs, in bed. She's drunk, like she always is. I'm working, and she's living off the money I make. Being able to get bombed in the afternoon and pass out before dinner is one of the delicious privileges of being married to me, I guess."

And then he slams the door in my face.

Liar, I think, as soon as I'm in the car.

She's not upstairs in the bedroom, nor is she anywhere on the premises.

The lights in the house are all on. Reminds me of the time my mom left with a suitcase and promised never to come home. Dad kept the house wide open, as if she didn't remember the address.

One question remains.

Why would he want to protect her?

Because it's what people around here do, I think. It's a way of closing the ranks. If he admits her absence, it opens a whole new folder of problems, of questions. And that's the last thing he wants.

Or maybe there's something a little more sinister to it. Maybe he *knows* what's going on and submits to his wife's Machiavellian schemes because he is afraid of the alternative.

Better to have her on his side than scheming against him.

Huh, I think. Mutually-assured destruction—what all great marriages are built on.

I pull away, wondering what to do next. It's not that I have nowhere else to go, I just don't have anywhere else I *want* to go.

I turn off the air and roll down the windows, letting the wind pull at my arm, stretched out the window to resist the breeze. It was how I drove when resistance was all I cared about. And this feeling, it takes me away from my own anxiety.

I'm drunk enough I shouldn't be driving, but it feels good, and I'm in the moment, so I allow my path to be dictated by feeling, rather than logic.

I *could* go to the police. I could, yes, but I would receive the same treatment I did back in high school. A bunch of officers giving me side-eye, wondering what I'd done to put myself in this position. That, or else they'd secretly relish the irony of my situation.

The mere suggestion of their skepticism deters me.

It occurs to me I'll need to go to the police at some point.

Just not tonight.

Tonight, I've got places *not* to be, and people *not* to see.

So, eventually, I end up with my mother. Sitting next to her bed, waiting for the deathwatch beetle to cease its interminable ticking. Not anticipating it, really, but waiting it out, guessing when it would happen, so the real grief could begin.

IT'S SO quiet in hospital rooms, like death is holding its breath.

I arrange the chairs so I can sit in one while propping my feet in the other. I'm not going back to the rental, and I'm probably not going to sleep, so it behooves me to find at least a little comfort in this godforsaken place.

My eyes never quite leave the door, but eventually I can steal glances at my mom without thinking an ax murderer might burst in at any moment. She looks peaceful. The lines of her face denote calm, and she snores quietly as the light frames her face with its industrial pall. I pray to God she makes it through this. I don't quite have the vocabulary for it—who knows when I prayed last—but the act itself seems to carry some weight, and I don't have much else to do but worry over the possibility that I'll be attacked in the night.

After I'm convinced I've said my peace with the Lord, I sneak my phone out of my pocket and surreptitiously flip through the pictures I'd snapped.

All I got was a few blurry images of the front of the house. I peer at them, trying to make heads or tails of the screen, but there is nothing to help me identify the intruder. I might as well have taken them while doing jumping jacks, for how blurry they are.

A voice, clear and crisp as a new recording, cuts through the darkness.

"Mary Ellen, sweetheart, what are you *doing* here at this hour?"

"Nothing, Mom," I say, looking up. "Just decided to come see about my best girl."

"Don't mind me," she says, smiling. "I hate to be a bad hostess, but I'm in the middle of a wonderful sleep, and I believe I'm going to get back to that."

"You do that," I reply. The corners of her mouth turn up in a second, more genuine smile, and not too long afterward, she's actually snoring again.

I continue checking the images on my phone. I'm not convinced I'll be able to establish the intruder's identity, but if I can at least discount some people, knock them from the ranks, perhaps it will make the whole process go a little bit easier.

Or you could call the cops, a voice that is both mine and not mine tells me. Technically, a crime was committed earlier tonight, and there has to be evidence—

I cut the fantasy off, mid-stream.

Nothing would come of calling the police, save for a fruitless investigation and a whole heap of publicity. It would be a hassle to go from mom's room to the car, let alone getting back into the rental property without being attacked by the media vipers camping out on the lawn.

I know how this works.

The irony is, it'd probably keep the one lunatic off the fringes of your life, this holier-than-thou voice tells me.

I keep staring at the photos, hoping for something to jump out at me like they do in the movies, but nothing does, and so eventually I'm drunkenly staring at pixelated representations of a stranger.

There are no clues.

There is no revelation.

However, I become convinced I know what happened.

. . .

AT SOME POINT in the night, I snap awake. The hum-and-whir of the equipment in the room had slowly lulled me into a light and fitful slumber. My head throbs not just from the alcohol but also the angle at which I'd fallen asleep.

But it's not my head I'm concerned with.

My screen flashes when I pick up my phone, and I notice that I have a voice mail from none other than Madeline St. Clair.

A new and blistering hot anger swells in my chest. It's like I've been inflated with pure venom.

Staring at her name on the ID, I can't help but feel cheated, somehow. This woman, she had every chance in the world to get in touch. But she chose a time she knew I'd probably be asleep. She never intended on actually talking to me.

This is her way of manipulating me.

It's the first step, and I find myself balking at it.

Oh, no, I think. You don't get to dictate the terms of our relationship like this, just picking and choosing when you speak to me.

Angrily, I delete the message without listening.

I call her back.

She's going to have to answer to *me*.

If she was the one at the rental property tonight—first of all, how crazy would that be? Secondly, if she was, then why in the world would she be doing this?

I argue with myself.

She doesn't *need* a reason, that self-same voice tells me. This is *Madeline St. Clair* we're talking about. She doesn't need a reason to do a goddamned thing.

What she doesn't know is that I'm no longer afraid of her. I was once the timorous little schoolgirl, grateful to lick her boots.

No more.

I've been through the wringer, and I am a different person. She might still draw power from those who have spent years under her heels, but I am not one of them.

She cannot hide behind her alcoholic husband. Not if she wants to do the right thing. If she truly is a different person—

(*I miss you*)

—she'll gladly apologize and listen to what I have to say.

Even if not, she still must answer to me.

I've got to know where Madeline's been tonight, and when she doesn't answer, I wait for the beep on the voice mail, and I let her have it.

"I don't know who you sent to do your dirty work, but it's not going to scare me. I'm not afraid of you, *Madeline*. In fact, you should be afraid of *me*."

And then, feeling a particularly potent rush of adrenaline, I hang up the phone.

11

The next morning, I eat some stiff eggs and soggy bacon in the cafeteria and bring a cup of coffee back to my mother's room.

"You don't have to stay here and wait for me to get better," she says, when I return.

"I want to," I say, sipping my coffee, full of sugar and cream.

"I know this isn't the time to say something like this, but I really wish you could find a way to move back to Nashville."

"Mom—"

"This is your *home*, darling," she responds. "Seattle is a place to get yourself together. Nashville is a place to *live*. Everyone you've ever known is here."

"That's the problem."

"And your job. You don't think you could make a living working in computers *here*? It's not like we don't have the internet."

"I know, Mom. But—"

"I mean, do they think we're all barefoot and sucking on hayseeds down here?"

"*Mom!*"

My hand jerks with the force of my response. Coffee splashes out of my cup and lands on my shirt front. I get up and yank some paper towels from the bathroom.

"Mom, I don't think this is a good time to have this conversation. Once you get better and I get back on my feet, maybe we can talk about it. But I work for a *start-up*. They don't allow people to work like satellites in different states. They need me there. I help make decisions."

"Uh-huh," she says. She's huffy. She might as well have her arms crossed, to boot.

I make it a point to talk about the future, to soften the blow of my mom's condition. They say talking about the future gives them something to work toward.

"Listen," I say, sitting down next to her, "I've got a lot going on in my life right now. I'd love to move back to Nashville."

A convenient lie.

"But this moment is just not right. I'm just reconnecting with old friends to see what that's like, and I think putting myself back in this city will complicate things. I mean, there's already been an article in the *Tennessean* about me."

Her eyes widen. "What?"

"I'm a perennial headline, Mom," I say. "That's just the way it is with the—"

"Don't say it."

"—Suicide blondes."

"Why can't they leave you alone? What about the others? When is it going to be *their* time?"

I sigh. "Never."

"Well, it just doesn't seem *fair*."

"It's never been about fair, Mom."

"We paid your tuition. We did all the things we were supposed to do."

"It was never about the money."

I get up. It's all too much for me to handle right now.

"Where are you going?" she asks.

"To figure some things out," I respond, placing the coffee mug to her food tray.

Sitting in the waiting room, the TV above me projecting a daytime talk show, I email back and forth with my boss, who wonders, in his own modern and sensitive way, where my work has been for the last few days.

I know you're going through a lot, he says.

Ian prefers emailing to texting. It imbues his nuggets of wisdom with a little more weight. He's always struggling with the concept of credibility.

Of course, I'd love for you to be doing the work right now, but it's important for you to figure yourself out. I see that you've logged in to the system, but don't stress yourself out. Just keep the boat moving down the river, so to speak.

His response is so even-keeled, I want to scream. I can't even be defensive and angry with him, and it drives me crazy. He gets the detail about me logging in wrong—unless I did that in a blackout—but otherwise, he's right.

The fact is, though, that work does circle the back of my mind. It's frustrating to be far away from home and not doing my work.

I'm not Madeline St. Clair.

If I were any other Suicide Blonde, I'd be all right. I could simply tell Ian to fuck off—because I'd have *fuck you* money—and live off the trust fund until something else came along.

None of them, not even Gillian, *has* to work. It's more like a hobby. Like playing stupid iPhone games on a bus. You're just waiting for your stop.

But what Ian doesn't understand about my predicament is, I *do* need a job. I need to *work*. What happens when I don't have a million things to do is that I go crazy.

Not *haven't-had-my-coffee-on-a-Monday* crazy. But actual crazy. *Legit* crazy. Like, committed to a psych ward crazy.

So, yeah, Ian, I do need to figure out work as well as *myself*.

But even then, I am stuck in a holding pattern. The other blondes have my time and attention in their hands, so work—both the concept and the actual thing—feel distant, like someone yelling a reservation name across a crowded restaurant.

There is nothing I can do about my professional life until I have this thing solved for myself. Then, perhaps, I can focus on all the code in the world. I can put in headphones and type until my fingers bleed.

But not yet.

Plus, I'm afraid of what I'll find if I go back to the rental property. Any number of things could be waiting there for me.

A ransacked house. A broken computer. A psychopathic killer.

Or nothing at all. Somehow, that would be most fitting.

Just then, I catch sight of someone in my periphery, which breaks the hold my phone has on my entire existence.

A very serious and official-looking man sits across from me. He has a bald head and very unstylish clothes. Suit coat. Button-down Oxford shirt with a loose knot on the tie. Sort of rumpled, kind of like a tortoise wearing an off-the-rack suit.

"Can we talk?" he says.

No introduction. No preamble. Just right to the chase. The perfect bum's rush.

I think he senses I see the gun in his shoulder holster, but I ask for formal ID nonetheless, and I am obliged to check every detail before handing it back to him.

He's a cop. Maybe FBI, but usually they clean up a little better. They're like the Mormons of policing. Local cops, they're football fans. Saturday night sinners.

"How can I help you, Officer...Ciccotelli?"

"*Detective* Ciccotelli," he says, nodding once.

"Not a lot of Ciccotellis down this way," I respond, "and—no offense—you don't sound like you grew up in Brentwood."

His eyes never leave me. He's not harsh, not intimidating, but he's as straightforward as coffee with no cream and no sugar.

"Brooklyn," he said. "I'm like ninety percent of Nashville now. I'm a transplant. I moved down here twenty-five years ago—"

"—Which does make you special," I interrupt. "That ninety percent you mentioned dates back to 2010 or so. *Maybe.*"

"I suppose you could say that," he responds. "I'm here so long, sometimes I forget I still got a little piece of the accent. Like a reverse southern thing."

My mind drifts back to last night, and I run through the options of what he might want to ask me. Did Colton end up calling the cops? Did I drunkenly run a red light? Has my house been ransacked by some mask-wearing lunatic?

"I suppose you want to speak with me about something?"

It's as even-keeled as I can make it, and I have to work to keep my voice from shuddering. Not an easy task when you're on the verge of breaking down.

"Listen, I don't mean to scare you, but I have a few questions, and I don't think there is a better time to ask them than now. You mind? It'll only take a few minutes."

I glance at my phone. Click the side button to check the time.

He notices this gesture. "It'll be quick. I promise."

"Sure," I say, trying to convey strength, but really I'm shaking so bad I think I can feel bones rattling.

He looks around, taps the ring finger of his left hand on the table. He's married, and the ring has some wear on it.

Turning back to me, he says, "Listen, I know you're in a bad way. I don't mean to intrude like this. There's just some things got to be done a certain way—"

"Just let out with it," I say. "I'm not fragile, and I'm sure you know my history."

He nods. He does. He's probably got a whole file on me.

"A friend of yours was found murdered last night."

"Murdered? Who?"

And then it dawns on me. Just my luck. Just my shitty fucking luck.

I say it before he has a chance to. "Madeline St. Clair."

He looks puzzled. "How—"

My voice doesn't feel like it even belongs to me. It feels like someone else's, some ventriloquist, using me as a sick little puppet.

"Because it's the way it has to go," I reply.

"I'm real sorry to have to be the one to tell you," he says. "Hazard of the job. But I *am* sorry."

The resulting silence is meant to give me time to react, but I don't. It's not that I don't recognize I should have some moment of teeth gnashing, eye wiping, hair pulling sorrow, but shock has robbed me of everything but limp-faced shock. I take enough anti-anxiety and anti-depression meds to tranquilize a buffalo, so I could be told my arm needs to be amputated and sold on eBay, and the best I could muster is a bewildered shrug.

At last, when he appears sure that I'm not going to cause a scene, he leans forward.

"What—what happened?" I ask.

"It was planned," he says, giving me nothing. "With the...nature of the crime, it is not consistent with robbery or breaking-and-entering. Officially, we are ruling it an intentional homicide."

"Oh," I reply.

"I find that, until we have a clearer picture of the case, there is no need to delve into the particulars. It...complicates things."

I can't help but place Madeline on the couch with me, her head resting on my shoulder, wanting to tell me her secret but somehow incapable. Now I'll likely never know.

"We don't have any solid leads on it, but I thought, considering your, you know, *relationship* with the victim, it was imperative I contact you first."

"I—that was so long ago."

With an even gaze, he says, "A nurse working the late shift tells me you wandered in late last night and begged her to let you stay here. Said you were frantic and wild-eyed, her words. Care to take a stab at that?"

I can feel my heart beating an imprint against my chest.

"What if I told you someone had broken into *my* place, too?"

He adjusts his glasses and rubs his stubble with one hand. It's so fresh I can't see it, but the sound is like sandpaper on corrugated metal. It's distracting, and I can only imagine what it's like to be in a legit interrogation room with him.

"If that's true—"

"Why wouldn't it be true?"

"—then I am going to suggest you keep a *very* low profile."

A few moments of strained, pained silence. Detective Ciccotelli has the look of a man who hasn't slept in years, and the silence only emphasizes the hang-dog countenance.

"Why don't we take a ride over to your home—"

"I'm renting a place."

He smiles, despite my *eat shit* tone.

"Your *rental*, then. It's not too far from here, no?"

"It's in The Nations."

"Perfect. Why don't we go take a look around, and then maybe I'll call in a crime scene unit. We'll just put *this* conversation on hold until a later date."

A HALF-HOUR LATER, and we're standing on the front steps of the house off 51st. Detective Ciccotelli is standing behind me, and I am numb with dread.

In momentary flashes of memory, I see Timothy Allred's body crumpled on my computer, a giant, living metaphor bleeding out on my monitor.

"It's all right," Detective Ciccotelli says. "I'm right here. No need to worry."

I unlock the door, and he asks for me to step aside.

"Better if I take a look around first," he says, pulling his weapon.

When I glance at it, he says, "Just a precaution."

As he disappears into the small foyer, I feel an acute need to scream. My whole body jolts with a kind of electricity, and I have to fight the urge to run back to the car and drive away, never looking back.

I anticipate the worst. If a guy *nearly* died last time, who's to say there isn't a dead body curled over my keyboard right now?

The detective's footsteps echo through the house and drift down to me. He's a big guy, tall and broad-shouldered, exactly the kind of cop you'd want protecting you in these kinds of situations. Always in control. Cautious. Seasoned.

"Ms. Hanneford?" Detective Ciccotelli calls from deep within the house. "I think you better come see this.

My mind cannot quite contain all of the horrors that *could* have occurred in this place in my absence. But what I see when I step into the main living room is worse than I could have imagined.

It's nothing.

I mean, Detective Ciccotelli is there, but he's already holstered his weapon, a *nothing to see here* kind of gesture.

He shrugs, as if to put a finer point on it.

"House looks clean," he says. "Nothing seems out of place, no physical evidence, and I don't see any form of forced entry. Do you?"

I don't fucking *know*, I think, and I tell him as much. "I know what I saw. In fact, I can show you what I saw. But no, it doesn't look like somebody ransacked the place."

"*Show me*? What do you mean?"

"I, um—I took pictures last night."

"You mean, like, you got photos of the suspect *in the midst* of breaking in?"

I nod, simultaneously going for my phone. A slight hesitation marks the movement, and I consider the idea that perhaps handing my phone over to a cop might not be the best idea. And yet, I find myself opening my device and tapping the Photos icon.

"If you look outside, you can see the owners' car parked in the driveway. I knelt behind it and—"

I stop. There's something wrong with my camera roll. All of my pics from the previous night—no wait, all of my pics *period*—have been erased.

With a flick of the thumb, I try to scroll up, but nothing happens.

"Everything okay?" the detective asks, and I nod, but internally, I'm freaking out. I know what's going on—even if I don't understand the how—but for some reason, I think that denying it will make it go away.

"My pictures. Something's—"

And then I find them. They have been moved to another folder entirely, a folder named *camera roll* that is not the actual roll from my iPhone.

My stomach twists as I open it.

Only, these are most definitely *not* the pictures I took. I don't recognize them, and so they take on a sort of blurry, otherworldly quality. I spin through them with a flick of the thumb. Detective Ciccotelli positions himself over my shoulder and peers down at my screen. I don't say not to because I don't know what the rules are here. Not only that, but I am too paralyzed to do much of anything else.

"Wait a second," he says. "Can I see that?"

Before I quite know what I'm doing, I've handed him my phone.

"That's not—I don't really know what that is," I say, my voice distant, even to my own ears. It's like I'm speaking to myself from someone else's body.

But I do know, because I recognize the person in the middle of the frame.

It's Madeline St. Clair—Queen Bitch of Belle Meade—and she is covered in blood.

MADELINE HASN'T BEEN KILLED; she's been *overkilled*. I catch just enough of a glimpse of her destroyed face before the detective pulls the phone from my sight.

Naturally, I reach for it, an instinctive gesture that only heightens the impression that I have something to hide.

"Not exactly photos of a burglary," he says, his voice even and calm.

"Someone—listen, I know this sounds batshit crazy, but someone has hijacked my phone somehow. It doesn't—why would I just *show* you pictures of..."

I trail off. My mind gets commandeered by the images on my phone. I feel my past rushing back up to smack me across the jaw right here in the present.

It's obvious—blatantly obvious—what's happening, and I am powerless to stop it.

The detective snaps his fingers. "Stay with me," he says. "This is—I'm sure we can figure this out, but I need you to calm down."

It's then I realize I'm hyperventilating. My breaths are coming in ragged, uneven pulses, and I suspect very soon I'm going to teeter over into catatonia.

Ciccotelli places me on the main couch—damn the evidence, I guess—and hurries out of the room. He comes back a few moments later with a glass of water.

"Drink this," he says, but he's also still holding my phone.

"I may need to hang onto this," he says, holding it up.

I shake my head, all the while downing the tap water.

"No way," I say when I'm done. "You can get what you need by issuing a warrant to my phone company. With the way things are going, there's no *way* I'm giving up my phone."

"I could—"

"But you won't," I say, my voice getting back to normal. "If you need my phone, you're going to need some pretty stellar evidence to crack it, not that I'd ever allow that. I'll be happy to cooperate, but not like this. I'm in shock. I'm in—"

My vision goes dim, and I have to fight to stay awake. The world is a series of flashes. The retro magazine rack. The scuff on the detective's right shoe. The sunlight reflecting off the hinges of the entertainment center.

A moment of darkness—just a moment—and then I'm surging back toward reality.

I manage only a single, sonorous syllable. "Unnnnnh," I say, pressing one hand against the spot on my temple just now beginning to ache.

"Almost lost you there," he says, smiling generously. "Your phone is, um, on the table there. I think we've done enough spelunking into your digital folders for one day."

He hangs around until he's certain I'm going to survive, and then he performs his more trivial duties. Promising to contact me again. Getting me a line on some protective custody. And on and on.

I have to leave the house so the crime scene unit can turn over the scene, check for fingerprints and whatnot, but Ciccotelli says it like he doesn't believe they'll find anything.

But it seems, for now, that I've been extended the grace of being excluded as a suspect, even if it is a temporary distinction.

12

Headlights appear in the driveway. Gillian emerges from a Range Rover and hurries to meet me.

When we embrace in the driveway, I can't help but ask her, "This is just the beginning, isn't it? Does it just get worse from here?"

She nods into my shoulder, and I sigh.

It's like a fault line has just shifted, and the resulting earthquake is going to bring everything down to dust.

Inside, the mood is no better.

"I wish I could say something like, 'I just don't know who would want to do this to her,' but that's just not the truth."

Gillian nods solemnly and sips the not-insubstantial glass of cabernet I've poured for her. She seems to be looking for something to say but can't quite find the words.

I decide to call her on it.

"This isn't the time to hide anything," I tell her, matter-of-factly. "One of us is gone, and you and I both know this is just the beginning. Plenty of people wanted Madeline dead in some passive way, but this wasn't random."

Gillian has never been one to mince words, so when she opens her mouth, I can't help but hold my breath.

"There is something no one has ever told you," she says. "It has to do with that night."

She slowly spins her glass on the table, watching the way the liquid sloshes against the sides.

"After you...left—"

"You mean 'was assaulted and kicked out,'" I interrupt.

"Either way," she continues, keeping a steady, steely-eyed gaze, "we were in my room, the computer humming in the corner when Audrey came up with the idea."

"What idea?"

"Like I said, we were just sitting there, kind of reeling from what we'd talked about in the chat room and also what had happened with you when she says it."

"What does she *say*, Gillian?"

Gillian, not one for inherent dramatics, pauses long enough that I begin to question whether or not this is some far-flung hoax to drive me insane.

"Well," she begins, and, thinking over her words, shifts uncomfortably in her seat. "I mean, I didn't hear it—"

"Just *say* it," I say insistently.

She nods this time, and the weight of the moment settles over the room. It's like twenty years are being vacuumed right out of the room.

"Apparently, they went downstairs, and one of them said, 'Let's go watch it. Let's go watch him die.'"

THEN

WHEN GILLIAN CLOSES the browser window, none of them can speak for at least a minute. They are like gymnasts manufacturing content- ment for some unseen judges. There is a crackling *pop* to the energy in the room, even if there is no sound, and at last Madeline gives what she probably thinks is a demure smile.

"I think we did it," she says. "I think it's actually going to happen."

All of them are possessed of a kind of exultant self-satisfaction. All but Mary Ellen, who is beginning to turn a very subtle shade of green.

"We need to tell someone," she says, the tone of her voice high and insistent. She's never heard these sounds emerge from her, but she thinks that if she is loud and frightening enough that she can somehow put an end to this.

"We did," Madeline responds. "We told Everett. Isn't that enough?"

"I'm serious, Mads," Mary Ellen says. "This isn't a joke."

"And yet, M.E., I feel like laughing."

And then she does, a risible, mocking sound. But it accomplishes its intended effect. It chills the rest of the room, and if either Audrey or Gillian was ever going to speak up, they certainly aren't now. It's all too late. Everything is too late. The wheels are set into motion, and they will carry this to the next horrid destination.

Mary Ellen stands, and Madeline stands with her.

"Where are you going?" she asks. "The night's still young. We have plenty of cigarettes and vodka, and we plan on getting *fucked up*, so long as the mood isn't killed off prematurely."

With that, Audrey's standing, her smile a detestable and somewhat sinister leer. "And you wouldn't dare do that, would you? Kill off the mood?"

Audrey's been waiting for this moment. Up to now, she's been a kamikaze pilot without a mission. That all changes when there's a divide in the ranks. Mary Ellen's defection provides her with a chance to go all-in for Madeline.

"This is murder," Mary Ellen says, though her voice sounds distant and constricted.

Madeline mocks her by pretending to search the room. "I don't see a gun in here. There are no *knives* or *bombs* or *baseball bats*, either."

"No fucking bats," Audrey repeats, her voice high and quavering. Gillian, meanwhile, just stares, half-lidded and contemplative. She looks like she's taken a whole bar of Xanax.

"It's not right," Mary Ellen tries again. "Listen, you got what you wanted. You completely *owned* a human being, took everything from him. Isn't that enough?"

Madeline steps forward, and she's so close Mary Ellen can smell the stench of cigarettes and vodka on her.

"It won't be enough until he's underneath his headstone."

Suddenly, none of this makes sense. She's gone along to get along, but she cannot figure out what has brought them to this moment. "But why?" she asks.

"I don't know," Madeline responds. "But really, who cares? It could have been anybody. Turns out, it was *him*. So what?"

Again, the silence is almost too much for Mary Ellen. The other girls just stare. It's as if they have some distant, burgeoning understanding of their actions, but they don't want to actually recognize it. Their eyes are glassy and unfocused, all but Madeline's, whose retinas burn with an anger Mary Ellen has never seen.

And, suddenly, she kicks her.

Just lifts a foot and kicks Mary Ellen right in the chest.

The backs of Mary Ellen legs hit the ottoman she'd been sitting on, and she rolls ass-over-teakettle back into the corner of the room.

Before she can gain a sense of what's happening, the other girls are on her. It goes so smoothly, almost like a choreographed dance. Almost like they'd *planned* it. Audrey grabs her wrists, Gillian her feet. And Madeline, of course, sits on her chest, pinning her to the ground.

When she leans down, baring her teeth, Mary Ellen can smell the nicotine again, but there's also something underneath that. Something more fundamental, more primal, like pheromones or hormones or pure adrenaline.

But nothing compares to the look in her eyes.

She actually sees death in them.

"What we are doing, that's not killing someone," she says.

And then her hands are on Mary Ellen's throat, pressing down with a vise-like tension. Her fingernails dig into the soft flesh beneath the chin, and she squeezes until it feels like Mary Ellen's windpipe will collapse.

"*This* would be killing someone," she says. "*This* would be murder."

Somehow, her grip tightens, displaying a strength Mary Ellen didn't know existed in her pot-smoking, un-athletic friend. The air is gone, floating around her but giving her no succor. Her vision weakens, turning a few unsettling colors, and she thinks she's going to pass out.

"I would kill you," Audrey says, from just out of sight. "I would fucking *gut* you, if Madeline asked. Do you want me to gut you?"

But of course she can't shake her head. She's too busy focusing on a single point on the ceiling, trying desperately to stay awake and present, because she knows if they let her slip into unconsciousness, they won't know how to bring her back.

So she just lets this happen. She just lets go. She focuses on the click in the back of her throat, the place where all of the tissue meets, praying for an opening that will allow even a sliver of oxygen in.

"What we are doing," Madeline continues, loosening her grip just enough that the blackness isn't quite so black, "is *freeing* him. We are giving him the out he so desperately deserves. We are in control of everything. We. Are. God."

And even though it is the most ridiculous, grandiose thing Madeline's ever said, to Mary Ellen, at least, it's also the most terrifying. Because it is true. Only a madwoman would say such things, and only a fool would discredit Madeline St. Clair's belief in herself.

When she finally lets go, Madeline pulls back and leans against the ottoman, an orgasmic expression slithering over her features. She moans just once, as Gillian and Audrey release Mary Ellen's limbs.

It is transcendent. It is amazing. It places her on another plane of existence.

Or at least it looks that way.

But Mary Ellen does not give herself time to drink it all in. She is up and scrambling away from them, rushing for the door.

Audrey begins pursuit, but Madeline waves it off.

"Let her go," she says. "She's served her purpose."

NOW AND THEN

"How do you know any of this?"

Gillian stares into her drink. A long time passes before she actually speaks.

"I didn't find out for a long time, not until we were adults," she says. "Not until they figured they could trust me with it, I guess."

"And what did they say?"

She shrugs. "They just kind of...told me."

And then she goes on to tell *me*.

***

Gillian enters the bar on Lower Broadway with a pit in her stomach. She hasn't seen The Girls in a while, and the truth is, she doesn't feel close enough to them to hang out anymore. The call from Audrey —ever the coordinator—came out of the blue, and if she didn't know better, she'd think she is being set-up.

It's the thing she thinks as she elbows her way past the cadre at the door and into the somber, darkened depths of this particular honky tonk.

She thinks it's like something out of a grainy old mafia movie.

Gillian Meitner now sleeps with the fishes, she thinks.

At the very least, this could be some weird kind of sting.

Or blackmail.

Somewhere, she expects cameras, a whole surveillance system. Maybe one of them is wearing a wire. They've been quiet too long not to have something planned.

When she spots them, she glances around, checking her perimeter. There's just something so...off about seeing Madeline and Audrey after all this time.

They used to be close. Used to go out drinking, partying until the wee hours of the morning, avoiding the old days like week-old sushi, unless it happened to be the general *We went through some fucked-up shit, didn't we* variety.

As soon as she sits down, they are feeding her lines.

"It's just been so *long*," Audrey says.

"We'd have invited Mary Ellen, but—"

"She wouldn't come," Audrey says, finishing Madeline's thought.

"What we mean is, she wouldn't fly across the country."

They struggle through the first drink, glancing around the bar and commenting on the tourists and new locals, before the hard edges begin to soften on the conversation.

"So," Madeline says, being inquisitive, "what are you up to these days?"

Gillian goes through her usual spiel about her job, and because it's kind of boring—and they look bored—she finishes before the band on-stage up front has finished their first song.

She rushes, in part, because she doesn't give a shit about her job. Her job *is* boring. She likes the boring-ness of it. Her job consists of numbers, and numbers, even with their complex calculations, are predictable.

She likes predictable.

It's not that she hates uncertainty. Uncertainty is welcome. Heisenberg had it down to a science, haha. She relishes when her job requires her to square a circle that seems impossible. That gives her a thrill, as much as she can be thrilled.

But unpredictable—Gillian wants none of that.

Her brain gets so far ahead of her, by the time she catches back up to the conversation, they've begun talking about something else entirely.

Gillian has never been good at conversation.

If not for her dad's relationship with Madeline's dad—something about finances—the two of them would have never been friends.

As Madeline and Audrey prattle on about their very glamorous, very public lives, she withdraws into herself. She's more comfortable like that, anyway. In her own mind. If the robots take over, and people are reduced to brains in jars, Gillian figures she will be *just* fine with that. She can spend all of eternity contemplating the spheres.

It isn't until their third or fourth drink that she is knocked out of her shell. It's when she hears something—a detail from their past—which is out of sync with the rest of what she knows about the whole *Suicide Blondes* situation.

Audrey is talking, and she gets halfway through a paragraph about *that night*—rehashing everything—before Madeline elbows her in the chest.

"What'd you say?" Gillian asks her.

Audrey laughs, her face a melting wax figure of drunkenness. "I said, 'Ow, my tit!'"

Both of them fall into a red-faced fit of laughter, all while Gillian watches on in a kind of solitary horror.

She is not amused.

She is massaging the wound her two...accomplices have opened up with just an offhand remark. She feels now as though she's been living a lie these past decades.

Gillian has a steel trap for a brain—it's the one compliment she accepts without attributing it to other people's obsequiousness—and so she is actively trying to recall every syllable uttered in the last minute, piecing it together into a mental tapestry.

"Oh, my *God*," Audrey says, "it was just a joke."

But Gillian doesn't find it funny. She has a very specific sense of humor, and not included in her list of things she considers hilarious is watching a teenager die of his own hand. She has grown up in the last several years, and death in all forms has become taboo for her. She doesn't even date musicians whose music focuses too heavily on death. (Her goth phase was short-lived.)

"Come *on*, Gil," Madeline says, after a time. "We *all* did some messed-up stuff back then. If we can't laugh about it *now*, then when *can* we laugh?"

"Maybe never," she replies, feeling her cheeks grow hot.

She doesn't know something. When she doesn't know something, Gillian freaks out. She has spent her whole life pursuing knowledge of things, so when she is in the dark on a particular topic—*any* particular topic—she loses her *mind.*

When she doesn't match their sense of levity about the whole thing, eventually they settle down, and the mood of their conversation dries up entirely.

Madeline eyes her from over yet *another* drink, her face twisted into a grimace, and then she says, "Do you really want to know?"

She does. Of *course,* she does. She wouldn't have chided them, if not.

Gillian takes this all in, as she does most things, analytically. Without judgment.

For a moment, she is possessed of the impulse to tell them about the sickness they very obviously suffer from, but she doesn't.

It's not her style.

Instead, she cogitates on it, trying to think through the logic of their decision. She supposes maybe it makes sense that they would keep it from her for so long, especially if they were somehow worried about prosecution in the matter.

Or if Mary Ellen somehow found out about it.

She would definitely have a claim for...something.

But first, she needs to know what *it* is.

"Tell me everything," she says, half a demand.

Audrey leans forward, her breath a cloud of liquor in front of her. "Only under an oath of secrecy. We need to know you're still...one of the girls."

"I am," she manages through gritted teeth.

She doesn't like the *rah-rah* girl stuff. It reeks of the same tribalism which got her into that jam all those years ago.

But she figures she must, for the time being, fall prey to it. She needs to know what they did.

Or, she thinks, what *else* they did.

"The night," Audrey begins, glancing once at Madeline before continuing, "we ended up leaving your place after...what happened with Mary Ellen."

She sips her drink, now more cognizant of herself—and maybe a little more reflective, too—and takes a moment to calm down.

"We were supposed to go home, but—and I should say this is *not* how I feel today—but we were so hyped from the *idea* of what we had done—"

"The actual *inception*," Madeline interrupts.

"—That we just couldn't let go without seeing it. We had set this thing into motion, and it was, like, we couldn't just turn our backs on it."

Gillian is already ahead of them, at this point, her mind racing up to the end of their whole scenario. She can see their teenage selves driving to the Coughlin residence and standing in the darkness of the family's garage, waiting for the right moment to peer in.

She is almost choking when she asks the next question.

"What did you do when you got there?"

Her hands quiver with the loss of humanity. It's as though something else—another person—is being taken from this world, from the mere insinuation of the story.

And these girls—not women, not at all—have no idea what they hold in their hands.

But as Audrey talks, Gillian sees something in Madeline's face, a changing countenance. There is now a darkness in her that was not present before.

Madeline was always cruel, but Gillian thinks she is witnessing something else.

Could it be—empathy?

"We chickened the fuck out!"

Audrey still has the fiery look of the anointed, as if she could do it all over again. Her face is wide and open and joyous, and though she is laughing, there is something grim about it. Like delirium.

Madeline—the voice of reason, for once—steps in and says, "Neither one of us could do it," she says, putting Gillian oddly at ease. "I mean, it was never really an option."

"You say that," Audrey says, "but you seemed pretty gung-ho about it that night."

"It was the adrenaline," Madeline counters. "I thought I was such hot fucking shit, that nothing would touch me. I was wrong, and that was wrong."

"You sure this isn't all in retrospect?" Audrey probes, an edge in her voice.

"It was fun in that way everything you do at sixteen is fun. Like nothing can kill you. But then something does. We were just lucky we didn't play those games with one another. It could have *really* gotten out of hand."

This is the first truly poignant thing either of them has said tonight, Gillian thinks. Otherwise, it's a couple of fried brain cells smacking against one another.

She is surprised Madeline is forthright about her monstrous behavior from back in the day, but maybe that's a case of *too little, too late*. No one from the Coughlin family would accept this disgusting show of attrition.

Why should Gillian?

"So, neither of you approached the house?" Gillian asks, refocusing their attention.

Madeline shakes her head. "We watched from the driveway."

Audrey, her eyes gleaming from the drinks, says, "We could see the light. But no. Neither one of us went even *near* that garage. Scout's honor."

She hiccups, laughs, and downs her drink. It takes every bit of Gillian's restraint not to slap her across her smug face.

Gillian is confronted with an immediate conundrum.

Does this information warrant relaying to the police?

Or to Mary Ellen?

She lives up in Portland or Seattle or somewhere now, so it's not like she will be coming home anytime soon.

It's almost like she's sublimated, gone from a human being to a phantom. Gillian knows she still exists—she suspects Mary Ellen has some fake profile—but she's yet to reach out.

There's never a perfect time.

Until now.

And the *now* of a situation like this is all that matters.

But then she comes to the realization that if she tells Mary Ellen right now, she might be playing into the hands of some complicated scheme of theirs. The way they're looking at her, they could absolutely eat her for dinner.

So she pulls back, thinks to think on it a while.

"Who else have you told?" Gillian asks.

Madeline holds up a big old donut, placing her thumb against her other fingers and looking through the hole. "No-fucking-body."

"Huh," Gillian responds. "So, there's no *there* there. You just went over there and then, I don't know, went to get ice cream afterward?"

"We stayed there for a while," Audrey admits. "I don't think either of us wanted to back away, so we just kind of stood there and prayed for the courage."

"Courage?"

"Yeah," Audrey says, clearly not hearing the horror in Gillian's voice. "The *cojones* to do it, to walk up and look in his frightened eyes as he—"

"Aud, that's enough," Madeline interrupts, the blush in her cheeks more than makeup.

Gillian allows Audrey's last outburst to linger in the air like old smoke, and then she frames her final—and most important—question as directly as possible.

"Why now?"`

BACK IN THE MOMENT, after her story, Gillian looks up at me, as if to beg me for the answer to that question.

I don't have anything of the sort.

I just have more questions of my own.

"What did they say to that?" I ask. "Certainly they had a reason, beyond *hey we're drunk*. That can't be it, can it?"

She shrugs. "It seems like maybe they felt the need to unburden their souls, even if it came off like two kids admitting to a childhood crush."

The thought of it makes my skin crawl. "Why do *you* think they did it?"

"I dunno," she says, sounding tired. "I've thought about that a lot. Like, they could have spent the rest of their lives without risking telling anyone about it."

"What's the risk?" I ask. "I already paid the bill for all of it."

"Yeah," she says, "that's the part I can't figure out. Maybe they thought there was some chance they could end up on the wrong side of a lawsuit."

"Or maybe they had buffed the scratches out of their personal lives enough that the shiny coat on the outside gleamed."

"Could be," she says. "They could be hiding it so they don't suffer any present-day consequences, but that doesn't seem likely."

She finishes off her drink. "Also, there's the issue of Madeline."

"What about her?"

"She looked...spooked about it."

"Like how?"

"Like she was being forced into saying it against her will," Gillian says.

"Maybe like she's been receiving threats?"

"Or like she genuinely wanted to get it off her chest. I don't know. You know how hard it is to read her. Everything is below the surface."

"And now she'll never be able to do it. To *unburden her soul.*"

"It makes me wonder if somebody else plans on doing it for her."

That thought hadn't occurred to me, either.

"Jesus," I say. "What am I supposed to do with all of this?"

"Do with it what you want," she replies. "I'm just the messenger."

"I wonder what Audrey thinks of it."

"I think maybe that was the beginning of the rift between those two," Gillian says, and I nod along. "Why else would they suddenly separate, when they've been so close for all these years?"

"Maybe it got to be too much for them to keep this mutual secret."

"Maybe the wrong person found out," Gillian says. "And this is the result."

I think about that for a while. "Everett's mother always seemed to have something inflammatory to say. You don't think—"

"I don't *know*," she replies. "All I know is, if somebody went after Madeline, then they could go after *us*, too."

My next thought about Madeline's death—her interactions with the cousin—is interrupted by my phone's ring.

I check the number, and by the time I answer, I've left Gillian behind, hoping she'll lock up on her way out the door.

13

By the time I get to Mom's room, she's unconscious. She's turned a sickly yellow color, like someone's doused the room with a bad Instagram filter.

They don't quite know what's wrong with her, but whatever it is, it's bad.

"Can you tell me what the fuck is going on?" I ask, when the first nurse is able to tear herself away to speak with me.

She runs through a whole list of possibilities, though none of them sound certain. However, one thing she says catches me off-guard.

"If I didn't know any better," she says, "I'd think she's been poisoned."

"And you can't do, like, a *test* or something to find that out?"

"Anyone who knows what they're doing could use any number of impossible-to-trace substances to get away with it. Polonium, for example, is what the Russians use when they—"

"My mother isn't a *spy*, for chrissakes," I say, desperation edging into my voice. I don't know jack shit about anything medical, but I do know that, whatever my mom has going on, it isn't some Russian plot to get rid of her.

The woman is a font of compassion. She smiles sadly and says, "Just know that we are doing everything we can to help her, but sometimes these things can be difficult to pin down, especially with someone as—"

"Crazy?"

"—*sick* as your mother obviously is. I'm not asking you to put your emotions on hold, but I do hope you can bear with us as we do everything we can to save your mom."

Once she's done, I'm left feeling better and more optimistic than before. Mom stabilizes, even if she looks like she's curled up on death's door, and I take up residence outside her room as I wait for updates.

As I sit there, a whole litany of possible outcomes become apparent to me, but only two make any real sense. Either she's going to survive this and be forever disabled, or she will die.

It's that simple.

I've been hiding from the truth of this eventual outcome for too long to prepare myself for it. The bridge is too rickety. The tires are too flat. The infrastructure has crumbled. I am brittle but also too distant from it.

And yet, I can still push it away for a little while longer. She needs me to be strong right now. There is no one else—no sisters or brothers, no remaining parents—so I am literally all she has.

I'd like to think Dad is looking down on us, that he is keeping watch over the two of us, but it's a blurry sort of wish, like the desultory career choices of children.

I want to be an astronaut.

I want to be President of the United States.

I want my dead father to make sure I survive my mother's death.

There is no solace. This last stretch of road is paved with misery, and I'm going to have to drive it, either way. Might as well throw the shifter into drive and pull forward.

Selfishly, of course, I want her to stick around. I always want my mother, though not in the urgent way most people do. I want her the way lapsed Christians want their gods: passive, present, and almost always in the background of their lives.

At a certain point, I nod off.

I wake up at dusk, desperately thirsty.

When I step out to pick up a soda from the downstairs vending machine, Detective Ciccotelli is waiting for me. Like I brought this on myself.

He looks older than the last time I saw him. Something about his face. The basset hound eyes and the high-grit sandpaper stubble. The gin blossoms. Eyes under cavernous brows. They shift to me slowly, filled with a grim perspicacity. As though he's seen everything and just needs it to be revealed to everyone else.

"Miss Hanneford," he says quietly, almost pleasantly, as if this is a chance encounter.

"Detective," I reply, eyeing the rows and rows of diet drinks in the machine.

I swipe my card and select a Diet Dr. Pepper.

He dispenses with the pleasantries this time, but his tone is flat and emotionless.

"How would you characterize your relationship with Madeline Ambrose?"

"St. Clair. She never actually changed her name."

"Oh yeah?"

"Yeah. She could use one when she wanted but rely on the other when it was convenient for her."

"Either way, what would you say about how you two got along?"

"Am I under investigation?"

"No," he says leaning against the Coke machine. "Just getting a sense of the case, as it is right now. It's like a broken mirror, the shattered pieces flung in all directions. Each one reflects something different—I just need to know what."

"How big is the shard you've got me trapped in?"

"It's not like that," he says, and for some reason, I believe him. Foolishly, I suppose, but I guess that's where we are.

"Nonexistent," I say, going back to his question. "She and I only picked things up recently, when I came back to Nashville."

"And she didn't mention any conversation, any communication, that might have provoked someone to act in a violent way toward her?"

"What, like she *deserved* what she got?"

I don't quite know why I'm defending Madeline, but there is an innate defensiveness in me when it comes to cops. It's like I've spent my whole life in solitary, when the opposite is true...mostly.

"No, like, did she say the wrong thing to the wrong person, and set a series of actions—Listen, I've spent a whole hell of a lot of time investigating cases. You remember the one story about the guy who stabbed his wife to death because she served him fried eggs instead of scrambled eggs?"

"I don't."

"Guy gets up at the ass crack of dawn to go to work. Never thinks about the fact that his poor, beleaguered wife gets up even earlier to cook his ungrateful ass some breakfast. Anyway, she can't read his mind, so she makes fried eggs and French toast. Son-of-a-bitch has some sort of psychotic break, takes one of them giant, Michael Myers type knives out of the drawer and stabs her until the cops arrive."

"Jesus Christ."

"Then, he just kind of drops it and walks over to us, explaining what happened."

I can only stare. He seems to have lost me back at the off ramp.

"My point is," he says, "sometimes people are victims of circumstance, and the random nature of the crime cannot be assembled from the disparate pieces and threads that make it up."

I nod. This part, at least, makes sense.

"Other crimes, though, they are the result of a direct line drawn from A to B. It might not be evident, at first—the way it was with the breakfast fellow—but eventually the thread becomes visible, and we can follow it to its ultimate destination."

"And you think maybe I am the thread?"

"I haven't decided that yet," he replies, looking me over speculatively. "Could be, in which case I should be demoted for telling you so much."

"I didn't do it," I reply.

"But my other instinct," he continues, ignoring me, "is that you have something to do with this, even if you're not directly involved."

I'm appalled, and I tell him so.

Detective Ciccotelli isn't perturbed in the least bit, however. He's chewing at something he feels like he can grind down into a kind of malleable paste. He just hasn't quite figured out how to get his teeth on it just right.

So I help him along.

"All right," I say. "She and I have talked—or just talked, past tense —a few times since I came home. Really only the once, I guess, when she—"

"Showed up past midnight at your rental home," he finishes my sentence.

He knows more than he lets on, so I have to be careful with what I have to say. Which is weird, considering the fact that I *don't* really know anything, at least not anything that would have any sort of bearing on the case.

Her exsanguinated corpse flashes through my mind. I can see the blank, half-lidded eyes, staring up at nothing. The growing puddle of crimson beneath her neck. The ragged, hamburger meat quality of the wound on the side of her head.

"Going back to my original line of questioning: are you aware of anyone who might want Mrs. Amb—I'm sorry—Mrs. St. Clair dead?"

"I don't know," I reply. "Can't you just check her phone? Wasn't it"—I refuse to say *found at the crime scene*—"at her house or something?"

"You have to understand where I'm coming from on this," he says. "I know you think it's my job to come in and give you a hard time."

He shifted his position and jangled the change in his pocket.

"But we have a woman in our midst who died in a very violent way. I have to explore each and every avenue as if it might be *the* one. Now, I know you aren't being cold about Mrs. Ambrose's—"

"St. Clair."

"Forgive me," he said. "I'm a little old fashioned, and maybe I've spent too much time in the South for my own good. Either way, I want to make something between us very clear: I'm going to go where the evidence leads me. Am I clear on that point?"

I nod.

"Because the most important thing to me is finding the person who did this. I don't like this aspect of the job, believe me. But it has to be done, and so that means you have to answer these questions."

Again, I give him the reaction he requires. In turn, he jangles the change again.

"Good. Now if we can go back to your relationship with...Mrs. St. Clair."

"I knew Madeline a long time ago, Detective," I say, "and though she was an angry, vindictive teenager, nothing about her tells me she'd provoke someone into killing her."

The detective seems to let that sink in. Then, he shifts his footing. He says, "Miss Hanneford, I'll be frank with you: We *don't* have her phone, as yet. We believe it to have been stolen from the scene."

"That seems odd," I say honestly.

His smile is more than withering.

"Funny you should say that," he replies, "because, even though we don't have the physical device, we are working on gaining access to the phone records. It's going to take a little while to get the actual texts and whatnot, if we even have to go that far. But the calls and the numbers, we have those."

"Oh." It's all I can say. Something in the pit of my stomach is suddenly very cold.

"These *records*"—saying the word as if he, himself, is skeptical of what they might portend—"indicate that you, Miss Hanneford, made a phone call the night of her murder."

"I don't—"

"And another thing," he continues, cutting me off. "I find this part *very* interesting. This call, it connected. Now, you can have someone call up their buddy, and the phone can ring and ring and ring. This one made landfall, and it seems like it was a voicemail message."

"Oh yeah?" I say, trying to keep my voice under wraps.

"You might, um, have an idea of what you said on the phone that night?"

I struggle for the words. They echo through my head.

I'm not afraid of you.

"Um—"

In fact, you should be afraid of me.

He gives me an even-tempered look that nevertheless tells me that he's got me. "I'll help you out here. People, they can get real clumsy, and they can accidentally get somebody on the line. Call it a butt dial. You ever experience that?"

I nod. My explanation—my excuse—is caught somewhere in the back of my mind, and there's nothing I can do to spit it out.

"Right. Of course. We all have. That what happened the night you called Madeline St. Clair? It was a big misunderstanding. What we might call...a *coincidence*. Am I on the right track?"

"I, um—"

"You and Mrs. St. Clair, you two had a difficult break in the friendship all those years ago, if I understand the situation correctly. Yes?"

If you call threatening to kill someone on the steps of the courthouse *a difficult break*, then yes.

"She and I patched things up."

"Is that what happened the night she appeared on your doorstep?"

"Sort of."

"And the late-night phone call. That was a further 'patching up,' yes? In that message on the phone, that's what you were saying?"

"Basically."

In fact, you should be afraid of me.

In my heart of hearts, I know they will find the message, and I will have to explain myself and that making a threat on the phone doesn't look good, but for now, I need to survive. I can't tell this man, this cop, that I threatened a dead person on the phone.

"You understand, I'm giving you the benefit of the doubt here. You can create your own...*narrative* about that night. Clear up any confusion for me right here, right now."

"I understand that," I reply.

"Because the next time we speak, you can expect it will be more formal."

"Everything happened the way I just told you."

His smile fades. I'm sure it's a look he's given hundreds—maybe *thousands*—of criminals. He's peering down the road several moves, predicting how things are going to play out.

And he's sad about it.

I think he sees me at the end of this situation, waiting in the back of a cruiser as my rights are being read to me. This is his attempt to forgo all of that, in favor of a less predictably depressing outcome. If it were up to him, I wouldn't be dragged screaming and crying to the cop car.

And with this moment passing, his gaze shifts one last time.

"You keep an eye out for the phone, now, okay?"

He shuffles off, favoring one leg, and it becomes apparent to me then, he's not just a cop but a war veteran as well. I convince myself to ask him about it the next time we speak.

WHEN I GET BACK HOME to the rental property, I pace around for a few minutes, trying to discern logic where there is none.

If this is Madeline's last big *fuck you*, then it certainly is a good one.

If she somehow knew she was about to be offed and used that opportunity to frame me for it, then *bra-fucking-vo*. Hats off for her ability to take an unsuspecting victim and put them in the worst possible situation.

It's ridiculous, but Madeline is—or at least *was*—the most vindictive and horrible person I knew. She could've changed, but my intense personal study of human behavior contradicts that theory.

In the house, I retrace my steps. There has to be *something* I missed. It can't be that out of my reach.

I hurry to the bedroom, lie down. Then, I get back up and sneak down the hallway to the front door, which I open with a nervous flourish.

There exists a moment in which I think Madeline might—just might—be standing on the threshold, waiting for me.

Haha, you crazy bitch, she'd say. Did you think I'd leave you like this?

But she's not. It's only the rapidly fading day of a bleak and meritless week.

Still, I don't give up. I continue the charade until something occurs to me. Something only marginally odd but just enough to make me investigate.

I don't know how I didn't notice it before.

I go to the bathroom.

It was the last place Madeline went before she stumbled drunkenly from the house.

The point of contention is the toilet. Not the lid or the bowl or the handle, but the tank itself. Now that I look at it—really look at it—I can see that the lid is *ever* so slightly ajar.

Like something out of a mob movie.

Sure enough, I find *it* in the tank, back of the toilet.

The inclination to call the police is quickly squashed beneath the weight of my own curiosity. There's no way I'm letting this out of my sight until I've had a chance to scan the whole goddamned thing.

It's a treasure trove. The Rosetta Stone of my teenage years. My own personal answer to the riddle of the Sphinx.

It's Madeline St. Clair's personal diary.

14

NOW

Some pages have been ripped out—while others are scribbled black—but the big picture remains intact. At first, I can only survey it from a distance, an archaeologist discovering a lost Dead Sea Scroll, uncovering an as-yet unpublished play of Shakespeare's.

The scope of this thing is huge. Madeline's reflective writings date back to high school, back to when she was queen bitch of DDA and the most vicious shark in the pool.

But it's incomplete.

Even a cursory glance through her journal reveals that Madeline was, at the atomic level, insecure about herself. Otherwise, why would she mark through so much of what she wrote?

It's obvious she thought she was in trouble. Otherwise, she wouldn't have stuck an artifact from her life in my toilet.

But now the question remains: Who was stalking her?

I thumb all the way back to a date that matches up with *that night*.

.   .   .

DEAR ME. Tonight I think I did...something.

THAT'S IT. The entirety of a kid's last hours on Earth boiled down to an *oopsie-doopsie* in her personal journal.

It would be embarrassing if it weren't so absolutely fascinating.

I check the date to make sure it all matches up, and when it does, I can't help but read and re-read the passage, hoping to divine some intended meaning that is clearly not there.

It is a single volume, a Five Star notebook that looks as neat as the day it was purchased. How she could put all of her thoughts down for twenty years and *not* fill it up is beyond me, but somehow she's managed. Either she didn't have that many thoughts, or what interested her about her life was not the day-to-day goings-on, but the things that made other people miserable.

Despite the uneven, sometimes stilted All-work-and-no-play-makes-Jack-a-dull-boy aspects of Madeline's journal, I do learn a lot about her.

She went through a considerable dark night of the soul following the death of Everett Coughlin. It is evident not necessarily in what she says but what lies in her silences. In the weeks following *the incident*—her words—she pens only a few staid phrases about it.

DEAR ME. It's done. I'm safe. I'm free. I'm really very sad and full of regret. One day, I hope M.E. understands, but for now, I have to be happy. Have to be.

EVENTUALLY, she returns to her vindictive, malicious former self, but this is a break in the narrative that helps humanize Madeline.

She wasn't all monster.

She just never wanted anyone to see beyond the mask.

I try to tamp down my own feelings—ignore my memories—so that I can try to embrace some kind of redemption on my old frenemy's behalf.

It's not there. I try, and maybe that's what she's looking for, but I just can't completely forgive her. Not yet. There's still something missing, something awful, about here. It just lingers amidst the messy details of her past.

I flip to the back, avoiding the redacted and excised portions, trying to find THE THING she wanted me to see.

If nothing else—if I cannot find the saint in the sinner—perhaps I can at least make things all right in the wake of her death.

It appears to me, as I scan the latter entries in her journal, that she hit a point where she was sick and tired of pretending to be everything and just decided to do what interested her.

And what interested her was fucking her best friends' husbands and boyfriends.

There are at least a dozen different men mentioned over the span of the last two years of her life, and though not every single one of them was named, it wouldn't be too difficult to figure them out, if I tried hard enough.

One of them is obvious.

It's the guy Gillian dated before this new one. This was not some temporary fling or mercurial sex type thing. It was going to be the real deal.

And then Gillian broke it off.

It would explain *why* Gillian broke it off, but not why she felt the need to keep it from me. Perhaps she has her own motive in all of this.

I am compelled to wonder to myself: Was her admission about speaking to Madeline and Audrey about *that night* and watching the garage door even true?

Just as I find some relevant passages in the notebook, my entire train of thought is sidelined by the zzz-zzz of my phone on the kitchen island.

I don't even have a chance to speak.

"Oh, my God, have the cops talked to you?"

It's Audrey, and she sounds frantic.

She never was able to handle stress.

"The lead detective thinks I killed her, but other than that, I think I'm doing okay."

I can't quite finish the thought, and Audrey apparently can't either, because the very slight hiss of the signal between us is all that exists for a few moments.

"Yeah," she says. "I'm sitting outside in my car. I need to see you."

I already hear the slamming of a car door, and I shut the journal and slide it under the couch before Audrey appears on the front stoop.

She hugs me like a sister. Like real family. Her tears stain my cheek.

When she pulls away, she looks like a human natural disaster. A state of emergency.

She loved Madeline St. Clair like I've never loved anybody, except maybe my dad, and he's also dead and gone. Maybe I'll love someone like that in the future.

"Who did this?" I ask.

"I think all of Nashville killed her," she says, "but who pulled the trigger, who choked the life out of her—that I don't know."

Already turning her into a martyr. No matter the fight they had, Audrey will always be her lap dog. Obsequious to the bitter end.

"But somebody *did* pull the trigger," I said. "Somebody *did* strangle her."

"They've taken Colton into custody," Audrey says, collapsing onto the couch. She's more drunk than I think.

"What?"

"It just happened," she says. "It's all over the news. He turned himself in. As fate would have it, he was in the midst of a pretty raunchy weekend with McKinley Nelson."

"She of the Nelson healthcare fortunes?"

"The same exact one," Audrey replies. "He's going to have a pretty tough road ahead, trying to prove he...didn't do it. I mean, what with his dick being stuck in every available orifice in Music City and whatnot."

"Did he do it, though? Do you think?"

"They had a monstrous relationship," she says. "He was always cheating—"

"And so was she, from what I heard."

"Yes, that too. Isn't it always the husband?"

"Or the jealous lover."

"Jealous *lovers*," I correct. "Usually. But when has anything normal ever happened to Madeline St. Clair? I wouldn't be surprised if it were a cult or some religious conspiracy. Simple jealousy isn't enough to bring Madeline St. Clair down."

And there's the old anger seeping through, I think.

Changing the subject, I say, "It's not Colton. It's not him."

"Because his family has a shit-ton of money? Come on, M.E."

It's true, though. Colton Ambrose is a *name*. If it were him, it would be the biggest murder since Janet March's disappearance in the 90s.

Colton's father runs one of the biggest brokerage firms in the city, and his mother is a professional socialite. Her name is on the invitation for any notable ball in Nashville, and the Belle Meade Country Club is like a second home.

Then, Audrey says, "They always talk to the husband first. It's, like, one of the rules of the game. It's always the husband. Don't you watch *Oxygen*?"

"So you do think it's him."

"I'm not saying *that*," she replies. "It doesn't seem like him to shoot and strangle someone. I mean, with the millions he stands to inherit, he would hire someone."

"Which could happen. This was a cold crime. I mean, the sheer, I dunno, *brutality* of it all makes it seem like more than just jealous rage."

Audrey shakes her head. "Colton's dad is dying."

"What?"

"He just got diagnosed with some heinous form of brain cancer, the same kind that killed John McCain. He doesn't have very long to live."

I'm confused. "What does that have to do with anything?"

"It just seems like a weird time for Colton to savagely murder his wife."

"When people get that angry—"

"Yes, but he knew she was fucking other people," she says. "If that drove him over the edge, then he'd have killed her *a long* time ago."

"I guess that's true," I reply. "Unless—"

"Unless *what*?"

"Unless it's someone that just got under his skin."

"Maybe," she replies. "But then we'd have to dig through all the names in Madeline St. Clair's nightstand, and that's not a task I feel like I'm up to."

We sit in silence for a minute, both contemplating the circumstances which have brought us here, when finally she says it.

"There's one thing we're walking around, and I can't tell if it's on purpose or not," she says. "I mean, I don't necessarily want to go there, but maybe we should."

"You think it has to do with the Suicide Blondes."

She nods. A single, quick gesture, but one whose implications I dread.

"I've tried to come up with any and every excuse for why it *wouldn't* be about Everett Coughlin's death—"

"I don't think it has to do with Everett Coughlin at all," I interrupt. "If it is indeed related to the Suicide Blondes, it has everything to do with *us*. Someone wants to punish *us* for what *we* did."

She thinks about it. "Maybe we deserve it."

"At least someone seems to think that."

"Sometimes, honestly, *I* think that," she replies.

I nod, looking down. "She came to see me. Madeline, I mean. She was drunk, but there was something weird about our whole conversation. Like she wanted to tell me something."

There's a moment where I almost disclose the existence of the notebook, but something prevents me.

"But she didn't? I mean, *say* anything?"

One corner of my mouth twitches. "You mean, did she tell me what you did that night? No, Audrey, she didn't tell me that."

Her face is a mass of confusion. "Then how—"

"Gillian dropped by," I interrupt, "and we had a nice, long conversation about things I *didn't know*."

She draws back—slowly—as if collapsing in on herself.

"Anything else you care to tell me? Anything else I didn't know about the night you thought about watching someone die?"

Her whole body is quivering. I can see it.

I should be horrified. I should be pissed.

But secretly I'm enjoying this. I shouldn't, with all that's going on, but I do, mostly because it is amazing to see Audrey panic. I've seen it before, but only at the hands of Madeline.

Not that *that* will happen anymore.

"We didn't—I mean, we just kind of stood there."

"And did nothing?"

She nods, hoping that it will end the issue.

But it doesn't.

"That's *worse*, Audrey," I say. "If you'd only shown up, you could have *done* something. But instead, you showed up and then decided to leave him to die on his own?"

Her face draws up a blank expression, as though the words had been smacked right out of her head. She's apparently incapable of embarrassment, but the shock registers quite nicely on her face.

"I didn't think of it that way," she says.

"You didn't *think*. At all. You wonder why in the hell you're getting threatening text messages. You're lucky that's all they *are* at this point."

"No, you're right," she says, her eyes welling up.

"I know I'm right," I reply. "Something very bad could happen to one of us. *Has* already happened to one of us."

"No, I know," she says. "I just—"

"Thought it would be okay to flirt with death like that and then avoid any consequences for it? You forget, Audrey: *I* am the one who had to pay for what you did. What *we* did. What we *all* did."

Her face blushes red. "Broken record, Mary Ellen," she says. "Get. Over. It. We've all had to suffer. You don't think we have to pay every single day for what we did?"

"I'm the only one who went to jail for it."

"Then you went to Seattle and hid for all these years. Do you know what it's like to face these people and have to ignore the fact that they *know*?"

"Well, *no*," I say.

"It's like being able to read someone's mind," she replies. "You just have to focus on what you have to say, knowing all the while that all they can think is *murderer murderer murderer*."

She's got a point, I think.

"But it doesn't help that you held a secret about what you did for all these years," I say, bringing the conversation back to my original point.

"We didn't *do* anything," she says, exasperated. "We went over there—it's shitty, I know—but we didn't know *what* to do. We were shitty teenagers. It didn't get real, not really, until *that moment*. And then we chickened out. That's *it*."

The last syllable slants up, reaching a pitch I've never heard, and then Audrey, whom I'd always thought was made out of bricks—gold or not—crumbles like a child's sandcastle, folding over herself and hiding her face in her hands.

For a moment, the shock is too great for me to abide.

Then, as if my emotions are on a hair trigger, all of a sudden I'm crying, too, even if I'm not entirely sure why. I should hate Audrey, should resent her for the way she's ruined my life and destroyed my potential, but the sight of her weeping—as well as the lingering feelings over Madeline's death—are much stronger than my bitterness over the past.

I need to feel less, and Audrey seems ready to abide by my decision.

Audrey looks up from her hands at some point and says, "Drink?"

I can't help but nod.

She gets up and fills two shot glasses with Tito's.

So much for a quiet evening in.

It's not long before the night elongates and grows hazy under the weight of a few stiff drinks. Audrey, who came to my place *already* wasted, still manages to drink me under the table. It doesn't take much for me to end up in blackout mode, and so when I reach my limit, she tucks me in before staggering out back into the night.

At least I think that's what happens.

15

NOW

"Did you know a woman poisoned her husband on the hotel's fourth floor?" Gillian asks nonchalantly as she and I order our usuals—vodka sodas—from the super trendy bar atop the Noelle.

I've spent most of the day fending off a hangover. The spontaneous wake with Audrey has left me dehydrated and achy, and I guess the only solution to that problem is more drinking.

"Where's the ball-and-chain today?" I ask.

When she doesn't exactly make the connection, I prompt her by mentioning the guy from Audrey's party at her place in the Gulch.

"Oh, Charley?" she asks. "He's clueless. If I had to guess his whereabouts—and I'm not—then I'd say he's probably stalking some poor, unwitting producer on Music Row."

"That bad?"

"He's...fine, I guess," she says. "He doesn't know how to play the game, but he thinks he does. It's pitiful when someone thinks they are being clever, isn't it?"

She leans back, surveys the expanse of downtown sprouting up on either side of us.

After a pause, she says, "It must be a treat to rediscover the town as an adult."

"Like finding a secret passage under the bed," I reply. "The new restaurants, and the restored neighborhoods—"

"I mean, you're staying in *The Nations*, for crying out loud. How much better has that area gotten in the last few years?"

"Exponentially better," I reply, but I don't follow up with more chit-chat about Nashville, because I understand what we've come here to discuss.

Gil sighs and kills her drink.

"So, what else is new?"

"Audrey tells me she has a stalker," I reply. "Says she started receiving messages right before—well, right before *I* came back."

"I see," she says. "So this *is* just the beginning."

"Seems like it."

"Did she say anything else? Any mention of Madeline in the messages?"

"It all seemed pretty vague, the kind of stuff I usually get—"

"When the documentaries start popping up again?"

I nod my head, looking over Gil's shoulder for our server. We make brief eye contact, long enough for me to tap my glass with a fingernail.

"You need another?"

"I'm good," Gillian says. "With all the anti-anxiety meds, I shouldn't be drinking."

"Same here," I reply, downing the rest of my vodka-soda.

"*You* never considered doing anything like that, did you? Sending us threatening messages?"

How do I answer that question? Of *course,* I did. I thought of everything, up to and including murder. I *hated* them. I *loathed* them. I wished them dead every day for *years*.

"No more than I had right to," I respond, finally.

Gil smirks. "Fair. Totally fair."

"Wait, do you think *I'm* sending Audrey those awful messages?"

Before I can say *I would never...*, I clip the sentence off and shove it back down, way deep inside, where I keep the emotional hangover associated with the whole *Suicide Blondes* phase of my life.

"Of course not," she says, though Gillian is too smart to complete endorse a lie, so it comes off like she doesn't entirely believe me.

I let it go, because distrust is just baked into this cake, I guess.

"Madeline thought someone was after her, too," I say, broadening the topic. "When she came to see me, right before her death, she was drunk and desperate, and it was obvious she was hiding something."

"Huh," Gil replies. "That's odd."

Then it occurs to me.

"Wait, have *you* been receiving threats, too?"

She doesn't answer, even when I stare without rephrasing the question. I can see the muscles working in her jaw, tensing up, and so I know the answer, but she's not ready to talk about it quite yet.

"You know you can talk to me," I say. "I've been going through the same thing."

"Has someone been threatening you?"

"Not through text messages," I reply, "but I could swear someone was following me at Percy Warner the other day."

"Did you get a good look at the guy?"

I shake my head. "I think maybe they turned off the path."

"*They*? Was there more than one?"

"No, like *they*, as in, I couldn't tell if it was a man or a woman."

"Oh."

"I mean, it sounds crazy to say this, but I didn't actually *see* them."

"What do you mean?"

"Well, when I turned to confront the person—it was someone else."

"How do you know someone was actually there?" she asks. "How do you know it wasn't—"

"Just my imagination?" I interrupt. "Because I *know*. Trust me. Someone was there. And that someone *wanted* me to know it, too."

There is another extended silence between us.

"Come on," Gillian says, at last. "Let's get off this fucking roof."

THE RICKETY ELEVATOR takes us down to the lobby level of the Noelle, and we bypass a wedding party in the main dining area before stepping out onto the street—

Where I full-on slam into a couple of people hurrying up the sidewalk.

"I'm sorry," I mumble, before I'm able to gather my bearings. I'm a little drunk, and so it all comes out a little more flippantly than expected.

Then, I recognize the woman I've just plowed into, and this night takes an unexpected nosedive toward the concrete.

The woman—it's Everett Coughlin's *mother*, and she doesn't take so much as a breath before her hand collides with my face. The force of the blow is enough to send stars floating out into the most distant point in my field of vision.

A woman stepping around us gasps. "Oh my *God*!" she exclaims.

But I'm not focused on her.

I'm focused on Myrtle Coughlin, whom I know only through the varied and expansive interviews she's given over the years, calling for my head on a spike. I've always been just out of reach, just beyond the length of her arm.

But not this time.

Here is her chance, and she doesn't hesitate. Her eyes glazing over with twenty years of sadness, she strikes me again and again, and I don't move to defend myself.

Neither does Gil, who keeps one hand on my shoulder but doesn't try to pull me away. She just kind of observes this smackdown with a detached serenity.

I deserve it.

Perhaps Gillian knows it, and that's why she allows me to get my just desserts from the mother of our victim.

I take another shot to the face, and the pain swells like somebody twisting a volume knob to ten. My face hurts, and I'll have to apply plenty of makeup to hide the bruising, but at the same time, I'm pleased to feel this. The hurt seeps up through the cracks of my drunkenness and wakes me up.

There is no way to be somewhere else.

I am trapped fully in this moment, and I could not be more compliant with fate's wishes. Predestination has drawn me here, and so I accept the consequences.

Mrs. Coughlin strikes me one more time, and it appears like she might be done.

In a talk with CNN's resident mummy, Larry King, she once referred to me as "The Deep South's Exquisite Harlot." She said this as I lay on a bunk in the common area of my juvenile dorm, where the CNN cameras either could not or would not tread.

And so I have spent the better part of my adult life with her words rolling around in my head like a marble in a sink drain.

I feel the pain stinging my cheek, but now that we're here, now that she and I are in the midst of an audience, I want it all.

Or, rather, I don't want it to end.

It would suit me just fine if she held me down and bludgeoned me to death with a stone from the Central Basin. Just put me out of my misery, right here for everyone to see. Then maybe I would be free of this curse.

I don't deserve the life I took from Everett Coughlin, but I'm too drunk to explain all of this to her. The words kind of fulminate and fight against being released, so I just stand there and stutter dumbly, like a junior actress who's forgotten her one and only line in the high school rendition of *Brigadoon*.

To my benefit and chagrin, Myrtle Coughlin is in shock. Full-blown shock. Her eyes remain fixed on me, but I can see the way she holds her hand, like it's a foreign object, a gun she didn't mean to fire.

And it's pointed at me.

"You deserved that," she says, her eyes brimming with tears.

"I know," I say.

Then the thing I don't mean to say, the thing that occurs to me in the moment, dribbles out like warm syrup. "You can do it again, if you want. I don't mind."

There is a sharp intake of breath from all those gathered around, all the hangers-on. They think I've insulted this poor, destitute woman, and judging by the look she's giving me, she does too. She's already begun backing away, her mouth open in a misshapen, stammering capital O.

And then she does.

She hits me again.

And again.

It isn't over, after all.

Some of the onlookers pull out their phones.

These videos will be on YouTube by the close of the hour.

When she strikes me again, Luther Coughlin steps in and wraps both arms around his sobbing wife.

"I think she's had enough," he says quietly, his own eyes lacquered with tears.

I can't help but stare at the way his bowtie has been knocked askew. It might be funny, if it weren't so sad.

My mouth tastes like blood. My ears ring like I've just left a concert. I struggle to keep my head up and my shoulders back. I want to collapse at her feet. I want to beg her for forgiveness, but the situation—and, I suppose, my own pride—prevent me from doing anything but standing there and taking it.

"He was our only son," she says as she is slowly led away from me. "I breastfed him. I changed every single one of his goddamned diapers."

All I can do is nod.

Now it is my turn to tear up.

But she doesn't stop. "It was the best, shortest time of my life. I'll never be a grandmother, never see my own child as an adult. You robbed me of that, and I hope you die a miserable, painful death."

"The way things are going," I respond, "you just might get your wish."

I can see iPhones flashing as people commemorate this moment with a photo. Or a video. It certainly is fitting, given why this is all happening.

Her last act of desperate ire is to spit on me. Flecks of wet speckle my face, and I can smell the nicotine in all of it. Her face, in that moment, is a contorted mass of anger and confusion, an impressionistic painting of a human being in agony, and that is the vision I am left with as she is hurried through the crowd.

"I think that's all, folks," I say to everyone standing there, and in turn, each of them films me as I stumble drunkenly away, daubing the back of one hand at the blood which has begun to trickle from one corner of my mouth.

∼

INTELLECTUALLY, I know it's a bad idea to search for myself on the internet. It's a bad idea for *anyone* to do it, but especially me.

The articles themselves are the worst, online "crime writers" or "internet sleuths" (or whatever they prefer to be called) portraying me as either monster or victim, with a tiny isthmus of pathos in between. They are viciously opinionated, believing themselves to be

But, then again, the internet *is* humanity. It is the *whole* of humanity. It is just what and who we are as a species. I recognize my place in the clamor to reach the bottom of the barrel, but I feel confident I've got it all pegged. There is a special place in Hell for all internet trolls, the seventh circle of a digital dungeon somewhere beneath Satan's cloven hooves, and I know I deserve to be there, but so do millions of others.

And so I brace myself for when I look for details of my...*situation* with the Coughlins from last night. There are several vids posted, many of them already above a thousand views. I watch them, each one, with a quiet sense that it is somehow my duty to do so.

It is the penance that I pay. The intellectual equivalent of self-flagellation. I walk into the firing line just to see how injured I can get and still survive the onslaught.

It's not that bad.

Oh, it's vicious, but vicious doesn't necessarily mean witty, so it doesn't actually hit very close to home. They call me a slew of mono-syllabic names—*bitch, whore, slut, cunt*—but nothing that reveals anything more than their latent (and lazy) misogyny.

In fact, when I see the videos and the vitriol people levy on me, I usually join in.

I can't help myself.

My online profile cannot be tied to me in any feasible way, and sometimes I spend hours going through my own comments about myself in online forums to see what I actually feel about myself.

It's not great.

These people in the peanut gallery on YouTube think they have it in for me. They don't have *shit*. They are mouth-breathing hypocrites, people who pine for civility when it comes to what I did, while nothing would make them happier than for me to jump off the Pinnacle Building or dive headfirst into the Cumberland with a pocket full of rocks. They'd watch the bubbles slowly stop appearing, if they could.

But they can't string together an insult that hits home. I'm inured to the uncreative jabs people take out on me, and even if one did somehow manage to hurt me, the anonymity ironically frees me to feel nothing about it.

This isn't honesty.

It's vengeance.

I begin to type. It's an accumulation of years of abuse—decades, really—rolled into a tight little ball, and I hurl it at myself.

CAN'T *this bitch just fucking DIE already? It's not like there has ever been a need for her to exist, beyond the target practice she provides for all of us. I hope her mother dies, just like her cocksucking father did. Better yet, I hope her mother lives and SHE dies, so we get what we want and her mother loses what the Coughlins never had—a child that lived.*

OUCH.

16

Detective Ciccotelli finds me at the hospital later in the day. He seems a little more relaxed than the last few times I've spoken with him, but then again, I can smell whiskey on him like cigarette smoke.

"Get you a cup of coffee?" he asks.

I don't like this particular ambush. I've got the jitters from two nights of drinking, and the day is looking bleak, despite my mom's slight uptick since her episode.

"I thought you had your man," I say. "Colton Ambrose is in custody, is he not?"

The detective smiles ruefully and shakes his head.

"If only I had more people like you on the force," he says. "There just isn't enough sarcasm in the world, is there?"

"I was being honest, but sure, if you want to take it that way, how do you feel about him being behind bars?"

"It's a start," he says. "We have some physical evidence, and uh, yeah, he's going to stay right where he is for now."

"You don't sound convinced."

"The wheels of justice turn quite slowly," he says, "so I do my best to speed them up whenever and wherever I can."

"Is that why you've dropped by? To tell me I'm lounging some-where under those wheels, that they're turning right for me?"`

His face falters to a microscopic degree, and I dread what comes next.

"This doesn't have to do...with the investigation," he says, at last, and then my heart really is thumping along.

"Well?"

It's hard to get the words over the lump in my throat.

"Believe me, there is nothing easy about this next bit for me. It speaks to all the worst aspects of the business of police work, and I—"

"Just tell me."

"Your old stalker—he's been set free."

The detective goes on to give me details about the terms of Timothy Allred's release, but I'm too freaked out to listen. Not that I need to hear about his role as the ideal prisoner or the work he did with the elderly and the physically disabled.

None of it matters. I have the answers I need to know why things have gone completely fucko since arriving in Nashville. It's like knocking over dominos.

The guy trashing my rental—check.

The person trailing me in the park—check.

The death of Madeline St. Clair—check.

After he's finished telling me the procedural and bureaucratic reasons for this fuck-up, his expression grows more pained than I've seen it. He's normally a fairly stone-faced individual, but he looks like he's been poked with something long and sharp. "There's one last thing."

"Oh yeah? Can it be worse than what you've just told me?"

"Allred's gone MIA."

Though I understand the words, I can't quite process them in a way that makes any sense. So, in turn, the detective continues through his spiel.

"His parole officer put pretty strict limits on his movement and communication, and when he didn't show up for a scheduled visit, the PO got worried. He checked in with the halfway house where Allred was staying and found that he'd been gone for a couple days. Once he realized Allred had split, he checked his files and contacted the authorities who contacted us. So here we are. On a manhunt for this guy."

I manage to receive all of this new information without screaming.

"Anything else I should know, officer?"

I can't bring myself to call him *detective*, and he doesn't bother to correct me. He's lucky I got the words out without calling him *fucking incompetent*.

"No, that's about it," he says. "You just keep your head on a swivel, and your eyes and ears open. I'll be in touch if anything else comes up."

"Okay."

"I don't suppose you've changed your mind about protective custody."

I shake my head. "If he wants to get at me, he'll do it, whether or not you've got someone posted on me."

"That's the most ridiculous thing I've ever heard."

"Is it? Do you think all of this is a *coincidence*?"

"That's why you should consider—"

"I'll consider no such thing," I reply. "If he sees me being tailed by a police officer, that gives him yet another puzzle to solve. It will *embolden* him."

"He's not a criminal mastermind, Ms. Hanneford. He's a criminal with a screw loose."

"We'll just wait and see about that, I guess. In the meantime, make sure you find him. If I do—or he finds me—things will get very bad very quickly."

WHEN I LEAVE THE HOSPITAL, I head back to the rental. My hands are shaking, and I can't quite escape the feeling like I'm being set-up.

I kneel down in front of the couch and reach for Madeline's journal. There's so much I need to find out, to figure out. I can't believe I've allowed myself to be distracted this long by other things. All the drinking and carousing with the other girls has left me rudderless, but it's time to get back on that track and ignore all outside pressure.

But even when I swipe deep under the furniture, my hand gets no purchase.

It isn't there.

The journal is gone.

I reach for it again, and again my hand manages to hit only dust and wood and air. There is no journal to speak of.

I stand up and pause there, numbly.

It's been stolen. It's been taken.

He has been in the house.

If it is not Timothy Allred doing this, it is the devil of Hell. It is the only possible solution, and the only one that gives me even a hint of comfort. In fact, I'd *rather* have the devil chasing me than that psychopath, at this point.

I'm not safe in the house, so I grab my laptop, my Seahawks hat, and my sunglasses, and I duck out of the Airbnb before I can drive myself crazy.

I don't know where I'm going, but I can't be here.

17

NOW

I end up at my childhood house, which looms over my memory like the home on Elm Street from the old Freddy Krueger movies. It is a shadowy and malevolent place, full of bad memories from my adolescence. It is where my father died, where I lived when the Everett Coughlin situation played out, and it is where my mother began her charade of death.

I still have a key, and when I unlock the door, I am reminded of why I decided against staying here for an extended period of time. Or at all. It is not the Radley home, or the place from that Shirley Jackson book, but it nevertheless feels as haunted as any evil location I've ever seen. The fact that it only applies to me—and perhaps my mother—doesn't matter. It's a bad, terrible, awful place, and only desperation brings me to darken its doorstep.

Oh, it's just a house, something built in the sixties and remodeled throughout the years. It is not covered in cobwebs or teeming with mice and bats, but there is something wholly terrifying about being in its presence.

And yet, I persevere.

My whole body trembles as I make my way first to the kitchen, where I spent most nights studying and doing homework as my mom cooked dinner—or, after dad died, threw something together after work. Nothing, not a single thing, is out of place, which makes me think of a museum. Or a movie or TV set. The walls are all cardboard. The doors lead absolutely nowhere. Yank on the wrong string, and the whole thing comes crashing down.

I pour a glass of water and drink it silently at the island, waiting for something—anything—to happen. I have no expectations, and I hope I'm alone, but I cannot say for sure why my attention keeps getting pulled in other directions.

The rooms around me are still and bare, and I can practically see the indentation on the one chair where my mother sits, where she whiles away the time as it slips through her arthritic fingers. Her life is a one-person meal, a single serving that leaves you hungry minutes later. It is only notable in the absent spaces. Where she *could* be but is not.

Seeing this—all of this—makes me feel as though the entirety of my soul has been scooped out and tossed aside. When I see the sad life my mother lives, devoid of friends and acquaintances, my whole body aches with a sadness I can't quite describe.

I resolve that this will not be my end, and I will do everything in my power to prevent it for my mother, too. Once this is all over, once Timothy Allred is back in jail and my mother's condition improves, I'm going to take a much more direct role in her life. Stop running from the past and making excuses to avoid engaging with her.

I make my way through the den to the main hallway. Mom's house is a ranch-style dwelling from a different time and place in Nashville. Now it's all prefab houses that look more at home in San Francisco than a southern town.

Mom's bedroom lies at the end of the hall, and mine is the first on the left. After I *went away*—her euphemism, not mine—she cleaned it up and left it alone. Since I never really came back home after my time in juvie—I moved to Atlanta for a brief stretch before sneaking away to the Pacific Northwest—my room is a time capsule to a very specific period in history, a paean to boy bands and long-forgotten trinkets. This place is a testament to the fleeting nature of childhood, the power that the past can have over a person. This is post-Lewinsky, pre-9/11 America, and if my mother has her druthers, it will always be that way. Over by the closet, there's even the—

Wait.

Something is out of place. My eyes are drawn to the thin black sliver between the door and the jamb in the closet. It's just enough to pull my attention from the 'N Sync poster tacked to the wall, but in that space is an infinite terror.

That door has been closed for two decades. Mother never comes in here, let alone to open a door that houses only a few old blankets and some discarded toys. It's little more than a time capsule to a younger and more hopeful time, and it is almost physically painful to look inside.

But I do.

He's been here, I think. I can tell. I know. I can smell it on the air, can feel it in my clothes, like smoke that has drifted up from a distant fire and attached itself to the fibers of a beloved sweater.

The worst part is, he might *still* be here.

Suddenly, I experience the terror of silence more so than before, feel its...absoluteness. As I step from room-to-room, I quiet my mind, try to quiet my own movements, but I can't escape the feeling that someone is standing behind me.

I can still see the blood pooling beneath him, the red liquid filling the pores in the monitor vents and seeping into the cracks between wood slats in my floor.

My imagination is strong with this one, and I have to actively fight it off, because I know this time—there will be a 'this time'—he will not turn his anger on himself. He is bound to turn the blade (or whatever he ends up using) on me.

The air shifts around me, and I turn and scream, thinking I'll find a bloody, ax-wielding maniac standing there.

But all I see is the room. There's something...off about it, though. Like in the movies, where the audience can see the ghost but the main character cannot. I expect a scare of some kind—maybe a well-timed cat jump—but receive nothing but the eerie silence. That *hnnnnh* hum of electricity (or whatever it is) fills my ears, and to fight it, I close the door.

Or I *almost* do.

One of the out-of-place things catches my glance, and before I know it, I'm no my knees next to a box of old belongings. I don't know how or why I'm rifling through my things, but once I get my hand on it, the rest of the world dissolves into darkness.

I pull the VHS from its protective plastic sleeve and sit cross-legged on the rug, inspecting the outer label. There is no writing on it, and though I've got a few other videos in the closet, they're mostly Disney movies and rom-coms from that era. They're all stockpiled in their own container in the back corner, far away from this lonely VHS.

And that's the point. There is just no reason for this to *be* here.

Part of me wonders what might be on it, but that part of me is fleeting and insignificant. The overwhelming majority of my brain is consumed with all the things I can just about *confirm* are on it.

I WONDER how long it's been in the closet, but in the end, it doesn't matter. All that really matters is that I've found this relic from the past.

When I am convinced my legs will hold me, I stand up and shuffle cautiously back to the living room, where mom's entertainment center is still adorned with photos. Not a single one of them comes from a time after the discovery of Everett Coughlin's body, so it's yet another reminder of how slow time moves in this house.

There are photos of me in cheer. On the softball team. Playing junior high volleyball.

There are even a few of me and my dad, but none of my parents.

What is missing are photos of me from senior prom—I didn't go. Wasn't able to. Just like I wasn't invited to graduation, because I was incarcerated. So, no pics in my gown and cap. I've never had any serious boyfriends or meaningful relationships, so it is kind of like I stopped living my life back in the late 90s.

How can I blame my mom for the very thing I *myself* am guilty of?

Shrugging off the guilt and the blame for a few moments, I open the cabinet where mom's seldom-used DVD player and rickety stereo are housed. But it's the VCR I'm after, and when I get everything set up and turned to the right input, I gently press the cassette into the machine and hit play.

In the intervening darkness, before the appearance of moving images, I can hear my own heart in my ears. I'm convinced I'm about to see something big.

And then it all kicks in, and I see the past brought to life. The camera spins once, and a flash, as Gillian's face appears on-screen.

"Oh my God, I think it's recording," she says.

Then, a series of cuts.

Gillian and Audrey and Madeline dancing to a mid-90s rap song.

Cut.

Madeline chugging a glass of wine, one eye turned toward the camera.

Cut.

Audrey and Gillian throwing eggs at the statue of Anne Dallas Dudley.

Cut.

Darkness.

Then, a whisper. Madeline's voice. "It's recording," she says.

This is it. Everything starts to come into focus for me.

It's the night. This is the secret, committed to video. Audrey and Madeline, surreptitiously recording at the residence of one Everett Coughlin.

"I hope we're not too late," Audrey says, her voice full of a kind of fevered excitement. Like the last person in line for a busted roller coaster.

"Yeah," Madeline responds, ever the cool cat. Somehow, she doesn't sound quite as thrilled about this prospect as her underling does.

Ahead of them, just now coming into focus, are the lights in the garage. Three perfect squares of illumination begging to be peered into.

"Do you think he's started yet?" Audrey asks.

"I dunno," Madeline says uncertainly.

And then she steps into frame. She kind of hovers there for a moment, her blonde hair a bright contrast to her leather jacket and the surrounding darkness. She blends into the light from the garage for a moment, and for a split second, they become one.

I desperately want there to be a chemical reaction that blows this into another timeline, so that maybe I can have another shot at my last two decades.

But of course she moves ahead, inching ever closer to the house, and their awed dialogue continues, though a little more stilted than before.

Audrey clears her throat. "There's, um, something I need to tell you," she says, just as the camera begins to zoom in on the back of Madeline's head. It's like a slow-motion bullet, headed for her pretty blond brain.

"Yeah?" Madeline responds, though the words barely make it back to the camera. Something's going on with the Queen Bitch of Belle Meade, and it's a little off-putting to see. She's not in her element, and though it should be comforting to find that she's not kicking down the door to see a dead body, it does give me this strange sense of pause about the whole video.

Like Madeline has been body snatched or something.

The video skips once, dragging for a moment, and then gets back up to speed. Most of what Audrey's just said is garbled and unintelligible, but it elicits a reaction from Madeline, who stops and turns *just* to stare at the camera.

"The fuck'd you just say?"

It skips again. This cassette is not faring well. It's had all of the George W. Bush and Barack Obama presidencies to sit and rot, so I should be happy that it works at all.

But the sinking feeling in my gut has begun. I think I might lose my coffee and honey bun from earlier that day. As the camera draws nearer to the garage, the lights at the end of the driveway growing bigger with each passing moment, the possibility of seeing Everett Coughlin's last few moments on Earth become increasingly definite.

It's a lie, I think. Audrey lied to me. They *didn't* stop at the driveway.

What else are they hiding?

Whoever brought this to my house, they placed it in my bedroom closet for a reason. The idea that this is all some major scheme is ridiculous—who could orchestrate me fleeing Nashville proper for my childhood home?—but this video is definitely here *for a reason*. I just need to figure out what it is.

Maybe I was always meant to find it. Maybe I was supposed to find it twenty years ago, I just never did. There's a possibility this was meant to grind salt in an open wound.

I use the remote on the stand next to the couch to pause the video. I hit rewind—this part is the whole reason this VHS is in the house, right?—and hope for the best.

It is a mistake I come to regret almost instantly. That high-pitched whine related to electrical equipment from the 90s precedes a few moments in which I think I might actually get to see the end game here. What Madeline and Audrey have been hiding all this time.

The video slows down. I hit play, and for a moment it seems like it is going to just resume without the horror movie effect of the previous attempt.

Madeline is back where she was before she stepped toward the house, and she is looking at the camera, her face as beautiful and unlined as it's ever going to get.

She opens her mouth to speak, and my guts cinch tight with a greasy pull.

But just as things start to get interesting—and move toward their inevitable end—the image on-screen jerks. Audrey's face expands, and then the screen blinks, turns blue. The VCR emits a high-pitched wail, the death rattle of a mythic beast, as something very terrible goes wrong inside the machine.

"No no no no no!" I scream, leaping from my seat. My first instinct is to repeatedly press the eject button, but that only seems to expedite this poorly-timed self-destruct mechanism. There is no magnificent unspooling of tape, but there might as well be. The machine whirs, then something catches, and then it grinds to a vicious halt.

I press and mash and beat the fucking thing, and finally—finally! —it ejects the cassette. I think, if I can just get the goddamned thing out, maybe I can get it to another VCR—surely there has to be one in Metro Nashville *somewhere*—everything will be all right. I need to see where Audrey was taking their conversation, what she intended on saying to Madeline in their brief, little exchange.

My heart skips a beat as I pull the black rectangle from the housing. I expect brown tape to dangle from underneath like viscera, but it seems to be intact upon first glance.

And then I see it.

It is busted. The tape—the actual stuff on the inside—has been stretched and ripped.

Even if I can get someone to splice it together—or do it myself— this specific part is probably ruined and unplayable. It's absolutely worthless. Might as well be a forgery filmed in front of a green screen. An imagined event on my part.

This thing doesn't even exist anymore, as far as I'm concerned.

In one feverish fit, all of my anger and frustration comes out, and I beat the ground with this home video until it's a thousand plastic shards on my mom's hardwood floors.

There is no time for reflection, no way to make it right. This thing is absolutely worthless to me, this definitive evidence proving Madeline and Audrey (and maybe even Gillian) to be the masterminds behind Everett's death.

But what's a little rage-induced destruction among friends?

I remain knelt there for far longer than is probably healthy, and it is dark, pitch black outside when I get back to my feet.

My first instinct is the most uncertain, but I simply cannot help myself.

I drag my feet over to my purse and retrieve my phone from within. Once the damned thing is on and functioning, I pull up Audrey in my contacts and dial her number.

The call goes immediately to voicemail.

Thinking maybe there are some crossed wires or multiple calls trying to go through, I try her one more time.

This time she picks up.

Immediately, I hear strained breathing on the other end.

"Help," she says, her voice high and thin and indicative of a definite, palpable fear.

"Aud?"

I'm frantic. "Where are you?"

Moments later, her voice returns. "Help me, please," she says, and then she hangs up, leaving me to feel the gooseflesh prickle every single cell in my body.

Before I'm fully aware of my actions, I'm back in the rental car and barking tires as I pull out of Mom's driveway.

THEN

THE OFFICERS, clad in dingy suits and threadbare ties, appear a few weeks after Everett Coughlin's funeral. They are long, haggard men, with neck skin that dangles under their chins like old blankets on used furniture. Their mouths smile when she opens the front door, but the gesture never quite reaches their eyes.

"Miss Hanneford? May we come in?"

It doesn't take long for them to get to the point. After the usual pleasantries about weather and high school and so forth, they dive right into the reason they've decided to perch on the Hanneford couch.

"I'm sure you've heard of the death of Everett Coughlin," one says from under his graying mustache. He could be played by Sam Elliott in the movie version of this whole southern spectacle.

"Yes, oh my God," Mary Ellen's mother says. "So tragic. Such a young boy. I'll never understand..."

And so on. It's kind of an amazing display, up until the cops—or detectives—stop her. Let her save some face when they reveal their true motives.

"I think your daughter might have something to tell you about it," the more country of the two says.

"What does he mean by that?"

"I don't know," Mary Ellen replies, trying to mimic the criminals she's seen on TV, thinking maybe if she says it forcefully enough, they'll just leave her be.

"I think you do," says Sam Elliott. "I think you have *plenty* to say."

"I don't," she begins. Her voice is reaching that quavering, I'm-about-to-cry register, but she continues. "I don't know anything at all."

Sam Elliott frowns. "Mary Ellen, do you happen to know what an IP Address is?"

She shakes her head, but the panic sets in more deeply, as she wonders if they somehow sent letters to the Coughlin residence. Why else would they be mentioning an address?

"It's, um, like a computer fingerprint," the official says, trying his best to sound like a *regular dude* and not a detective with a stick up his ass. "Whenever you log onto the internet, the IP Address creates this digital number, and it can be tracked just like hair or blood or clothing fibers from a crime scene."

And it's then she sees exactly what's happening. Her whole body begins to shiver, as she sees the bloody writing on the wall.

"I don't mean to be rude, *detectives*," Mary Ellen's mother says, "but could you please get to your point? I don't see what any of this has to do with my daughter."

"Oh, we *are* getting to that," the other detective says, "but I think Mary Ellen knows *exactly* where we're going with this. Don't you, young lady?"

She doesn't want to, but she can't help but nod. If they have tracked the computer back to Gillian's house, then they no doubt know what's going on.

And then Sam Elliott goes in for the kill.

"We spoke to each and every one of your friends," he says, "starting with the one who has the fancy computer—"

"Gillian," Mary Ellen says, hoping somehow—desperately—that it will be helpful and thus get her out of this nightmare of a predicament.

"Yes, her. And then we moved on to the Winstead girl before finishing up with Madeline St. Clair."

"Oh." It is Mary Ellen's turn to be her mother, incapable of finding the right words for the moment. She provides a kind of gobsmacked fish mouth but offers up no real comment of substance.

The officers do her a solid and fill in the silence.

"And I am here to tell you, young lady, *they* had plenty to say about *you*. I don't like to throw around the word *ring leader*, except when it comes to racketeering cases, but this whole scenario feels like something straight out of a mob movie."

"I don't—"

"It is imperative that you are careful with the statements you make next, because they very well could seal your fate."

She glances forcefully at her mother, imploring the woman to do something, anything, to stop this from happening. It's all going too fast, and she can't apply the brakes, no matter how fast her mind goes.

Finally, the woman inside her mother's skin sucks in a breath and declares, "Why, I think we'll need to consult with a lawyer over this."

Mary Ellen's mother sounds like she's been submerged in ice cold water.

It is effective in that it moves this scenario along.

Sam Elliott looks at his partner. "Well, I think that just about does it for this interview," he says. "Once you invoke the evil of jurisprudence, we have to get on our merry way."

The two cops, moving like living corpses, get up and shuffle out of the room, assuring the Hannefords they'll be in touch before the week is out. (In truth, it will be a matter of hours before the wheels of justice spin toward her.)

When the door closes, Mary Ellen fears what will come next. She's never seen her mother so frazzled, so distant, and she wants to reach out and touch her, but she doesn't dare. She has never done anything quite so horrifying to her mother—has anybody, other than those involved?—but instead of wrapping her hands around her daughter's throat, Mary Ellen's mother sighs, her eyes filling to the brim with tears.

"I think I'm dying," she says.

And that's just about it.

Two days later, Mary Ellen is in a juvenile holding facility, and her mother is sitting in a doctor's office, complaining of a lump in her throat she thinks is a tumor.

18

NOW

While speeding down Charlotte, veering around cars in an attempt to turn onto White Bridge Road, I dial Audrey's cell number twice, only to be sent to voicemail both times. Each time I hear her saccharine greeting, I hang up, cursing myself.

Maybe she knows, I think. Maybe she knows *I know*, and she's actively avoiding me.

Beating on Madeline's front door didn't work for me, but for some reason, I think doing the same to Audrey will somehow do the trick. She and her husband, Jenkins Finnell, live in an estate off Belle Meade Boulevard.

I *have* to figure out what happened that night. It's just something I need to know, and I need to know it *now*. If *he* has gotten to Audrey before me, then I may *never* find out. I'll die with the uncertainty of their actions spinning around in my head.

When I pull into the Finnell residence, I can see that there isn't a single light on in the house. It's like someone's cut the power, which gets my heart going.

I turn the car off and sit in the darkness for a moment, trying to convince myself to call the cops and wait it out.

This internal struggle lasts...maybe twenty seconds.

The next moment, I'm out of the car, taking measured steps toward the house. It's eerily reminiscent of the video I just watched, and I can't help but notice the parallels.

Maybe it's planned, I think, before I scoff at the idea.

How the fuck could someone have *planned* this?

But, as if on cue, my phone dings.

A text from Gillian.

> HAVE you talked to Audrey today? I texted her a few times, and she hasn't hit me back. Just wondering.

ODD TIMING. I stop and look around, checking the distance for any hint of a glowing blue cell phone screen. If Gillian wants in on this action, she's more than welcome to step on up.

Seeing no light—not even a flicker—I move stealthily along the edge of the driveway, where a fountain blocks both BMWs parked just on the other side.

It's so dark, I can't see a thing. I don't believe there's someone stalking me, but if there were, I wouldn't be able to see it anyway.

After digging my phone from my back pocket, I flick the control panel up with my thumb and turn on my light. My path inside becomes instantly more manageable, and I hurry along, stepping lightly but quickly in the grass next to the house.

It's then that I notice.

Not *all* of the lights in the house are off. A single, bare bulb has turned the single square on the garage door a bright yellow, like a highlighter made of sunshine.

There is not enough money in the world to bet on this being a coincidence, so I back away and struggle to keep from toppling over on my already shaking legs.

I could *guess* what is in the garage, but I think I already know. It is my intention to get as far from here as humanly possible before the same fate befalls me.

Just ahead of me, I see the *beep beep* of a car unlocking. It's not one of the BMWs, so I search until my eyes find the vehicle in the darkness.

It's a sedan of some kind parked under a tree, and a figure dressed in black is skulking toward it.

I glance from that car to *my* car, the rental, and realize that this person will likely see my car in only a few moments. Part of me wants to scream, but I have neither the strength nor the inclination to follow through. I just want to get the fuck out of there.

The shrubs are big enough for me to hide behind as I hurry toward the front door. I figure if I can get inside, I can lock it behind me and call the cops, find a space to hide until the cops arrive.

That is, until everything goes upside down.

When the car's headlights turn on, I am caught right in the midst of their glow.

And I am not alone.

In that illumination, there stands the figure, his silhouette and nothing else visible to me. Of course, I can't tell for sure, but it certainly appears to me that he is looking *directly* at me. He is not moving, and the blinding white bulbs on the front of his car remain fixed in my direction.

There can be no other explanation.

That's when I panic, the fear a hollow ring in my guts.

I just have to run.

I can barely make myself go, but somehow I do. The light from the headlights flashes as I flee towards the front door.

He's coming for me.

I can't let that happen.

My eyes catch details in an order but without any real rhyme or reason: the stairs leading up to the front door. The dueling sconces on either side, like sentinels hiding from their duty. The sliver of black between the door and the jamb.

Then I'm inside, and I close and lock the deadbolt behind me. It's imperative that I lean against the door, at least for a few seconds. I need to catch my breath, to get a sense of my surroundings. The wrong step could send me right into the grasp of my tormentor.

The door behind me rattles as *he* slams into it. I scream. I can't help it. I can feel my muscles going watery, and this time it seems like it'll be permanent.

And yet, the screams don't accomplish anything. They only embolden him, for every time I let loose, the door shakes under his force that much more.

I need to find a hiding place, call the police. Then, maybe, he'll be scared away.

The violence being wrought upon the door stops, but I do not. I shriek one last time and make my way into the kitchen, around the den, and into the main bedroom.

The smell almost knocks me down. It's blood mixed with something else, something even worse and more visceral. I ignore it the best I can, because I know now there's nothing preventing what will happen next.

Their closet is big enough to fit my Seattle apartment on one side of it. I'm scrambling, scrambling in that direction—

And suddenly, my feet are no longer beneath me.

I'm on the ground, my sternum burning from the force of my fall. It only takes me a moment to find the object that tripped me up.

Jenkins Finnell lay in a heap next to me, his body so eviscerated I can barely recognize anything from the neck up as human. It looks like one of those creepy Asian dolls that people live with and marry.

But I don't have time to discern more detail of this horror show.

From below, I hear the sound of a closing door, the whoosh of shifting air pressure.

He has made it inside.

And *he's* coming for me.

I've got to find a hiding spot.

My hands doing their own thing, they manage to drag me forward, and then I'm in the closet, closing the door and locking it behind me. I stumble into the far wall of dresses and press myself against it, praying desperately for some miracle.

It is silent and dark, and right about then—when I try to call 911 —I realize something. My phone isn't with me. It's not in my pockets or my hand.

I must have dropped it.

The fear is real. I am stuck here with no phone, no plan, no hope.

And there is also no Audrey. Jenkins lies face-up in the bedroom, but there was, in that fleeting moment, no sign of Audrey.

Where could she be?

You know the answer to that, I think.

The garage. The garage. It's all in the garage.

Suddenly, there is a presence near me. I can't hear the footsteps or see their shadows under the closet door, but I know he's nearby. He has to be. It wouldn't *feel* this way, if not.

A slight shift of weight causes the floorboards to creak, proving definitively he—fuck it, it's Timothy Allred—is standing not fifteen feet from where I'm curled up. There is no sense in delaying or denying the obvious. I've been found. Discovered. Cast into the same well as before.

I've just got to survive, I think. Just live long enough to make it out of this closet, and then daylight will come soon.

As my eyes adjust to the darkness, I am able to make out the sight of the doorknob. The seconds tick by, and I brace myself for the inevitable shock of the gold object rattling as my stalker breaks the door down.

My imagination sends me to a million different scenarios, each of them ending in death. It's not like I haven't thought these things before, but time and distance have not mellowed the worst of my nightmares.

But instead of the ax scene from *The Shining*, I get...nothing.

Just more darkness.

Of course, I do see *something*. Allred takes my phone. It must have landed camera side *down*, because its light intensifies in the space between the door and the carpet before spreading out and then disappearing.

He's standing just on the other side of the closet door.

And he's not moving.

I can't see everything, but I see enough. I see the shadow of both his feet.

I hold my breath. I fight every urge to cry out. I manage to keep myself quiet.

Somehow.

After a few minutes, the light from my iPhone recedes, and I am left all alone in this room. I don't want to ask myself why he would take my phone, but the question circles my mind as I wait and wait and wait, hoping for the cavalry to show any minute.

But they don't, and so I am stranded there to account for the whereabouts of a deranged killer, whose sole mission appears to be wiping out the Suicide Blondes.

Halfway there. Two down, two to go.

All these years, I've thought myself to be the isolated one, having moved all the way across the country, but it's really the other girls who are alone. They live these lives in the city where they grew up, and though they are surrounded by people, they are more cut off from the world than they think.

I actually feel a little sorry for *them*.

My train of thought is broken by the central heat clicking on.

Time to go, I think.

No matter how much I want to run, I force myself to step gingerly through the bedroom, avoiding Jenkins's body with my eyes *and* my feet, and descend the stairs. I want to scream, want to make myself known, but that's just the intrusive thoughts coming back. I used to fantasize about suicide. It wasn't like I thought about it constantly, but if a situation presented itself, I was likely to choreograph a series of moves that would end in my death. While driving, I constantly surveyed the car's proximity to the center line, thinking how easy it would be to jerk the wheel left into oncoming traffic. If I happened to be on a tall building, I contemplated leaping off, pondering what that first step into the void would be like.

I actively avoid those thoughts now, trying desperately to push them back into place. I do not want to give up, do not want to let go. Now that I have something to live for, to fight for, I don't want *anything* bad to happen.

I *must* know what happened the night of Everett's death.

My phone goes off as I reach the downstairs kitchen. At first, I hear it, but I can't quite make out the sound's location.

I track it to where I feared it would be—the garage. The iPhone is leaning against the door, just beneath the chair wedged under the doorknob.

On the last ring before voicemail takes over, I kneel down and pick it up. "Hello?"

Nothing at first. Just an airy kind of breathing. Something straight out of a 70s horror movie.

A rage, which has been slowly building to a visceral crescendo, bubbles to the surface and spews into my phone's receiver.

"You know they can trace this call right, asshole?" I say. "They'll be able to locate the tower and the phone and every goddamned thing, and you won't be able to hide. You hear that, you fucker?"

Click.

The blood rushes to my face, and I want to throw my phone, go run screaming into the yard. But I don't. I can't. This isn't over. Because I haven't seen what's actually *in* the garage. Whoever was here is leading me toward that room, *the* room. Not that I need it. I already know this place is the end-all be-all of the Suicide Blondes saga.

So I grab the doorknob and turn. The chair topples over. Car exhaust billows from the opening in the door, and I advance into the room with no idea of what I'm going to see.

The tableau before me is clear, though: it's vengeance served ice cold.

Audrey is seated against the driver's side door of a Lexus that is currently running. That's where all the exhaust is coming from, and it's been going for a while, because the room is filled with the stuff.

I hurry over and see that the window is down and she's been handcuffed to a door handle inside the car. It's an elaborate message, but an effective one.

"Audrey?" I say, kneeling next to her.

She's a sickly shade of green—not that green looks good on anybody—and she has slipped into a dangerous-looking unconsciousness.

I check her pulse and don't feel anything. I'm no nurse, but I don't get so much as a single beat. All the exhaust. It's suffocating her. If she's not in a coma, she's probably already gone.

Standing up, I find the button for the garage door and punch it with the side of my fist. My other hand is already doing the work of calling 911.

Almost immediately, the sound of approaching sirens cuts through the panic inside my head. The higher the door travels, the louder the wailing becomes.

I return to my former spot and place one hand on my old friend's cheek. Death has made its introduction to her, and she seems to be succumbing to it.

"Stay with me," I say, repeating the only thing I can think of. Nothing could be more cliché, but then again, nothing could be more necessary. If she drifts too far from reality, she's a goner. "We've got to survive this, find the guy who attacked you. Come on, now. Don't go too far. Please stay with me. Please."

"Hold it right there!"

The sound shocks me, and I yelp in response.

It's Detective Ciccotelli, standing under the glow of the single bulb outside the garage, pointing his service pistol at my head.

19

The cops detain me in the back of a cruiser until Detective Ciccotelli can deal with me. When at last he does make it over to the cruiser, he leans against the side of the car.

"She's alive," he says. "Barely. She's in a coma, and her vitals are pretty shitty."

"And Jenkins?"

"The husband? He's—no. He, uh, he didn't make it."

"Oh."

He turns away from me, places his hands on his hips. In that silence, I am reminded of how kind Jenkins Finnell was to me, how absolutely welcoming he was, when I turned up at their place for the "little" party of theirs.

When the detective turns back to me, his face sags with a heavy professional weight.

"I *almost* don't want to know how you ended up here at this exact moment," he says.

"I could say the same thing to you," I reply.

"This isn't the time for fucking *jokes*, Hanneford," he says.

"I'm not joking," I reply. "I have a good reason for why I'm here, but—"

"What is it?" he cuts me off.

"You first," I reply.

"I'm not the one in the back of a cop car."

"Fine. I came to see Audrey to ask her some...questions."

"What about? Interior design? Relationship advice? The state of the Titans season? Please, do tell."

"It has to do with that night."

"Oh, doesn't it always," he replies. "I'm gonna need more than that."

"I don't—"

"Unless you want to leave this crime scene in handcuffs, you're gonna have to tell me everything."

I glance from him to the house and back again. He's not pleased, and the lights from the cop cars and ambulances are enough to make me dizzy.

Something tells me I'm not getting out of this unscathed, so I dive into a truncated summary of the last few days.

Not all of it, though.

He doesn't need to know about the video, for example, but I don't find it controversial to let him know that I dug through some stuff at my house and found it necessary to speak with Audrey.

During the whole of my shaky-voiced monologue, the detective does little more than listen, one hand cradling his chin. Occasionally, he nods, but for the most part he is an unreadable mask, an indifferent judge.

Once I'm done, the words swirling out into the ether and disappearing into the night air, Ciccotelli nods once and removes his hand from his face.

"This...motivation to come and see your friend—could you tell me more about it?"

"Like, how did I come to the conclusion to drive out here to Belle Meade?"

His smile is brittle and appears uncomfortably placed. "Indeed," he says. "Was it something particular that drove this sudden burst of curiosity?"

"I don't think I follow," I respond.

Ciccotelli scratches his stubble, blinks. "It can be like a game of ping pong, these things," he says, "but you don't strike me too much as the duplicitous type, so I'm going to just come out and say it: Do you now or have you ever been in possession of the journals of one Madeline St. Clair?"

It has to show on my face, because he reacts in a way I've never seen before. He looks unrelentingly disappointed.

I just cannot help myself. "Here's the thing—"

"Just the truth," he replies. "No stories. Just the truth."

Jesus, I think. I can't tell him *the truth*. The truth sounds stupider than any lie I could make up on the spot.

I mean, what can I say? That Madeline St. Clair appeared on my doorstep in the middle of the night, and between downing drinks she dropped her personal diary in my toilet tank, protected only by a resealable Zip-Loc bag?

Or, more to the point, someone then broke into the house and stole this item from me, this thing that should have been turned into the police when Madeline St. Clair turned up dead in her home?

Is *that* the truth I should tell the good detective?

So, naturally, I try to stall. I hem and haw and give half-answers, but he's not buying it. Ciccotelli stops one of my stammering replies by saying, "Whatever you come up with, it needs to end with her journal sitting under the seat of your rental car."

I've heard of people talking about the color draining from their faces, but in this situation it's no joke. I can actually *feel* my face turning an improbable shade of white right before his eyes.

"You don't have the right—"

"I have probable cause," he replies. "And besides, you left the driver's side door open, so it wasn't like I broke in. I mean, is that really the hill you're going to die on?"

I shake my head. My mind does backflips to come up rational explanations, but nothing is readily available to me. Instead, I choke on a bad lie and end up sitting silently in front of the detective.

"Listen, I want to believe you, I really do. But these...coincidences keep happening, and I'm afraid they're not doing you any favors. So tell me: how did that notebook end up in your car?"

I adjust the blanket the EMTs gave me. "*He* did it. He put it there. I don't see why that's such a controversial statement."

"Miss Hanneford, there is no—"

"He said he wanted to kill me," I reply. "He's maintained that since the day he was arrested. If he gamed the system, then that's entirely on them. But he is here, and he did this. If you are unwilling to believe that, then..."

"Then what?"

"Then this is happening to me all over again."

"*What* is happening?"

In the moment I'm having trouble saying it, but it's the thing I've been thinking for twenty years. The reason I went away. The reason I did not graduate high school. The reason my whole life was ruined.

I was railroaded. I was sandbagged. I was made to be the scapegoat.

And it's happening *again*.

"Miss Hanneford?"

"Someone put it there," I say, at last.

"Someone took Madeline St. Clair's journal and placed it in your car, *under* the seat," he says, skepticism creeping into his voice.

"It's true," I say. "Someone's—"

"Trying to frame you?"

It sounds ridiculous, but I'm too far gone to say anything else right now.

"Yeah," I respond. "Must be."

His eyes go from me to the ground, just a flicker of a gesture, but I know exactly what it portends, because I've seen it from police officers before.

"You ever heard of Occam's Razor?" he asks, and despite his best intention, it ends up coming off as patronizing as it sounds.

"No," I respond with an equal amount of petulance.

"It's an old, I don't know, saying. Shit. I'm not a philosopher. I don't know what to call it. But it says that, in any given situation, the good money is on the thing that most likely happened being the truth."

"So you're saying you think I did it, then?"

He makes a face and sighs. "Let's run through this thought experiment together," he says. "On the one hand, there's this idea that a woman—troubled, to say the least—returns to her hometown around the twentieth anniversary of this terrible event in her life. She feels scorned by her friends—maybe a little jealous and angry—and it's been festering for all this time, so she decides to take them out, one by one."

He shifts his weight and runs one hand through his hair. "And then on the other," he continues, "we have the idea that some little gremlin of a man is killing each member of the famed Suicide Blondes and is planting evidence to make it look specifically like *you*. How close am I?"

"Pretty close," I respond. "It's far-fetched but not impossible."

"For you to be believed, it would have to be an amazing coincidence. Would, in fact, have to be *several* coincidences, all strung together."

"Occam may be right in a lot of cases, but he's *wrong* here."

"Could be," he says. "But either way, we are going to be extremely thorough with every single piece of evidence we recover. If you're free and clear, then there's nothing to worry about. I've made my reputation in this town on being diligent but fair. I'm not going to railroad *anybody*."

"That's comforting."

"But if you've been jerking me around, then I'll have no choice but to come down on you with the full weight of the Metro PD. Do you understand that?"

By the time I reach the hospital, it's the middle of the night, and the nurses don't want to let me in, but I think they're pretty much terrified of me, so of course they do.

I shamble in like the walking dead and seat myself next to mom. She sleeps peacefully, and under the light in this moment, she doesn't look nearly as sick as all the tests and the doctors' somber discussions make her seem.

Eventually, though, her eyes flutter open, and she seems aware of my sorrow, because she speaks in a plaintive, gentle voice.

"You were always such a sensitive child," she says, and I am momentarily dismayed by the need to be comforted by her. She's the sick one, after all.

She reaches up and touches her face, as if she's forgotten what it feels like, and then she gets a distant look. "It's that ugliness with the St. Clair girl. It changed you, changed the whole way you carried yourself. I expected you to go to an Ivy League school, you know that?"

I shake my head. Mom never mentioned college, in part—I believe—because of everything that happened with Dad. When he died, all the fight just seemed to slowly seep out of her, until she was nothing more than the silhouette of the strong-willed woman of my early childhood.

"And now here you are, afraid for your life. It should have never gone this far."

"This was the way it was always going to go," I say. "Wherever I am now, it's where I was always meant to end up."

She plucks at the bed sheet, like a dress she hadn't expected on wearing. "Which means I was always meant to end up *here*," she says. "So sad. So sad, indeed."

I draw a deep breath and try to muster the strength to contradict her, but I can't. I believe my life has led inevitably to this point, and so instead I just let the night slip away from the both of us.

Before long, she's asleep, and so am I.

It isn't until the next morning that I realize Audrey and my mom are in the same hospital, so I swirl enough sugar into my coffee to stand a spoon in it, and then I head down to ICU. A stern-looking nurse stops me before I can make it to her room, and the whole time she denies me, I can see recognition in her eyes.

She knows who I am.

"If you're not family," she says, "you cannot be allowed inside. I'm sorry."

The last bit is so sarcastic, I can practically see the shade she's throwing at me.

"I just need to see her," I respond, adding, "I'm the one who found her."

Somehow, that does it, and moments later I'm standing outside her little pod, staring in as if she's the most pitiful kind of zoo animal on the planet.

Her beauty is in the fragile nature of her existence. She's barely hanging on, and for some reason, it makes her look *stronger*. Even unconscious, she has the air of a fighter, of someone who will not give up, and suddenly I'm embarrassed by my own previous perceptions of her. She's as strong as anybody I've known, and I only hope she makes it to the other side of this so I can tell her that.

She has done what Madeline St. Clair was unable to do: survive.

I'm not much of a pray-er—as in, one who prays—but nevertheless, I close my eyes and say a few private words on Audrey's behalf. I muster all the dignity of a lapsed Catholic and give my godly side a stretch. I don't know if that sort of thing works with God—don't know if He'd even listen to someone like me—but then again, it can't hurt.

Then, I go outside for a cigarette. I've started smoking again. I haven't had that many cigarettes, but I make the decision that it's time I start in earnest again, not just when I'm stressed or when I drink. I am a smoker again, and all I want to do is just smoke and smoke and smoke. Stare off into the distance, maybe, and wonder how things will turn out. But mostly just smoke.

When I reach the hospital's front entrance, however, I'm mobbed by reporters of all persuasions, each looking for an angle for their shitty news story.

Do you know who did it, Mary Ellen?

Is it someone connected with the Coughlin family?

Have the cops contacted you about the crimes?

Can you speculate as to whether or not there's a serial killer on the loose?

It's not speculation, if you know it's true. Someone *is* mowing down the Suicide Blondes, and he's basically halfway there. Maybe he'll circle back around to Audrey, once he's finished me and Gillian off.

I push past them and hurry to my car, as if that were the whole intention all along. I get in and light a cigarette and just *drive.* No idea of where I'm going, but I know I've got to get the hell out of there.

Eventually, I end up at Gillian's place.

Gil's waiting for me with a half-gallon of moose tracks ice cream, and I sort of half-collapse in her arms for several minutes before I can regain my composure.

We sit on the porch of her swanky digs, looking out over the Nashville skyline's recent facelift. I'm not really hungry, but I plow through the ice cream like I haven't eaten for days, and then I smoke a cigarette, all in silence. Gillian only watches, paying attention to the broad strokes of my movements without commenting on them.

Finally, she asks, "Want to talk about it?"

I shake my head *no*, like I don't, but then I do exactly that. "Privately, I made fun of Audrey," I say, "like her fears about being stalked had more to do with *her* mental state than the truth. I thought, you know, it was just Audrey, being her dramatic self."

"I think we all engaged in a little bit of that," she says. "It's totally understandable."

"The irony is, I had all this disdain for her because of *my* stalker. Now, it is entirely possible that Timothy Allred is *her* stalker, too."

I avoid her eyes because she's staring at me. This is how Gillian operates. She doesn't leap to conclusions. She processes things. She's like a human computer chip, moving information from one format to another.

After a lengthy pause, she says, "That's just speculation, though, right?"

"What do you mean?"

"Don't get me wrong, M.E. It's obvious the guy is out of prison. That much we do know. But it seems to me, I don't know, that you've created this whole narrative about him tracking us down out of whole cloth."

"He was *released*, Gil," I reply.

"That's true, but do you have any evidence that he's *here* and not hiding out somewhere in Washington state?"

I roll my eyes. "Because I *know*, all right? He's here, and he's behind this. If he's not, then I'll treat you to a dinner at the Catbird Seat, my treat."

"If we make it through to the end."

"Gillian!"

"We're down *two*, girl," she says. "It's not unrealistic to think that maybe one or both of us will not see Christmas."

"You sound oddly okay with that."

She blows out a long, discontented breath. "I'm just facing facts. We cannot go blindly into the end game of this thing. If it keeps moving toward its inevitable conclusion, then one or both of us will be targeted."

"Detective Ciccotelli—has he talked to you yet?"

"Briefly."

"Well, either way, he's offered to place me into a protective custody. I'm sure he'd do the same for you. Maybe that's the way through. Be surrounded by cops one hundred percent of the time."

"Like we're Taylor Swift or Beyoncé or something," she says, smiling. It never quite gets to her eyes, but it's a nice try, either way.

"So should we go into witness protection or something?"

Briefly, as if it's a physical tic, Gillian glances at her door. The deadbolt is locked, so I'm sure she can breathe a sigh of relief, but the gesture brings up something.

"How bad is it, Gil?"

She avoids my eyes.

"Oh my God, you're getting them, too, aren't you?"

With a quick shake of the head, she attempts to push the idea away.

"What is it? Threatening texts?"

A single tear forms in the corner of her eye, but she wipes it away before it can fall. She is not the type to allow tears in front of people. She thinks it a form of weakness.

"Tell me, Gillian."

"I—"

"Just say it."

"He—if it's your malevolent phantom—hacked into my computer."

A lump settles way down in my chest, like I've swallowed something dry and big, and it's stuck way down in my diaphragm.

I have a sneaking suspicion that someone's been peeking around in my work computer, that maybe whoever broke into the Airbnb might have gained access somehow. If they were able to get into the computer, there are ways of them accessing my stuff remotely. I could see the same thing happening to Gillian, truth be told.

She gets up, pours herself a glass of wine and returns to the couch.

"I have this—thing," she says. Her voice is shaking. "It's a folder in one of my cloud drives, where I keep some...*risqué* images—"

"No."

She nods. "Just, you know, private things. Some videos, too. It's no *One Night in Paris*, but I don't want this stuff getting out. It could ruin me."

The words *revenge porn* flash across the front of my mind as she talks. It's the worst kind of digital violation, and yet it's consistent with what our unnamed stalker—

(*Timothy Allred*)

—wants to accomplish. To humiliate us and then end our lives.

This would be step one, and a fitting one for one of the Suicide Blondes.

It just happens to be Gillian's turn.

"And not just me," she says, continuing. "I've been involved with some guys who have careers. None of them will end up in the Rock n

Roll Hall of Fame, but they can fill venues. If any of the stuff in that folder gets out, it will be some hashtagable material."

She buries her face in her hands.

"Could it be a jealous ex? Someone you've dated who might have a grudge?"

It's my attempt to give her the benefit of the doubt, to pull this out of the realm of the entirely speculative.

"I don't know," she says. "I genuinely don't know. All I can say for sure is that someone's been in that folder without my consent."

"But so far you haven't seen any of it outside the folder?"

"No," she says flatly. "It's just swirling unnecessarily in my head."

"There's a chance nothing will come of it."

She nods, but there's no weight behind it. She knows I'm just being nice.

"You know," she says, "it's almost like I always expected this to happen. As if I created that folder for the sole purpose of having it turn around and bite me in the ass someday. Perhaps the guilt made me do it."

Maybe, I think.

But in reality I hedge.

"We've all put things on the internet that we regret."

"Oh yeah?" she asks. "Do *you* have a half-dozen sex tapes floating around on Dropbox? Is that something you have to worry about?"

"Well, no," I reply.

I can't remember the last time I had sex. Not that it was that long ago. It was just that unmemorable. Definitely not something worth filming.

"Then keep your fucking mouth shut about it," she says, and then her face twists up into a godawful pained look.

"I'm sorry," she adds, "I don't mean it. I'm just—God, I'm just so *stressed*."

"Don't mention it," I reply, thinking about the source of the hack. If it's an ex-boyfriend, I'm in the clear.

If, however, it's The Man From My Past, then I should be apologizing to Gillian.

"Anyway," she says, "maybe we can talk about it when I have more perspective on it. Right now, it's just so raw that—"

"I get it," I reply.

"I mean, the folder was password protected and everything. I'm just—I feel so *stupid*. I know better. I do. I know better, and yet I left this window open so that someone could waltz in and take whatever they wanted."

She sighs heavily and finishes off her wine, as if signaling the end of that part of the conversation.

After another generous pour for the both of us, she changes the subject.

"You know," she says, "I think I can pinpoint the moment it all started to go to shit between Madeline and Audrey."

She shrugs. "Not that it matters in any objective way," she adds. "It just might give you something else to contemplate as this whole nightmare plays itself out in front of us."

"What is it?"

"Amelia Wessinger told me at a birthday dinner—place called 404 Kitchen—that Madeline and Audrey got into a screaming match that ended with them swinging their handbags at one another. Full on catfight."

It prompts an uneasy giggle from me, which then fades into a kind of weird sadness. One of them is dead, and the other is barely hanging on, all because of me. Because I came back to Nashville.

It's like feeling that I've murdered someone all over again.

"What else did Amelia say?"

Pretending I know who she is.

Gil shrugs. "In the moment, it was just a tick-tock of *this happened, that happened*, and then we had a good laugh about it. I mean, this was right during the Kavanaugh nomination, so we had more on our minds than our old friends' particular brand of crazy."

"The details matter," I reply. "What else did she say—anything?"

"The only thing she said she heard was them arguing about regret."

"Regret?"

She smiles. "Madeline was making this big production up about how she regrets the past but that there's nothing she can do about it. That there's nothing any of us can do about it."

"That sounds like it could be anything."

"Really does. I mean, shit—"

"We're all full of the stuff, right? Regret, that is. Not shit."

"Although most of us are full of that, too."

She smiles sardonically and then adds. "M.E., you know the both of them, know how they are. Were. They've always gotten into the middle of everything. If I personally litigated every issue that came between them, I'd have no time for a life of my own. That's what's good about you. You've never interfered in our private lives."

She sees my expression, and it causes her to krinkle her nose, a gesture I haven't seen since we were teenagers.

"What is it?"

"I have to be honest with you," I say, incapable of holding it in any longer.

"Shoot," she replies, her voice uneven under the weight of the conversation.

Blood warms my cheeks, as I feel embarrassment rising to the top, and I can't help but sigh before going into the whole ordeal.

"So, after everything...happened, I felt isolated from the world. Trapped on the west coast, with only myself to keep me company. But that solitude slowly cracked the foundation of my life—and then Facebook happened."

Gillian nods, following along, though a crease appears between her eyebrows.

"Yeah, the private account," she responds. "That might have fooled some people, but not me. I don't just friend people I don't know. I did a little research on you, M.E. Your profile name is just your mother's maiden name topped off with a random first name. It's not exactly rocket science—"

"And yet no one else figured it out."

"It's just the nature of being my friend, I guess," she says.

I let that thought sink in. She's about to learn what it's like to be *my* friend. "Well, anyway, for a time that was enough. I felt like I was getting away with something. And then I didn't feel that way anymore. It became rote and predictable, of course, because it always does."

Gillian is no dummy, and so the truth of what's happened dawns on her face before I relay the information to her.

"You spied on me."

It's not like that—my description is much less generous than that —but I have no choice but to keep going.

"I did a little research of my own, Gil, and somehow I ended up with your social media passwords."

"Which ones?"

I smile, despite myself. "All of them."

Gillian isn't vicious, but she's also no pushover, either, so her anger manifests itself in a righteous scowl.

"That's my private account," she responds. "That's my private information. I set up two factor authentication. I used a secure password."

"Apparently not secret enough," I say.

It's a sad attempt to lighten the mood.

"You fucking monster," she replies.

Yup, I think. I earned that one.

"We're the last two," I reply, as if that will do anything at all. "We need to—"

"*We* don't need anything," she says. "I thought I could *trust* you."

"You still can. I mean, I'm coming clean now, and I just hope you'll give me another chance. I've changed all that. I'm—I'm not that person anymore."

"When?"

"What?"

"When's the last time? When's the last time you sifted through my profile? Maybe checked my direct messages?"

"Last night," I reply.

And that seals it.

"I'm sorry," I say, hoping to undo some of the damage of my previous statement, but it doesn't seem to have worked. Gillian looks *pissed*.

"Get out," she says.

"What?"

"Get the fuck out of my place."

"But Gil—"

"I'm not saying it again. If you're not out of here within the minute, I'm calling the cops. That will...complicate things for you, or am I wrong?"

I get up and back out, but not before laying one last statement on the table for her.

"Please consider getting some protection," I say. "The detective will no doubt contact you. But we all need to be safe, at least until—"

"Shut your fucking mouth," she says. There is no ire in her statement, but she is emphatic enough that I trail off, because I don't know how to react.

She nods once but turns away, heading out to her balcony so she doesn't have to see me leave.

20

As soon as I leave Gillian's, I'm trying to get this Amelia person on the phone, because I feel like something she has to say can be critical in understanding the break in Madeline and Audrey's relationship.

When I finally get up the nerve, I call the number Gillian gave me, but there is no answer. The call goes to voicemail, and why wouldn't it? Some rando with a Seattle number showing up on her phone?

However, a few minutes later, it is *my* phone that lights up.

"Hi, is this Mary Ellen Hanneford," I say, once I answer. "Gillian Meitner told me to call you about something you witnessed between Madeline St. Clair and Audrey Winstead?"

When I fill her in, she instantly knows.

"Oh, yeah," she says, "I remember that. It was in East Nashville, right near Mas Tacos Por Favor. I had stuffed myself on quinoa and sweet potato tacos, and I saw these two girls kind of screeching at one another."

"Did you hear what they were saying?"

"Oh yeah," she replies. "I should say I heard it *before* I saw it. There was this loud sound, and you know, when you're not expecting it, these arguments come off like noise. Honestly, I thought it was homeless people having it out at The Pharmacy. It's a local burger place—"

"I know what it is. What were they saying? I mean, when you could finally hear it."

She takes a moment. "Honestly, I don't remember. Me and my friends, we felt like slumming it, so we went to a few places and drank cheap beer, and what I mostly remember is the hangover. I'm sorry I couldn't be—"

"Just tell me what you *do* remember."

When there is just more silence on the other end, I reply with, "Just think. Anything. Fragments of speech. Anything. It will help, I promise."

"What are you even doing this for?"

I think of a thousand different reasons, but I settle on the truth. "It has to do with...what happened to Audrey."

"Oh my God," she replies. "You don't think *she* had anything to do with this, do you? Wasn't she just attacked, too?"

"She was," I reply, "and she almost died."

"It was just awful," she replies.

The effort to relitigate all the fact surrounding Madeline's death and Audrey's attack just isn't enough to sustain me right now, so I feel the annoyance creep into my voice.

To stay calm, I try a different tack. "If you can't remember anything—"

"Oh, wait, there is something," she interrupts.

"What is it?"

"Just before they started swinging, one of them asked the other, 'Is it true?' Something like that."

"And that's it? No response? They just went to swinging?"

"That's close to it," she replies. "There was just, like, this standoff in the middle of the street, cars passing by, and then the next moment they were swinging handbags at one another. Until Audrey's husband—"

"Jenkins."

"—pulled them apart. And then Audrey turns and hits him, too, before storming off. He kind of turns and shrugs at Madeline before trailing behind her."

"So do you think—?"

"I don't know *what* to think," she replies. "I'm just the witness to the whole event. Two-thirds of them are now dead, so I'm not sad to say I'm glad I didn't see more."

There's a pause, as I try to think of a follow-up question, but the woman on the other end gears up to speak before I can manage to come up with something.

"And that's about all I remember," Amelia says. "Now if you'll excuse me..."

She's off the phone before I can respond, and I am left to contemplate just how this little nugget of information fits into the whole of the Suicide Blondes saga.

I RETURN to the rental property, where a smattering of media waits in the street for me. I push through by waving apologetically and gently pressing the gas so they can't stop me. I've learned it's best to be polite but firm in these situations.

An unmarked car is in the driveaway. As soon as I pull in, a hulking figure gets out, and I recognize him immediately.

In a single, fluid motion, I park and exit the vehicle. The "journalists" from the TV stations and newspapers remain out by the road.

"Detective Ciccotelli," I say, sounding more hyper than expected, "I was just on my way to speak with you."

"That so?"

His tone is a little...off, and I suddenly feel the need to look around me. My whole body clenches, and I keep the keys handy, just in case I need to jump back behind the wheel. I can't handle the way he's looking at me.

But, perhaps sensing my anxiety, he keeps his distance, stopping several steps from me and crossing his arms.

"I've been doing some research," I say, "and I want to catch you up on it."

For some reason, I expect him to be ecstatic about the possibility, but his face doesn't change. He's impassive, and there's a sadness to his expression I can't quite get over.

At last, he makes a half-sighing noise and slicks his hair back with his dominant hand.

"Miss Hanneford, I'm afraid I'm not here with good news."

"What is it?"

"Would you mind coming with me? Maybe we could go inside for a minute?"

"For what reason?"

"I insist." He glances toward the street. "The, um, *vultures* are out in full force, and I don't want to give them the show they've come to expect."

I turn my attention toward them and get what he means. They're keeping a safe distance, but it seems like the tide could burst at any moment.

"Okay, let's head inside. Want some coffee?"

"You read my mind."

After the coffee is poured, I draw the blinds and lean against a nearby counter.

"Okay," I say, "I don't suspect this will be easy. Go ahead. Let's do this."

He clears his throat, but he never waivers. "We did some testing on Madeline St. Clair's journal, and your fingerprints were all over it."

I feel relief wash over me. "Oh, I can explain that," I say, think that it might be a little tricky but knowing that there isn't going—

"That isn't all," he continues. "We submitted a request for Mrs. St. Clair's phone records, and as it turns out, you made a call to her home the night of her death. Is that true?"

You need to be afraid of me.

"Yes, but—"

"And the neighbors, they distinctly remember a woman matching your description driving a car exactly like yours here showing up drunk and angry the night of their deaths. Is that true?"

"I—"

"Making a scene and arguing with the husband, Colton Ambrose?"

"Yes but—"

"And then there's the internet records. Is it untrue that you've been following her social media habits—how can I say this —*obsessively*?"

Shit. Mentally, I try to calculate how many hours I've spent trolling through Madeline's personal messages. Then I multiply that by three and come up with an ungodly number.

"Miss Hanneford?"

"I don't have a good response to that."

"Well, there are...records of that sort of thing, and we will be checking in on them. We had no idea but we happened to receive a call from—"

"Gillian Meitner," I finish his sentence. "I figured as much."

"Any idea of why she knows such intimate information?"

"I told her," I say, sounding even more depressed than I feel.

"And you didn't feel any such need to avail us of the same information? Don't you think that would have been helpful?"

"I don't know—I *didn't* know—that it would turn out like this."

"In checking on our friend, Mr. Allred, we've found that his name isn't on any flight manifest for a flight coming into Nashville *since* he walked out of his previous facility."

Just hearing this information makes my stomach go acidic.

"That doesn't mean anything," I say. "He could have flown into another city, or used a different name or—

"But is any of that likely? Remember Occam."

"*Fuck* Occam," I reply. "There isn't anything likely about any of this. What self-respecting cop would say any of this shit?"

"Miss Hanneford—"

"Really. I mean, come *on*."

"Miss Hanneford, I'm going to place you under arrest for the murder of Madeline St. Clair. I'm going to save you the embarrassment of frog marching you out of here—we have a car parked on an adjacent street—but I am going to have to take you with me."

My initial instinct is to run. My brain teems with potential locations where I could hide out until I get my thoughts together, but both Detective Ciccotelli and I know it's not going to happen. Instead, I allow myself to be directed out the side entrance to a waiting unmarked police cruiser.

The throng of reporters and camera crews hustle around to the side of the house to hurl questions at me, but I'm both too afraid and in too much shock to do anything but stare straight ahead.

I'm sure that it'll look good for the evening news on Channel 5.

As we pull away, I turn to see the house just off 51st surrounded by paparazzi. Infested by them, like cockroaches who have discovered a crack in the foundation. Very soon, I am lost in my own head, waiting for the next phase of this charade to kick in.

THE NEXT DAY passes in a blur. I spend most of it in my cell, awaiting arraignment. They're really going to have to dig to put together a list of charges and a clear indictment. All they have is some flimsy physical evidence and some search histories. None of it seems enough to hold me, but here I am.

But the fantasy bubble in my mind pops, and I'm left only with the sounds of loud people talking to the loud television in the common area. Occasionally, my face appears on-screen as the grisly details related to my crimes, both real and imagined, are read loud for the masses to see and believe, but otherwise, I am left to my own devices, to suffer inside my own head.

Beyond the claustrophobia, though, jail isn't that bad. Some people howl and cry at night, and someone's always asking you for something—cigarettes or the food from your tray, for example—but they're not altogether bad, so long as they keep their distance.

The real problem with jail is the solitude, and not just because you are separated from friends and family. It's the way that being alone highlights your deepest insecurities. I could spend that time thinking about a million different things and it would pass the time, but instead I am driven to contemplate the life and death of Everett Coughlin.

It is pure torture.

Over the years, I have spent an inordinate amount of time trying to blur the memories associated with that fevered, manic school year, but eventually they push through my imagined boundaries, and I become a captive audience to them. Thank God for the ravages of time and drinking, or else these memories might sting like alcohol on a fresh wound. Instead, it's like watching TV at the bottom of a river bed.

But the guilt remains, and so during the first twenty-four hours of my stay, I am treated to visions of the past that I've tried to suppress with the entirety of my being.

~

THEN

THE LAW OFFICES OF ALLEN, Garrett, Donnelly, and Edmiston are large and inviting, though not for Mary Ellen, who sits curled in on herself on a couch in the corner. Her mother sits next to her, idly crocheting nothing in particular.

Once the birdlike secretary leads them beyond the threshold, they are taken to a conference room and seated on one side all by themselves, while Madeline, Audrey, Gillian, their families, and their lawyers are seated on the other side.

They have a lawyer, but he is not present today. He is not able to attend this little meeting, and despite his dire protestations, Mary Ellen and her mother do. Mary Ellen is under the naive impression that truth matters and her friends simply want the same things she does. They all want the truth to come out, and in the wake of Everett Coughlin's death, it seems most important for all the lies and rumors to be outed and cast aside.

But still, she can't help but be nervous.

Point of fact, she hasn't spoken to any of the other girls since the night...of the incident. She's tried a few times to get in touch with them but has had little success. Zero, in fact. She had recently come to the conclusion that she may never actually see Madeline and the others again.

That is, until the representative lawyer for the St. Clairs contacted *her* and insisted they meet in an informal way and talk this through. On the phone, the jerk even emphasized the informality of it all. Maybe he did expect for her to bring her lawyer, but she didn't hear it that way. He made it seem like a cordial invite, a palaver of no particular consequence.

Even if not, perhaps her mother could have taken it upon herself to be responsible and insist on getting representation involved, but Mary Ellen's mother is in no shape to be a parent. She is convinced she is a walking cancer cell, and no amount of logical intervention can disabuse her of her wild and—frankly—idiotic notions. She claims to be able to feel the cancer growing inside of her, even though that seems ridiculous on its face.

So, with her mother slowly drifting out to sea on the force of her convictions, Mary Ellen is required to be the sound, thoughtful adult in this scenario. It makes her miss her father dearly.

And Mary Ellen is not stupid. She may be naive, but she's not stupid. As she sits here, across from the Murderer's Row of lawyers on the other side, she realizes she should take leave until she can get her own counsel here, but she just can't pull the trigger and say it. In part it is because she feels silly, that somehow asking to do the right thing will somehow make her look *more* credulous and unprepared, but mostly because she harbors the ill-conceived idea that they eill come to some kind of tacit understanding without lawyers and family.

Maybe she *is* stupid, she thinks.

But she persists in believing she will get herself out of this situation.

"Miss Hanneford," the hawkish gentleman to Madeline's right says. Since her parents are seated to her left, it only makes sense to assume this is the same lawyer who contacted her. "We are so thankful for this opportunity to speak."

Mary Ellen nods. Since her mother is still crocheting, she gently elbows her to bring her into the conversation. She returns her hooks to their former position in her bag and gazes blandly across the table.

"Can I ask what this is all about?"

Madeline's lawyer, Mr. Schnell—he introduced himself when he called her—smiles graciously. He glances from his client back to Mary Ellen, and that's when Mary Ellen notices it.

Madeline St. Clair is *glaring* at her. Not *looking*. Not *staring*. She is giving Mary Ellen the stinkeye to end all stinkeyes.

The rest of the crew refuses to engage her in eye contact. Gillian and Audrey are both staring down into their laps. In their faces, some semblance of embarrassment and shame has begun to form, but it's not enough. Not enough for them to stand up. Not enough for them to tell the truth. Not enough for them to take responsibility.

That's when her heart sinks.

This is the performance. This is how she is going to get out of this scot free and foist it all on Mary Ellen. She has the backing of her parents. Of her high-priced lawyer. Of her sycophants. She is the mastermind, and she is in complete control.

"It is my understanding that you were, at some point, acquainted with my client and also with the other clients at this table. Is that true?"

Years later, Mary Ellen will realize how shady—and potentially illegal—all of this is. But by then it'll be too late. Being a teenager, she trusts the system to work. She believes in ideas like justice, and she expects law and order to mean exactly that. She believes this because of all the movies she has seen, and just how passionately her 8th grade teacher praised the ideas brought up in *To Kill a Mockingbird*.

This moment, it is the first time she's ever questioned the way things work, and even though she hopes for the best, she can't help but expect the worst.

"This situation...it's complicated, isn't it? Some horseplay entered into by one party, followed along by the other parties, ends in an unfortunate accident. Very messy. Quite unnerving for all those involved."

"Yes, sir."

She can't believe it. She wonders: is Madeline actually going to admit to wrongdoing?

"Well, I'm glad we can agree on that. Absolutely ecstatic. Now, onto the more...sensitive portion of this discussion."

"O—kay," Mary Ellen replies.

Meanwhile, her mother remains silent. She has a look of utter confusion on her face, but otherwise she is motionless and mute during the proceedings.

"These things can get out of hand very quickly," the lawyer, Schnell, continues. "Therefore, it is necessary that we all be proactive in these matters, and my—our—clients are prepared to testify in the upcoming trial, if there is to be one."

"Good," Mary Ellen says, feeling like a mechanical version of herself.

"They—each of them—is willing to state that they engaged in these activities under duress and fear of reprisal from you, one Mary Ellen Hanneford."

Her heart skips a beat.

She looks first up at her mother, who seems to be somewhere else right now, and then to her left—where her lawyer *should* be—before letting out an exasperated sound.

"That's—that's not true. That's not the way it happened."

She can't get the words out fast enough, and they seem to get lost behind her rage and sputtering anger.

The lawyer, Mr. Schnell, smiles that alligator smile of his, all teeth and eyes. "I'm afraid you might be in some trouble there," he says.

Out of a folder in front of him, Schnell retrieves several typed sheets of paper, and he places them on the table in front of him, careful not to let them get too close to Mary Ellen.

"These," he says, tapping one index finger on the pages, "are signed, *sworn* affidavits from our clients, stating in no uncertain terms not just your complicity in these matters but also your role as the leader in them."

She glances from Gillian to Audrey, and then her eyes settle on Madeline, who smirks at her from across the table.

This is the first moment she sees the details of the long con.

She was meant to be on this side of the table the entire time.

"And because they are sensitive to the suffering on all sides of this issue, they are prepared to take care of any legal costs incurred during the whole of your...situation."

"But that's not—"

"In addition," he continues, cutting her off, "they would donate a sizable amount of money to the family of the deceased, as a means of offsetting any potential liability stemming from your prank."

Liability? Is that how they see the life and death of Everett Cough-lin, as some risk that needs to be dealt with? She can barely contain herself, and she feels the heat boiling over deep inside herself, in the place where she tries to shove all of her sadness.

"I see how you're reacting. It's written plainly on your face. However, I'd caution you against saying—or doing—anything you regret at this point. Indeed, it would behoove you to check yourself. A family in your position could do with a quiet settlement from—"

Finally, she erupts. "I don't *want* your goddamned money," she says. "I'm not looking for a payday. I was under the impression that we'd all face this together, because we were all involved in equal parts."

"And if you want that to be true," the lawyer replies, "then you will have to convince someone else—perhaps a judge or jury—of what occurred that fateful night. The statements issued by our clients are...ironclad. Think, maybe, of what your father would suggest you do in this situation."

That's it. The final straw, yanked free and snapped in two.

"I might as well be dead," Mary Ellen says, through choked tears, as she stands up and exits the room without looking back.

But then again, she doesn't need to.

Look back, that is.

She can feel her ex-friend's eyes burning a hole in the back of her cheap blouse.

"You're dead to me," Madeline St. Clair says from somewhere behind her, and it is the last thing she hears before she slams the door. She doesn't need to see her to know the Bitch of Belle Meade is actually *smiling* at all of this.

21

NOW

The next morning, before the sun's faded rays pour through the bars in the windows, a squat woman with the beginnings of a mustache opens my cell and informs me to gather my belongings. I want to protest, but my joy is so great I cannot. Instead, I allow myself to be escorted from station to station in the jail, as various documents are signed, and I get closer and closer to freedom.

Instead of being released, however, I get escorted to a small room with a table, two chairs, and a window. It's an interrogation room, but so far as I know, I'm on the verge of being cut loose, so I bring it up to the female guard.

"I think this might be a mistake," I say, but I'm met with an equal and opposite reaction.

"I'm only doing what I'm told," the mustachioed female guard says before slamming the door behind her.

I take a seat, and a few minutes later, Detective Ciccotelli ambles in and retrieves the chair across from me.

He lets go of a long and disquieting sigh. "I think you are owed an apology," he says, his eyes flicking from the glare on the table to me.

It's not something he wants to say, but he does anyway, and he doesn't shy away. I am struck by the fact that this man has delivered about as much miserable news to the people of Nashville as anybody alive.

"What does that mean?"

"It means I got something wrong. One of my hunches backfired."

"I'm sorry, I—"

"You are cleared, for the time being. It seems your friend, Mrs. Winstead—"

"She's alive?"

He nods. "And in a state, to be sure. She's going to be unwell for a very long time, but one of the first things she did upon waking was identify the person she claims is responsible for all of this. So, yeah. You're going to be walking out of here in a matter of moments. I just wanted to make sure I pulled you for a formal apology."

"Well, that's—I don't need anything. But I do need to know..."

His eyes drop, and he breaks his gaze for the first time. He sniffs—an affectation—and then says, "Timothy—"

"Allred."

He nods. "That's right."

"Where is he? Have you arrested him?"

"No official word just yet. We're still sorting out the details."

There's Kleenex on the table, and he takes this moment to slide them across to me. I take it out of instinct, and yet I don't feel the tears the way I probably should.

Instead, I pull a few free of the box and wipe the corners of my eyes. The shock is still settling in when Detective Ciccotelli continues.

"It appears that Allred did his time quietly, but a few days after he was discharged, he boarded a plane under an assumed name."

"Huh."

"Yeah," he replies, almost sheepishly. He opens his mouth to say more, but he doesn't quite get there. Instead, he closes it and clasps his hands on the table in front of him.

So I help jumpstart the conversation.

"And Audrey said—"

"She said a man showed up at their house, broke in, was slinking around, and then he attacked them. Shot her husband and then tied her up. Kept talking about 'unwinding the clock.'"

The exact words Allred used once upon a time to threaten me.

He once sent a long diatribe about time that mentioned a philosopher named Heidegger, among other things. He believed it was possible, somehow, to undo the damage of the past by reclaiming the present. A pretty crazy way of framing vigilante justice, but one he was committed to.

"You all right, Ms. Hanneford? You look a little pale."

"No, it's just, I mean, that sounds exactly like something he would say."

"You couldn't apply any of that insight regarding his whereabouts, now could you?"

"Isn't that supposed to be *your* job?"

"Fair enough," he replies. "But I don't know this guy. I don't have a read on him at all. He's invaded my ecosystem and is wreaking havoc on par with a Bundy or Ramirez. Unless he's stalking you right now, I have no clue where he might be."

"In which case, you're all flying blind."

"More or less. I don't want to give up the ghost, but if he don't want to be found—and he doesn't make a stupid mistake—then he can ride under the radar for some time."

The pure horror of that statement sinks in, as I contemplate living life as a target. Then, something occurs to me.

"Has Audrey's awakening from the coma been reported out yet?"

"No, not yet."

"And there's no one who would leak it to the press?"

"There's a pretty tight lid on this thing."

"That doesn't answer my question. It needs to be ironclad."

"It's ironclad," he responds, not unkindly.

I can't believe I'm about to say the words that come out of my mouth. "I think I should try to lure Timothy Allred out of hiding."

"You sure about that?"

I nod. "But first, I need to speak with an old acquaintance."

Audrey looks like a science experiment, full of tubes and hooked up to all manner of medical equipment. Her skin is even paler than usual, and the dark roots in her highlighted mane reveal traces of gray. My own hair has faded to a dirty blonde over the years, but even with all the stress I've managed to stave off the beginning of middle age.

Audrey, though, has evidently been holding herself together with makeup and blowouts, because she is old well beyond her years. Perhaps it was the attack which has brought her to this point, but I'm thinking maybe not.

When she opens her eyes, she has a broken doll quality that makes me want to look away, but of course, I can't, so I just smile and make the best of it.

"How are you doing, Aud?"

It takes her a moment to focus, but when she finally sees me—really puts her eyes on me—she begins to cry uncontrollably.

"It was horrible, M.E.," she says. "He looked like a wild animal. I'll never forget the way he looked at me."

In my mind, I can see the moment I discovered him, naked and bleeding, on the floor of my apartment, having made a living metaphor of himself. Then, I try to imagine what a few years of detention in a psychiatric facility might have done to him, and I can't help but shudder. She's definitely lucky to be alive, even if she doesn't quite look it right now.

"Coming out of a coma is a fucked-up thing," she continues. "I've had hallucinations, you know. It's so irrational. I know I'm here, and not back at the house, and I know—I just *know*—he's not actually coming for me, but then I *see* him. He's standing in the doorway, holding his gun. Right where you're standing, as a matter of fact."

Somehow, intangibly, I feel the outline of the man and the murderer surrounding me, and so I step aside. And then I say the thing I came here to say, the thing I've been thinking about since Detective Ciccotelli told me what Audrey says happened to her.

It's the last thing I want to say, but I have to. Common decency would have me do the thing *they* wouldn't back when we were in high school.

"I'm sorry," I manage to say. "I know that this is all my fault—every single bit of it—and I'm sorry."

"Yes, well. You couldn't have known that the psychopath would follow you here. And I'm sure it's difficult to live with this on your conscience. I get it. I know how hard it must be for you. And to think, you might be *next*."

I try to hide my shock.

Then I remember: This is Audrey. She is the star of her own show, and she doesn't quite possess the same sense of empathy as most human beings.

It's not that she's malicious. She's just not very self-aware.

"My mom always told me that I'm a survivor," she says.

"You are," I reply, the bile rising to the back of my throat.

"We all are, I guess."

She has the glazed over look of an astronaut speeding into the eye of God.

"Is there anything you...remember about the other night?" I ask. "Anything you haven't or didn't want to tell the police?"

Her face goes blank for a moment, and I think maybe she's having a stroke when a single tear appears on her cheek.

"I refuse to tell that one detective, what's his name?"

"Ciccotelli."

"Yeah, right. It seems like he's just *looking* for something, and I'm afraid of what he'll do if he finds out something he doesn't like."

I nod, but really, I don't know what she's talking about. She looks a little loopy, so maybe the drugs, or the coma, have done some damage to her.

It's the eyes. They glisten with a new kind of intensity, and so I prompt her. "What were you going to tell me?"

She looks away. "There's something about *that night* no one knows about."

In the stillness of the room, the sound of the beeping machines and the nurses' voices from outside are amplified. I can feel my breathing, can feel each molecule of oxygen reach its destination. I focus on it, because I'm afraid I'll pass out.

Instead of pushing her, I let her linger there. If she doesn't speak now, while she's in this state, she may never get around to it. She'll come to her senses and realize she's doing something rash, and she'll keep this—whatever it is—to herself.

Forever.

"After we...after you left Gillian's house," she begins, "we all hung out and continued saying things to him."

"Everett Coughlin."

She flashes a sad look at me. "Right. Yeah. He has a name. I get it."

"Just saying," I respond.

"Anyway, *that* night. After you left—"

"I was assaulted and kicked out of Gil's house."

"Please let me tell you. After that, you can berate me to the end of time. But for now, allow me the space to say what I need to say."

I have to force down twenty years of anger over this point, but somehow I manage. When I nod, she continues.

"The night—that night—we went to his house."

I feign shock.

"All three of you?"

"No, just me and Mads. We got this idea—Jesus, it sounds so cruel —that it would be...fun to watch it happen. To see him do whatever he was going to do. God, it's just so sick."

I nod.

"But we did it. Madeline brought Gillian's camera, and we made this big production about filming it. But then Madeline got spooked by something, and she went home."

"And you?"

There is a moment, just before she speaks, in which I think maybe the reel-to-reel of reality will strip away and be flung off into the darkness, and I will never find out what happened that night.

But then the moment passes, and the two of us remain.

She seems to clench the sheet, to hold tightly on it so as not to float away, and then she shakes her head. "I stayed."

All of a sudden, I feel weak. The chair by her bed is too close for my comfort, so I pull it a few feet back and sit down, trying not to topple over onto my face.

"And that's it?"

Another shake of the head. "I felt like I had something to prove."

"To whom?"

"Madeline, of course," she says. "Don't pretend like you didn't see how she treated me. She might have scapegoated you for the death of Everett Coughlin, but she *always* tied me to the whipping post. And no matter how poorly she treated me, somehow I always felt the need to get into her good graces. To win her favor. I was her *dog*. Her little *bitch*."

"And you felt like that would be the ultimate gesture of loyalty."

She nods. "I assumed videotaping the last moments of his life would make things different between us. I thought she and I would reach a kind of *détente*, and then she would respect me."

It almost makes me smile. "Guess we were all naive back then."

"*I* was more naive than most," she replies. "I craved her attention, and all she gave me in return was the back of her hand."

"And you thought witnessing someone else's death would somehow make that relationship *less* complicated?"

"I guess I figured she would see what I had done for her—for our friendship—and come around to the fact that *I* was her best and most loyal friend."

"So—that night..."

"Madeline freaked out," she replies. "It *was* weird, but it was the thing we had been talking about all year. Now that it was coming to fruition, Madeline..."

"Chickened out."

She glances away. "Lucky for her."

"Wait a minute," I reply, thinking of the video. "Tell me you didn't. Is *that* the fucking thing you left in my house? Fucking *evidence*?"

"I was a different person back then."

"But that didn't stop you from keeping it a secret all these years."

My voice is as cold as the icicles in my guts, and God help me, all I want to do is slap her. Somehow, I manage not to, but the urge continues to circulate through me like cheap booze.

"When did you finally fess up to Madeline?" I ask.

"...Years ago."

"And did you never, not even once, consider discussing this with the police?"

Audrey gives me a look like I just landed on this planet. "Well, *no*. It's just—no! Oh my God, no. What would that accomplish, Mary Ellen?"

"It would maybe give the family some solace. Some closure."

"Would it? To dredge this all up now?"

"Or at least clear me of some of the guilt in all of this. I went to *jail* for all of you."

"Haven't you ever heard of letting sleeping dogs lie?"

I bite my tongue. Then, I say it. "No. But there *is* such a thing as common decency, Audrey. It doesn't have anything to do with who is on Instagram or how many FaceBook friends you have."

She smiles. It's the biggest *fuck you* ever. "Then you obviously don't understand how the world works. The *only* thing that matters is who you are and—more importantly—who your *friends* are. My whole *life* is built around the people I know. If that suddenly went away, then I'd suddenly cease to exist."

"If you don't tell anyone about any of this, then I will."

"No you won't."

"Yes I will. Detective Ciccotelli is waiting downstairs, and I'll—"

"*Think* about it, M.E. If you go downstairs and run off at the mouth about this thing, just how will it make you look?"

"I don't care how it makes me look. The truth is—"

"The truth is, you are on the hook for it. No matter what story comes out, you will always be the girl—the monster—who led the charge in Everett Coughlin's death. To a good number of people in Nashville, you're nothing more than a murderer. If you come out with this story now, it will come out that the man who wants to kill *you* actually started with *us*. Do you think that will garner any sympathy from the public?"

"That's not what I—"

"Yes it is, Mary Ellen. You know that's true. You, more than anyone, want to be vindicated. And that's okay. But this is not the way to do it. Maybe when this is all over, once they've caught that psychopath of yours, then you can sit down with someone on *60 Minutes* and tell your whole story, and some people will shed tears for you. It might even erase some of the past. But if you think that doing this now will help your cause, honey, I know the public better than you do. It'll be better for both of us if you just keep this a secret for now. Just between us girls. You know—The Suicide Blondes."

It's then I realize I've been played. Audrey knew this whole time what she was doing, and she drew me in to wrap me up in my own insecurities.

I don't give her the satisfaction of seeing me upset, however, because I walk out before the tears come.

When I appear in my mother's room, she's sitting up, and for once she's smiling. It's good to see one of the members of the Hanneford family to do something besides grimace at everything life has to throw at them.

It's so unlike my mother, but she manages to surprise me. Her smile is wide and unselfconscious. She looks hale and hearty, like she's ten years younger.

Like a weight has been taken off her.

"You're looking spry," I say, nudging her with an elbow. "What did they give you?"

My eyes go to her hands, and she's thoughtlessly picking at a thumbnail with one finger. There's something she wants to say.

"Another chance at life," she replies.

"What do you mean?"

Her eyes seem to grapple with the question, but eventually she tells me.

"I—may have jumped to conclusions about my prognosis," she says. "And I totally blame myself, but I think the doctors had it in for me, because they made it seem—"

"Like you were dying?" I interrupt.

She takes a deep breath, expels it slowly. "Maybe it's just my luck, that I spent most of my golden years damning myself, and then when it comes to pass—when I think Death is knocking at the door—I end up suffering some kind of miraculous recovery."

My eyes drift from her face to her hands, where she works over the skin surrounding a nail bed until it bleeds. She only does that when—

She's lying.

Her eyes become wet with tears, and it's then I know. I don't know how she doesn't know I know, but that's where we are.

Reaching out with one hand, clasping hers, I sink into the seat next to her bed.

My whole body trembles, but she's so earnest in getting me to believe, I have to give her this. She's trying, for God's sake. She's *finally seen the light*, as the old folk are fond of saying. All these years, she's been looking for something, and it seems, in the dimming twilight, she's appeared to have found it.

And I can't take this away from her.

It just wouldn't be fair, otherwise.

"I—I should stay with you," I say, feeling the lead in my limbs slowly take hold. The words can't or won't come out right, and I struggle around them to try and sound normal.

Smiling, all the worry gone, she shakes her head. "Baby, you need to go. I'll be out of this place in a few days, and then you and I can plan the rest of our lives together. Heck, maybe I'll come for a stay with you in Seattle, once this is all said and done."

My throat closes up at the thought. I have to choke the words out, working them around the grief knotted up just behind my tongue. "That'd be nice," I reply. "I'd love to see you in my neck of the woods."

Her face drops, but only for an instant. She reaches the hand not holding my own up, and she wipes the tears from my chin, where they seem to have come to rest all together.

"Don't be sad now," she says. "The hard part is over. It's all sunshine from here."

It takes more than my remaining willpower to nod, so I just allow my head to droop. "I know. I'm just so...happy to get you all to myself."

"Things get bad sometimes, but they end up righting themselves. Don't ever forget that, darling."

"I won't, Mama," I reply, calling her the name I hadn't used in more than thirty years. I gave up *mama* with *y'all* when I realized they both made me sound common.

And even though she doesn't understand—doesn't know that I know—I can't help but level with her in the only way I know how.

There's no time like the present, I think.

"Listen, Mom," I begin, mapping out each word as it occurs to me. "I'm not sure where the next few days will take me—or what's going to happen when I get there—but just know I love you. It's been a long, tough ride for the both of us, but I am a fundamentally different person. I know you struggled with who I was, but I hope you're proud of the person I've become."

She doesn't quite chide me, but offense is definitely taken.

"Oh, baby, you have no idea how proud I am of you. Always. As long as I live, you will be the light that brightened the darkness in my horizon. I love you, sweet girl."

A sound of some kind is prepped to escape, but I shove it back down, along with the feelings that I cannot let escape.

I owe my mother that.

So I smile.

And I lean forward.

And I kiss her on the cheek.

But I do not cry.

"I'll see you soon," I say.

And then I leave, because I know no such thing to be true.

I make it to the family bathroom by the elevators before it all comes up. I sob until there's nothing left to let go of, and then I move on.

22

I don't have a foolproof plan to get through to Timothy Allred, but I have ideas. While the cops and other local officials attempt to find him through traditional detection, I am going to use the one thing I have at my disposal—the internet.

It's simple. I begin the way I would draw in any demented weirdo. I make my profile public and change my name and picture to the one everyone knows me by.

Mary.

Ellen.

Hanneford.

If it is him, then this first step will draw him out of the woodwork. It's not enough to step out of the digital shadows, but it's a start.

The effect is not immediate, but I can feel myself becoming something else. Someone else. I am transforming into a different person, or else I am finally leaving my own personal cocoon to become the most curious butterfly of all-time.

Moving on.

I use all of my social media accounts to make myself vulnerable.

Nashville is a very public (and publicly visible) city. There are plenty of places to go and be seen, so it's easy for me to taunt my stalker.

My first stop is Lower Broadway, where thousands upon thousands of people gather each and every day to experience the wonderment of Music City. Honky tonks, pedal taverns, bachelorette parties, and day drinking are part and parcel to the experience. At night, the city overflows with people looking for a good time, stretching from 1st Avenue, along the Cumberland River, all the way up to Printers Alley, which used to be the city's Red Light District. Sad wannabe starlets and grungy finger-pickers ply their trades in the bars along the side streets, but during the day, it's a whole different atmosphere. There's almost a family friendly quality to the debauchery when the sun is out, and the sound of misery and heartbreak coming from the voices inside the bars does nothing to ward off the tourists with their mid-summer vacation plans.

Today, I am one of the city's main attractions.

I feel like one of those people on Hollywood Boulevard who dress up as Spider-Man or Marilyn Monroe and take pictures with credulous out-of-towners for tips.

Only, I'm selling something completely different.

I am trading death for attention.

People stare and take pictures, and when they do, rather than shy away from the attention, I approach them and ask if they'll use a specific hashtag, the one that I've included in all my own posts.

#SuicideBlondeOnTour

Almost instantly, Instagram lights up with people who have just experienced a brush with the macabre. Their Insta stories and Nashville posts are enlivened with the visage of a killer, and they are none the wiser.

This is helping me catch a killer.

Once the news media gets word, I am bombarded by journalists and TV anchors of all stripes. They hurl questions at me.

And I speak with each and every one of them.

Not only am I accommodating of their tasteless and trivial requests, I smile the whole time, as if I'm actually enjoying being put on display. It's like something out of *Black Mirror*, and I can't help but think of how those shows usually turn out.

But still, I persevere.

Each time I'm interviewed, I make sure to mention for the cameras that I am, indeed, *the* Mary Ellen Hanneford, that I intend on speaking up, not just about my own experiences with online bullying, but also about the stalker who attempted to take my life a few years back.

I even dare speak his name.

"Timothy Allred became obsessed with my case, and though he may have had a point about my role in Everett Coughlin's death, he proceeded to stalk and harass me to the point I had to change addresses."

And then I provide my own little tag to my soon-to-be-televised comments. "I know I'm the last person who deserves sympathy for this sort of thing, but I'm tired of his antics. He is a scared, sad little boy, and I might be afraid if the whole thing weren't so silly and pointless."

It's the headshot in this whole scenario, and my hope is that it works. Timothy Allred is nothing if not easily manipulated.

People are astounded. It's like a mermaid has washed ashore in the midst of this concrete-and-neon city. But it felt necessary, in some way. People have always used *me* for their own entertainment, so why can't I use them for a little justice?

Once I feel that I've made my point, I sneak away to the rental car and venture back to my place in The Nations.

A few hours into this little experiment, I get a message from Gillian.

> What the fuck are you doing?

I ignore it, at first.

But when she posts the *exact* same message ten minutes later, I can't help but respond.

> I'm doing the thing everybody wants me to do. I'm sacrificing myself for the greater good.

> You don't have to bring everybody else down with you. No one else deserves to be painted with your brush.

Ouch.

Another ding of my phone.

> I know there's a good person in you, Mary Ellen. And this isn't it. Step back and consider what you're doing before it's too late.

I read it but don't respond.

If it happens, if it goes the way I expect it to, then she'll be thankful I threw myself on the pyre for her.

For all of them.

For now, though, she just sees me as an asshole.

Which I am.

Then, before I can think of a clever response, my phone dings again.

I check the message. It's a message from a rando.

Bingo.

I've got him.

> SEEMS A LITTLE DESPERATE.

I'd forgotten—he's one of *those*. An ALL CAPS writer from way back.

But still, I keep the facade rolling.

> Who is this?

The response is immediate.

> YOU KNOW WHO THIS IS.

And, just like that, I am speaking digitally with the man who wanted to wear me like a bearskin rug.

And I'm in his sights again.

> Oh.

Letting it linger gives him the impression that I'm just now figuring this out. Even if that's not true—even if he's convinced that I'm bluffing—it never hurts to play the cards in your hand.

I decide to be a little cavalier, because that is what will pull him from the shadows.

> Did prison do anything to re-thread the loose screw in your head?

But he doesn't miss a beat.

> DID GETTING YOUR FRIENDS KILLED DO ANYTHING TO WARM THAT COLD, BLACK LITTLE HEART OF YOURS?

A pause. Then—

> OR WILL I HAVE TO RIP IT OUT AND SEE FOR MYSELF?

> Maybe. You certainly haven't tried yet.

> YOU DIDN'T SEE ME BECAUSE I DIDN'T LET YOU. DID IT EVER OCCUR TO YOU THAT MAYBE I HAVE *YOUR* PASSWORDS?

Admittedly, that one gets through the armor, but I can't slow down, can't think, because if I get this just right, I won't have to worry about him ever again.

And neither will Gillian.

> Not much to see there.

> OH, BUT THERE IS. AND IT IS GOING TO END UP SPLATTERED ACROSS ALL OF THE INTERNET.

> Like my blood?

> YOU SAID IT, NOT ME.

My heart is thrumming, and I want to scream, but somehow I maintain my composure, try to think of something else to taunt him.

He's winning.

It floats around and around the inside of my skull.

He's winning. He's winning. He's winning.

> HURT YOUR FEELINGS?

> No, I'm just thinking of how much like him you are.

> WHO?

I turn on all caps, just for him.

> YOU KNOW WHO.

I don't hear back for a few minutes, and there's a split second in which I *think* I can hear someone typing. I spin in my chair and glance, only to see...nothing at all. Perhaps it's psychosomatic, or maybe I have really lost it.

> Did I hurt YOUR feelings?

> NO. I'M JUST RECORDING VIDEO. I'M NO MULTITASKER.

> Video? Of what?

And then, just because I can't let him get the upper hand, I wave.

If he's here, I'm already dead, I think. Might as well play along.

> NOT YOU.

> Then who?

> AN OLD FRIEND.

> SHE AND I HAVE SOME UNFINISHED BUSINESS.

> CHECK YOUR PROFILE.

I don't want to—something tells me it's a *huge* mistake—but I can't help myself. I open my laptop and head over to my FaceBook page.

In my messages, there is a video.

And the video is live.

The window fills with a rectangle of moving images. The footage is grainy—how old is the phone Allred is using?—but I can see his subject just as clearly as is needed.

It's not me. He's not standing behind me like some horror movie villain.

But he is standing near someone.

Apparently, someone has gotten out of the hospital a little early.

Audrey is walking unaccompanied to her car. She looks a little green, even in this phone shot, but she is clearly able to leave the hospital on her own authority.

> I'LL TELL HER YOU SAID HELLO.

And then the window indicates he's left our chat.

"HELLO?"

I have to struggle to keep from bursting into tears the moment she answers. "Aud, oh my God. Listen!"

She sounds a little weak but otherwise okay. "Mary Ellen, your voice is shaking. What's going on?"

"He's there. Get in your car and drive to a police station. *Now.*"

In moments like this, in which information is at a premium, and the only way to convey it is quickly, very often the person on the other end has to play catch-up in a hurry, which slows down the whole process.

"I'm...not in the car," she says.

So the video wasn't live.

Good play, I think.

You really had me.

By the time *I* catch up, Audrey's already on some other thing.

"I'm already at home," she says. "Well, not home. I'm staying at The Hermitage until they..."

"Lock the door and stay there. And listen to me—"

"You're scaring me, girl."

"Good. Call the cops. Tell them to come to *you*. Do not—and I repeat, *do not*—open the door for anyone. Make the cops, even, slide their badges under the door."

"It's him, isn't it? He's made contact."

"He's begun to."

She pauses and then says, "Things will move quickly now. Be careful, M.E. I'm going to call the cops."

And then she is gone.

I CONTACT DETECTIVE CICCOTELLI, tell him the details of what's happened. He listens mutely to the whole monologue, and I hear a sharp intake of breath as he's prepared to speak, but I interrupt it.

"Can you track phones?" I ask. "Like, if I can keep in contact with him?"

He seems to measure this question. "Yes, I think so," he replies, "but that would take some time. It probably wouldn't help you in the short term, especially if you're taunting him across all of the internet and television."

"He's tracking Audrey," I reply. "He's started chatting with me on social media. I think he knows the end is near. I'm afraid of what he might do."

"We've got some units heading over to The Hermitage. They're *en route*. Are you in a safe place?"

I glance through all of the windows and hope against hope I don't see anything in the distance. Shadows swish all around me, but I cannot name my fear aloud.

"Yeah, I'm safe."

"That doesn't sound convincing."

"Well, it's going to have to do for now."

"Listen," he says, "get in your car, and drive to the nearest police precinct. They just built one on Charlotte, between a pawn shop and that pizza joint next to the abandoned Goodwill. It's right before White Bridge. They can keep you safe there."

"Uh-huh," I reply.

"Don't dismiss me. And do not—listen—do *not* try to solve this on your own. You've already placed yourself in enough danger."

"It seems like the danger has sought *me* out."

"Get somewhere safe. Actually, how's about this: I'll come to *you*. The responding officers can check in at The Hermitage. It's downtown, lots of lights. I'll be over to 51st in a few minutes. Don't move. Maybe lock yourself in somewhere safe."

My phone bleeps. I check the screen.

It's a message from an unknown number. I think I know who.

"Sure thing," I reply, and then I hang up.

I can see from the message format that it's a video and not a text. Somehow, I don't even need to see it in order to understand what's going on.

It is perfectly framed—like something out of Kubrick—and dead set in the middle is one Gillian Meitner. The image is mostly silhouette, but I can tell it's her. She's in her room, on her computer, with her back facing the frame.

And then a message from the anonymous source appears.

> DID YOU HONESTLY THINK YOU COULD BAIT ME INTO ATTACKING YOU? NICE TRY.

A silent beat, and another.

> HOPE THE COPS FIND AUDREY. I PUT HER SOMEPLACE SPECIAL.

> HA HA.

Then, a text from Gillian. Two simple words, no doubt typed by Allred himself.

> *Help me.*

The irony is, he's drawing *me* out of the darkness. He's taunting *me*. This is his end game, and the only way to beat it is to stay home.

I'm out of the door before I can get my shoes on right.

23

I leave the car running and get out to see that Gillian's place is completely dark. No lights on at all. Just like I imagined. She lives on an affluent street, but her place, hidden away on a private drive in the midst of trees older even than her family name. It sits back from the road, and you have to climb stairs steeper than the ones in Percy Warner to get to the front door.

My phone buzzes in my pocket, and because my nerves are shot, I can't help but check. I need to know who is on the other end.

I almost pray that it's a wrong number. Anyone else might break my nerve.

Detective Ciccotelli's number flashes on my display.

My stomach twists into a tight little knot. There is no way this conversation goes better than the last one I had with him.

"Where are you?" he asks.

"I'm at home."

"No you're not. I'm *at* your house. Where are you?"

"Why do you want to know?"

"Because we just checked with The Hermitage. Audrey Winstead isn't there."

"Oh."

"So, where are you?"

"Right now? I feel like I'm in Hell."

"Which Hell, specifically?"

I see something in Gillian's house that sends my heart into my esophagus, so I hold the phone close to my mouth and say, "I've got to go, detective. Thank you."

I can hear him protesting on the receiver when I end the call.

Maybe he will find me. Maybe not.

But either way, this is ending right now.

I MAKE it inside and close the door quietly. I half expect a bloody scene to greet me, but no, the dark is my only companion so far.

Holding my breath, I head into the house's inner sanctum.

There is a chef's knife the size and length of my forearm in a block on the main island in the kitchen. I slide it free and then retreat to the darkest corner of the house. I need to catch my breath, because I feel like I'm going to scream.

I try not to think of that last scene in *Silence of the Lambs*.

Once my eyes can make out the details amidst the darkness, I step tentatively into the residence proper. A guiding beacon draws me through the house, pulling me toward a final destination.

It begins very small, like the aural equivalent of a pinhole of light. It is a single sound, reaching through the empty darkness and tickling my inner ear. Years of isolation have prepared me for this.

I can't quite make out the sound, at first. It is too small, too minuscule, to discern among the natural sounds of my environment and the hum inside my head.

But it *does* exist. That much I know.

My mind goes wild with the possibilities.

I'm halfway up the stairs leading to the second floor when I make out the sound. As it becomes clear, my stomach drops.

It's a voice. At first, I'm convinced it's Gillian begging for her life, but that's mere projection. A few more seconds tell me it's not Gillian at all.

Can't be, I think.

It's—Madeline St. Clair.

The voice seems *odd* somehow, and I can't quite wrap my head around it.

I am at a loss.

I try to think of how this could happen. Body switch? Faked death?

"Gillian?"

My voice echoes in the darkness. I can't focus on what I should be doing, only on the force that is inexplicably pulling me forward. The tractor beam from an alien spacecraft, the supernatural tug of a possessed person.

I am Regan from The Exorcist.

I am Jack Torrance from The Shining.

There is only the mystery now, and I have to bring it to a halting conclusion, even if it means my life. I come to this on my own, as a matter of course, because this will never end. As long as I live, it will follow and haunt me, so I might as well see what lies in Room 217.

Once I reach the second floor, it all becomes clear.

The bedroom at the end of the hall is dark, but the scene is punctuated with dizzying flashes of light. Like a techno club with only two sad and frustrated patrons.

"Gillian?"

Though her name is on my mind and on my lips, I don't suspect I will receive an answer. Unless it's from Timothy Allred himself.

Walking on stiff legs, I reach the doorway. *The* doorway.

The room is illuminated by a single, bare light bulb from the desk lamp beside the computer, as well as the flashing computer screen.

It doesn't take long for me to realize what's happened.

Gillian is propped in front of her desktop. *Slumped*, really, is the word I'm looking for. Her shoulders sag, and her head is tilted to one side like a badly-propped doll.

The sobs escaping my throat seem to come from a very distant place, somewhere outside my body and down the hall behind me.

But no, it is me. I am the one screaming, and yet inside my head, there is a crazy sort of calm. I need to see this through to the end.

I reach Gillian's desk and spin her chair gently, as if waking her from a nap.

Her head flops to one side, and that's when I see the blood. She's been spared the postmortem indignity of having her face blown off—like Madeline—but it's still not pretty.

I scream, but rather than run from the room screaming, which is what I imagine ninety percent of people would do, I shut the door behind me and turn the lock.

Because something else has grabbed my attention, and I need to see what it's all about. If Allred has plotted this out for me to view, then I am duty bound to witness it.

There is a video. At first, I can see nothing and can only infer that it is, in fact, moving pictures. A blurry set of images wavering shakily on-screen.

But then I recognize the house. It's Everett Coughlin's place, and I don't need to know the date or the context to understand that *this* is the night. It is happening right now, and it is like seeing your own life from a completely different angle.

I can't help but notice the video's on a loop, picking up from right around the point where my old VHS—the one someone left in my house—actually crapped out.

I get another chance to see how the night—and the life of Everett Coughlin—ends.

There is the rustling sound of the camera being passed off, and then the frame whirls around. Madeline can be seen walking away from the camera, and just as she reaches the edge of the driveway, she turns and glances once over her shoulder.

The look of shame is evident on her face.

It is the last moment of her life as it *was*, as everything transforms into what it would eventually become. In this fleeting passage of time, she is still Madeline St. Clair, heir apparent to Nashville's upper echelon. The golden apple was just bound to become hers. In a few minutes, though, that will all change, and she will become one of the famed and loathed Suicide Blondes, forever associated with the death of a misunderstood kid in a wooded neighborhood in Nashville.

And then, something...changes. Madeline disappears from the frame, and the camera's attention returns to the Coughlin household.

It becomes something else entirely. The opening scene of that old horror movie, *Halloween*, maybe. We are forced to see the world through the eyes of Audrey Winstead, and it is a chilling thing, indeed.

The camera stops, and the attentive listener can hear the sound of Audrey breathing. It's not tired breathing or stressed breathing. It's...excitement. The kind of inhale one takes before walking into a job interview or asking the cute guy at the office on a date.

Very quickly, it becomes evident why that is.

The camera returns to the house, and the lens focuses in on the scene playing out just on the other side of the garage door. The room is filled with exhaust, and so it is impossible to see anything but a blanket of white. It could almost be called a letdown, if the future hadn't already supplied the audience with certainty about the night's events.

From behind the camcorder, she says, "Mads, I hope you know what this proves, that it shows I am your *best* friend. No one else would do this for you. No one else would take this step. I—love you."

Then, with a flourish, Audrey spins the camera around and points the lens at herself. Her eyes, wild with the rush of a newfound mission, are the eyes of a madwoman.

She says directly into the camera, "If something goes wrong, and I get caught...in the middle of it, I hope this video finds you so you can know exactly why. Okay. Okay. All right. This is it."

Audrey cautiously shuffles along the side of the house and makes her way to the door, where—miraculously—it opens.

"I don't think his parents are home," she says aloud, maybe to herself and maybe to the audience members.

I glance once over my shoulder, just to make sure the door is still closed and locked, and then I continue watching. I can't *not* see it through. Timothy Allred will have to appear and hack me to pieces to prevent me from learning about my legacy.

By the time I get back into the video, Audrey is standing outside the door leading into the Everetts' garage.

She reaches down with one hand and, turning the lock, says, "Here goes nothing."

Out of context, it is perfectly ridiculous, but in the heat of this unalterable moment, it is chilling. Not half as chilling as what comes next, I'm sure, but pretty close.

Inside the exhaust-filled room, Audrey finds a pale and desperate Everett lying on his back, moaning deep in the back of his throat.

Apparently, he's second-guessing his plan.

There is nothing I can do. I want for him to get up and flee, to stagger into the kitchen and call 911, but this is it. This is the reality of it all.

And it is much more morbid than I could have ever dreamed.

"Who are you?" he asks from his spot on the concrete.

It actually draws a laugh from Audrey, who says, "I'm your dream girl."

Never dropping the camera. Never breaking character.

She has gone full-on Squeaky Fromme.

She whispers to herself, "I'd do anything for you, Madeline."

Everett's eyes, dark against his sickly pale face, grow confused. "Who is Madeline?"

And that's all I can watch. As I scramble to find the mouse so I can stop this bloodcurdling scene, on-screen it gets worse. The camera drops to the concrete, but it faces at such an angle that viewers can still see Audrey mount Everett Coughlin and place the edge of one forearm against his throat.

He tries to fight back, but he's incapable. The exhaust and what-ever he's ingested have rendered him mostly paralyzed. He flaps one arm against Audrey's side, which doesn't amount to much of a defense.

Through teary eyes, though, he utters a single plea: "*Help.*"

Audrey leans down, sporting a grim smile. "This *is* me helping you, freak," she says, before leaning forward with the whole of her weight.

Then, the video stops.

It's over.

It's done.

The screen goes black, and I find myself staring into darkness.

Only, it isn't completely dark.

A white mask floats in the blackness across from me, where the door to the room's only closet has opened up.

He has been watching the entire time. The video was the preamble; now the real show begins, and I am the headliner.

"Timothy," I say, trying to get a reaction, but nothing happens. Only the sight of that fright mask glowing against the backdrop is evident.

The figure doesn't move, doesn't react, but the zombie thing's face smiles malevolently back at me.

I am momentarily distracted from the mask by the sight of something else in this pitch black room. The light from somewhere glints off the barrel of the gun my tormentor is holding. It's the same weapon that took Madeline's life—And Colton's and maybe even Gillian's too.

"You were right, Timothy," I continue. "We were bitches. We fucked up, and we did some fucked up things. But you have to admit it, now—at least to yourself—that we weren't the ones, me and Gillian. It was Madeline and Audrey. They were the ringleaders, and we were just the fall girls. Gillian did the tech stuff, and I was just stupid enough to believe I could ever be friends with them. That's my crime."

I take a tentative step backward, slight enough that someone in the dark shouldn't be able to notice it, but enough that it will bring me to the room's only exit.

"You see," I continue, "for the longest time, I thought I was too poor to be friends with them. I thought they only kept me around for pity's sake, or to make fun of me behind my back. I learned that it was all of that, combined with the fact they needed a scapegoat when they couldn't wiggle out of it."

Another step.

"I take all the blame for my part in it. I admit it. I tried to stop it, but I didn't do enough, and he's dead. But so are multiple other people, people who weren't involved."

Another step. A deep breath. A long pause. I can almost feel the door handle.

The figure matches my step this time, showing me that he notices. The mask continues to grin, and I am oddly mesmerized by its presence.

"But you do not have to do this."

I blink.

The figure seems to jerk, and then the gun raises as the masked tormentor fires a single shot. I duck just in time, and I listen for something behind me to explode, to be destroyed, but nothing happens. The shot must have gone *way* wide.

I scream—it's the only feasible reaction—and run straight for the masked figure. I have no idea what I'm going to do when I get there, but I know I'm going to do *something*.

He lowers the gun, and I expect to get shot, but nothing happens. I'm moving too fast, maybe, and then the next thing I know, I'm plowing into this figure.

I scream again, but this time the act is entirely more triumphal in nature. I am not dead, and somehow I've managed to wind up on top.

Allred has lost weight since the last time I saw him. He was never a big guy, but prison must have really taken it out of him, because he feels small and bony.

I just *know* I can take him. I bring one hand back to punch him, to put this whole thing to rest, but in the darkness I get confused by a pain that seems to come from nowhere and everywhere at once. It starts on the back of my head and moves quickly to every synapse in my body.

Blinking does nothing to prevent the blanket of unconsciousness that overtakes me, and soon I am in another world entirely.

24

Groggily, I open my eyes. The pain reaches like bony fingers through my body and squeezes the nerve endings and open wounds.

Looking around, I see I'm now in a living, waking nightmare.

I am on the floor in the middle of a garage—dare I say, *the* garage—and there is a fine, cloudy white substance to my left.

Car exhaust. It is just *pumping* from the tailpipe of a nearby vehicle.

The first thing I notice about myself, beyond the pain, is my hands. They've been tied behind me. Above me. I am bound to the driver's side door of an old car, one that seems familiar but one I don't quite recognize.

Then, it hits me: it is the exact type of car Everett Coughlin drove back in high school.

For a moment, I'm caught in the moment, wondering who in the hell would take the time to track down a car like that, with such specific details, when I realize it's not a car *like* the one Everett drove back in high school.

It *is* the car Everett drove back in high school.

It is covered in dust, and though it is, in fact, running, it doesn't sound like it will be doing so for very much longer.

I try to find my feet—they're somewhere beneath me—but I can't. Nothing seems to work. Whatever I was given, it's still ping-ponging around in my system, and I feel like I'm in a living watercolor. Everything is blurry. The shapes don't quite make sense.

But one thing does.

Timothy Allred is in here, too.

"It took a while to get that puppy up and running," he says. "New battery. New spark plugs. But eventually it turned over. The wonders of German engineering, am I right?"

He's standing just in front of me, close enough that I have to tilt my head sideways to see his face. The man is nothing special to look at, but the wild, frenetic energy in his eyes is enough to make me want to turn away.

"Where are the Coughlins?"

Somehow—distantly, I suppose—I hope they're still home, that he's somehow forgotten about this one little detail so that I can scream and plead until they call 911.

But he's ready for that question. His eyes drift toward the ceiling.

"They're upstairs sleeping," he says. "Well, I mean—in a way."

His smirk is horrific. The sort of thing you might see in a comic book, the wide, jagged-toothed grin of a monster about to attack.

"You killed them? You *killed* them?"

I can't wrap my mind around the reality of it.

"But they were nice people. They...didn't deserve this."

"I mean, you could argue that I actually *helped* them. You should see their bedroom. It's just one big memorial to the pain and suffering they've endured."

He takes the gun and places the barrel against his cheek. He doesn't seem to notice how dangerous that is.

"And they owe it—all of their pain and suffering—to *you*.

I hope desperately for him to have an accident, to pull the trigger and end this whole thing. But he doesn't do that.

"Oh," he says when he notices me looking. "Safety's on. You didn't think I'd accidentally shoot myself in the *face*, now did you? Silly girl."

"That was you in the house, wasn't it?"

He only stares.

"I mean, that night. The night I came home from the party. You followed me around and then broke into the house. Didn't you?"

He shrugs. "Old habits die hard," he says, a smile stretching out one side of his face.

Prison has done something to him. He's leaner, harder. Tattoos peek out from beneath his sleeves and above the neck of his shirt.

He's been broken.

Wherever he was, it broke him.

"I don't want to die," I tell him, though the lingering effect of the pills causes me to slur everything into a single word, a winding syllable that fades away rather than ending.

But he seems to catch what I'm saying, because his face droops, as if the grand prize from a second-rate show has been taken from him.

He makes direct eye contact, and then he says, "I love you, Mary Ellen."

It looks like he wants to tell me something else, to explain himself, but he doesn't get the chance. A loud *pop* interrupts him, and in a kind of slow-motion horror, blood and bone and brain matter spray all across the room's interior.

The smile on Allred's face remains fixed for a moment before his slumps to one side.

It is an accident, I think. He's gone and shot himself in the head, and now I'm going to die all alone in this fucking garage.

Speaking of irony.

But then reality sets in, and I hear someone talking.

"Jesus Christ, that was like the end of a really bad *LifeTime* movie," says the voice. "Two crazies find love in an old garage."

The voice's owner steps out from beside the car.

"And then one of them gets shot in the fucking head."

I look up.

It's Audrey Winstead, and she's so drunk she's lopsided, holding the gun precariously in her right hand.

"You know, this is turning out even better than I had planned," she says. "It's going to be utterly believable you two were in a death pact."

"What are you doing, Audrey?" I ask, hoping against hope that what I'm seeing is just not true. "Help me out of this. Come on."

There is a part of me that thinks maybe she really will help me, and I have to take that chance. But she only smiles and totters over, still holding the gun.

"Man, you are way tougher than I expected."

"Then let me go," I say.

"No, I'm afraid I can't do that. God! I've been waiting all night to say that."

I see flashes of how the night will turn out. My body crumpled over in the garage, the air filled with exhaust. A production carefully laid out in specific detail.

A more adult version of Barbies. *Ken, your body goes here. Barbie, I'm going to place you next to the pink Corvette in the garage. Ooh, yes, let's put the top down! It's so cute! Now, who's going to call 911?*

Audrey walks over, nudges Timothy Allred's body over onto a side, and then trades her gun for his. She presses the handle against his palm and then gently places a finger between the trigger and the guard.

"Give a guy a cross-country plane ticket, and he thinks suddenly everything is about him. How insane is *that*?"

She giggles. Her laughter is meant to be sardonic, but it only gives her an absolutely insane look, and for some reason I think she knows it.

"Besides, I have the sneaking suspicion he'd have confessed at some point before this was all over. I can't quite take the chance on that, now can I?"

She's wearing latex gloves, so I suppose she thinks there will be no fingerprints on the weapon. Her hair is tucked in a net fast food workers wear, and she's even got little booties over her shoes.

For once in her life, she isn't wearing high heels.

"Do I not look the part?" she says. "I got the booties idea from the end of that movie *The Departed*. Did you ever see that one, a few years back? Oh, it's a *great* movie! No spoilers, though, just in case you ever wanted to get to it.

"Anyway, Timothy here responded well to my uneven scribblings. See, the way I wrote him, he thought I was *you*. When it wasn't *the* Mary Ellen Hanneford who met him at the airport, he got seven shades of pissed, let me tell you. But that quickly ended when he figured out what I really wanted to do. And then he was all over it."

She takes a few steps back, watching bitterly as the blood seeps out of his body and onto the floor of the garage. There is an inhuman, animalistic hatred in her eyes, and it is compounded by the violence surrounding her.

"Still, he wasn't a keeper," she says, looking pitiably down at him. "Great with a computer, hell with research, but one hundred percent out of his fucking mind."

"Then why would you work with him?"

"I needed a scapegoat," she says, matter-of-factly. "Just like we all did with *you*. It's like the story has come full circle, Mary Ellen."

She pauses thoughtfully, then flips the safety off on her new pistol. "See, if he kills you and then himself—a super morbid murder-suicide—it closes the circle. The motive is there. The *motivation* is there. I mean, there's no *way* I could let him live, right?"

She nudges his body again.

"In the end, he wasn't trustworthy. Not like the girls. Girls really know how to keep a secret. Especially Madeline and Gillian. They took the secret to their graves. Literally!"

"Never a slip-up? Not once? I mean, you almost said it *to me* in the bar that one night."

She rolls her eyes and affects a drunkard's posture. "Oh, you mean how *dr-dr-drunk* I was the night you saw me?"

She straightens up. She's actually drunk—I can smell it on her— and she doesn't even have the slurred speech of a two-martini lunch yet.

"That, honey, was my way of stringing you along, getting the motor revved up. I knew it would start that big brain of yours cooking on the quote-unquote unsolved case of Everett Coughlin"—she makes those bullshit quotation marks in the air—"but it was all just like everything else in this, an act."

She curtsies and almost stumbles, the gun dangling from one freshly-manicured hand.

"In all the years since it happened, not one part of what occurred in the garage with me and Everett Coughlin ever got out. We made a blood pact over it, and it worked."

"And all you had to was betray me."

She almost finds that laughable. She says, "All we had to *do* was promise to sink one of us, and, well, it's obvious who that turned out to be, am I right? I mean, one of us had to be sacrificed so the others could live."

"You could have just let Everett Coughlin, I don't know, *live*, instead of killing him the way you did. That was a sick thing to watch, by the way. I can't believe you."

"Stop talking to me like that."

"I will—"

"I have the fucking *gun*, Mary Ellen," she interrupts, "and you will listen to every word I have to say before this is all done."

"Why?"

"After tonight, after I list it out for you like some dimestore villain, I'm never going to speak of it again. This is where the hatchet is buried, or whatever the proper metaphor is. I need to have all my words in the ether so that I can go on without speaking them ever, ever again."

Audrey's face contorts as an unexpected sound cracks this little scene of ours in half. It comes from just on the other side of the garage, and for a moment I believe—truly believe—that reality is folding in on itself around me.

All of a sudden, the door leading from the garage to the house opens and a figure steps inside. It's Detective Ciccotelli, and he appears to be sweating from every pore on his face.

"Put the gun down and step away from the young lady," he says.

Audrey makes a face. "*Young lady?* Asshole, she's middle-aged, *at best*. She doesn't even get botox."

"Drop the fucking gun, or I blow the back of your head all over the far side of this garage. I mean it. Drop the fucking gun."

She doesn't give him time to respond. Her gun goes off, and his gun goes off, but it is she who is still standing when it is all over.

Ciccotelli spins like a top and goes down.

Audrey bellows, a dissonant, unsettling sound. "Fuck!"

She raises the gun, looking like she might empty the clip into his unmoving body, but at the height of tension, she lowers it and screams again.

"This ruins everything," she says. "How in the hell am I going to explain this now? There is no feasible narrative for why the cop showed up. Wait, are you crying?"

Blood seeps from under the detective's body, and I have to strangle back tears. He is my last hope for a positive outcome, barring some kind of miracle.

"Did you have a *crush* on that old tub of lard, or do you just see the last moments of your life slipping, slipping, slipping away?"

For a few moments, Audrey has lost her pincer's grip on me, as I glance over and dwell on the *other* corpse in my midst.

"I mean, I can probably make it look like—shit, I wish I hadn't downed all that cinnamon whiskey. Really clouded up the old freight train, know what I'm saying?"

She burps. "Phew! Maybe that made some room!"

At this, she paces around, trying to plan for how to reconfigure this bloodbath to her advantage.

"Maybe," she says, biting her lip, "maybe the detective shows up because he's figured something out about you, and he—*goddamnit!*"

She's clutching the gun like a talisman, and for a moment I fear—really fear—that she is going to turn on me and fire. That is the whole inevitability of this situation, right? That she kills us all and then gets away scot-free?

"This isn't going to work. It just isn't going to work now. Too many moving pieces. I mean, the detective *has* to have briefed somebody on all of this, hasn't he?"

I open my mouth to say something, and Audrey senses it, because she steps over and places the gun against my face, pushing, pushing, until the barrel is jammed between my teeth, sliding against the back of my throat. I have to tense my jaw muscles to keep from gagging.

And she notices.

"Guess that's why Madeline never accepted you," she says, her eyes cutting into me, and suddenly I can see her finger trembling on the trigger.

She wants to do this. Wants to just get it over with.

But she hasn't wrapped her head around it, and so she can't.

Not yet.

And so suddenly, the gun slides back out, leaving an oily, metallic taste in my mouth.

Still, the question remains, the one that I have to ask, just to put it out of my mind and into the air around me, because I cannot die with it still in my brain. It will live on with me, interred with my bones, and I will have to spend eternity contemplating it.

"Why are you doing this?"

The question stops her in her tracks. She smiles like a pageant girl being asked a question about world peace.

She pulls back, momentarily lowering the gun. She smiles unevenly. "So glad you asked that. You see, I've already *survived* the awful wrath of the revenge killer. I'm the lone survivor. The final girl. The hero in all of this. When this is all said and done, as they say, I'll be seen as a hero. No more living in the shadow of the Suicide Girls."

She saunters forward, her eyes wider than usual.

"I can already see the headlines: *Suicide Girl Goes on Murder Rampage.* You see, coming back home just triggers all the old emotions, and they come flooding back, too much for you to handle. That, and the fact that your cuckoo mama just seems on the verge of keeling over. So you take it out on the rest of us. First, Madeline, of course, because she's the ringleader in everything. She was the boss bitch, and so she deserves what she gets most of all."

She stops herself, places the edge of the gun's barrel against her lip.

"And on and on. No need for *all* of the details. You get the idea, right? Now, on with the show. I need to set everything up and get back to the house before I'm missed."

"It doesn't make any sense, though," I say. "You're killing me because I was finally moving on with my life?"

"No, silly," she replies. "I'm killing you for my career. And to get back at the bitch who took my husband away from me."

And there it is.

It's a land dispute. Madeline took what Audrey had claimed was hers.

"So this is about Madeline sleeping with your husband?"

I see the mask slip for the first time tonight. "She wasn't just *sleeping* with him," she says. "She was *fucking* him, and she had planned on leaving Colton for him."

"You're crazy."

"I'm highly motivated. There's a difference."

She really has thought about this for quite some time, hasn't she?

So I have to dig deep for something that might knock her off her perch. I say, "You will *never* be me. And you will *certainly* never be Madeline St. Clair."

She leans close and says, "You're so wrong. You're so absolutely wrong."

"You were always clinging to Madeline's coattails, like the rest of us, and now that she's dead, no one will care about you, either. Your stock will plummet after this is all over. You'll barely be able to get your name on a billboard in a few months."

She laughs, and I can smell the vodka. She stumbles, and it takes her a few tries to stabilize herself.

The next moment, her hand snaps out and pops me across the jaw. I can taste blood, but I don't give her the satisfaction of reacting to the fiery pain in my face.

"You deserved that," she says. "You haven't been here in two decades, so what the fuck do *you* know? Secondly, this isn't high school. I am a successful woman. I've done things to separate myself, up to and *including* Madeline St. Clair. She was *lucky* to get the send-off she did. She was a faded starlet, a sad hologram of her former glory."

"And when you went to the hospital, there was barely a mention in the *Tennessean*, so what does that make you?"

She lunges for me again, and this time she strikes me with the butt of the gun. Right on the top of the head. It is a white-hot, absolutely blistering pain, and something inside me seems to break loose. Like two ends of wire don't quite connect.

"There's no way this works," I say, trying not to slur my words. "You're not Gillian. You can't pretend this plan is airtight. There's going to be a full investigation. They're going to collect DNA evidence, check all the—I don't know—bullet fragments, and they're going to conclude another person was here, orchestrating all this."

She seems to think about that.

"Doesn't matter," she says. "Even if they do, there's no way they'll think it's me. I'm the sweet survivor. Check this out."

And just like that, her face changes. She puts on her sad mask, and she says, "I—I just can't believe someone would do that. My only hope is that my friends find the peace in death they weren't able to in life. I'll miss you all. Dearly. Truly. Honestly. I will. Oh, God."

And then she whimpers as if surrounded by cameras.

I'm tied up, but as she's putting on this little performance, I pull one wrist toward me and feel how loose it is. When they find my body, it can't look like I was tied up. There can't be ligature marks.

She's thought of everything...except what I do next.

"What are you doing?"

Her face becomes a cartoon version of itself, all wide eyes and crystalline teeth. A malfunctioning Stepford Wife. She sees the way I'm twisting my wrist inside the restraints. She is a pre-planner. She has never been able to account for variables.

Me, I'm the variable. If I don't play nice, her plan will go upside down on her.

And yet, I have to keep an eye on the exhaust, which creates an ever-present haze that will soon drag me into a permanent slumber.

"The big problem is," I continue, "once we're all dead, you won't have anyone left to impress. As shitty as Madeline was to you, she was the only person who ever mattered in your life. Not your parents. Not all the terrible, disinterested frat guys you bedded. Nope. Just Madeline. And she's fucking dead. You killed her."

"Stop it!" she says, a tone of desperation creeping into her voice.

She kneels down and begins to untie me, then stops mid-action. She knows what will happen if she does, and also what will happen if she doesn't.

To drive the point home, I saw my forearm side-to-side to create an ugly red rash at the point of contact. It burns like hell, but this is literally the only way I can think to save my own life.

When my hand is *just* free enough, I yank down, sending a spatter of blood to the concrete floor next to me.

But I'm no longer tied up, and so things move very quickly.

Audrey lunges for me, but I've got a plan.

Before she can react, I snatch the hose running into the car and point it at her face, sending a spray of carbon dioxide into her open mouth.

She howls and coughs and flails towards me, still holding the gun. She claws at my face, sending tendrils of pain across my cheeks. I can't quite push the hose in her face—she's bent it sideways—but then again she can't see well enough to shoot me, either.

Then, she manages to get the upper hand.

She swings the gun butt down in a wild arc and catches the side of my head. It's not a direct hit, but it's a devastating one. The world goes wobbly on me, the fine lines of my normal reality turning hazy and uneven under the light of the garage.

She doesn't try to shoot me, doesn't even try to pistol whip me. Instead, she yanks my other hand free of my bindings and pulls me to the ground. On the way down, I somehow manage to dislodge the gun, sending it skittering across the floor away from us both.

But she's not focused on that.

Before I can really get a sense of the situation, Audrey is strad-dling me, her hands clamped around my throat. I can smell the sickly sweet odor of the cinnamon wafting off of her. She's huffing and growling like a caged animal.

"You're fucking wrong! I'll fucking kill you!"

And she is well on her way. I can't breathe, and a whole galaxy of stars begins to spread out in front of me. The darkness is coming, and it's closer than I imagined.

I've only got one chance at this, so I have to make it count.

Gathering all of my remaining strength, I thrust my hips up and sideways. Audrey's not expecting it, so she goes tumbling drunkenly over to one side.

I suck in a cold, smoky breath. The car's exhaust has filled the room, and I don't think I have much time left to do this. The world is a dull shade of yellow, and the hard lines of reality have begun to soften and sag, like an artist erasing her own drawing.

But there is life in me yet.

Rolling sideways, I manage to find my knees. Audrey sits up, but I scramble forward and bowl into her with my shoulder, knocking her flat on her ass. My body doesn't feel like my own, at this point, but the adrenaline sends me toppling over on top of her.

It's not ideal, but it's more than I can hope for.

I press my elbows into her chest and push down with my whole weight. She screams in a sort of enraged agony. If I wear her out, then maybe I can flee into the street and call for help. That would ruin the hell out of her plan.

She swings and manages to catch me in my right temple, and though it sends stars dancing across my line of sight, I keep my focus on Audrey. My life depends on it. If she gets me sideways again, it's over.

I thrust my head down, cracking it against her nose, and hear the distinct *snap* of a bone shifting sideways. Blood pours immediately from the wound in her face.

But she's not giving up. There's a wild look in her eyes, and she smiles as the blood reaches her lips. I slam my head against her face again, but there's less force this time, and I catch her in the chin.

She pushes me off of her, and I land *hard* on my shoulder.

Audrey gets up and steps over toward the chair, but she's wobbly, so I'm able to stick a foot between her ankles and send her stumbling forward. She recovers, but it gives me time to think of my next few actions.

She turns to face me, and I kick her on the inside of one knee. It's not a heavy blow, but it's enough to hurt her. She cries out and drops to the floor.

I kick her again, this time in the chest.

As she falls backward, I drag myself to my feet. I can barely hold my head upright, but I do it, because the alternative is death.

Audrey reaches for something next to the chair, and I see it's the gun.

Her fingers touch the barrel, and I see the flashes of a terrible few seconds stretching out before me. It's a world in which she wins, even if she loses. A world in which she gets to tell *her* story, and I have to rely on a characterization from fragments of the truth.

And then the redness overtakes my vision.

Raising one foot as high as I can, I bring it down on her elbow, and I hear a shotgun-blast *snap*. She shrieks, pulling the limb back and then reaching with the other arm. She uses her good hand to move forward, but I'm quicker than she is. I scramble ahead of her and kick the gun into the corner of the room.

Sensing the fight is over—Audrey is cradling her broken arm—I lean forward, hands on knees, and try to catch my breath. I'm fairly certain I've got a cracked rib.

I don't see her next move.

She's quick for an injured person. The next moment, she's got me pressed against the driver's side door and is using a length of twine she must have grabbed from the ground to choke me. With her full weight against me, I can't move, and the twine cuts off my circulation.

The stars return.

My arms pinned beside me, I can't get enough momentum to hit her. I feel my legs weakening, and I think maybe this is the end.

Then, my hand touches something.

A plastic tube.

The car hose.

With one last burst of energy, I grab the garden hose and point it at Audrey.

It doesn't do much, but it's enough to distract her.

"Fuck!" she says.

The light comes back to me, and I use my body to slam into her again, and we both go tumbling.

She screams, and I scream, too.

But I'm still hanging onto the garden hose.

I push myself on top of her, and she scratches at my face with her good hand. I feel the blood, warm and stinging, slide from the wound.

She slaps me, and I nearly fall. I'm on top of her, but my grip isn't strong enough to hold her down.

So I do the only thing that comes to mind.

I bring one fist down on her broken elbow, and when she screams, I shove the hose as deep into her mouth as humanly possible.

Her eyes widen, and she stops fighting back.

I scoot forward and put one knee on each of her arms. Smoke pours from her mouth and her nose, and though she fights, she can't spit out the tube. I manage to change my grip and get a better hold.

Tears stream from her enraged and desperate eyes, and though I'm crying, too, I can't let go. The struggle continues for a full minute or more before she finally releases her grip. Her eyelids flutter before unconsciousness finally overtakes her.

Once she's out—for sure out—I roll over and weep until I have the sense to call 911 on Audrey's phone.

EPILOGUE

This is not a happy ending.

I spend a week in the hospital, maybe a little more than suggested, in part because I can't seem to find the emotional strength to get up and out of bed. But I'm in the same hospital as my mother, and so the first few days the nurses wheel her into my room so that we can talk at length about the past and the things we miss about Dad. The conversations are short, because I'm on a lot of meds, but talking to her like this feels like being visited by her in dreams, and sometimes I think our conversations might be imagined constructions of the things I've always wanted to say.

She dies in her sleep a few nights later.

I'm not with her when she passes, but somehow it hurts less than I thought it would. In a way, I became just like my mother, living in a fantasy world of my own making. I ran away not just because of the Suicide Blondes fiasco, but also because I was afraid of dealing with the pain associated with my mother's mental illness. Her pretend sicknesses infected me, too, and so I couldn't quite bring myself to confront them interpersonally. The further away I was from everything, the more content I felt in my own life.

But as I learned by coming back to Nashville, time does not stop, nor does it slow to a crawl, just because you're away. The years marched on, and my mother aged, and finally, when it was her time to go, she just...let go.

The drugs make it easier to go through the process of burying her than I thought. *Easier* meaning less panic-inducing. I sleep at the old house while I make all the necessary arrangements, and she is laid to rest next to my father in a cemetery I never visit. I lean on the help of police officers and strangers who have stepped in to assist me, and the funeral itself is mostly a blur. My focus is broken by the hordes of reporters who follow me around. The *narrative* surrounding the dramatic end of the Suicide Blondes has become a national curiosity again, and I live in a turbulent eye of the storm.

Luckily, I have help.

Detective Ciccotelli is there for me.

He survived the ordeal in the Coughlin garage, and after spending a few days in the ICU, walks out of the hospital of his own free will. He takes on the task of personally directing my security while I bury my mother.

How he came to step foot inside the Coughlin residence that night seems, at first, like magic but ends up being the result of a tenacious, logical cop's process.

When I ask him about it, he shrugs. "Each of the crimes took place in a significant location. After we eliminated the remaining residences"—euphemism for *found Gillian's body*—"there were only a few locations where he—they—might have taken you. We sent officers to a few different places, and I ended up with the Coughlin residence. That's it."

That's not all we talk about, though.

He and I have conversations about it—all of it—at night, when he escorts me back to my mother's house. He works through the details, sipping at a few fingers of whiskey his doctors tell him he should give up, and I listen, mostly because I'm interested in the way his mind works.

"The details are off," he says. "We've got some computer forensics guys connecting the dots between Audrey Winstead and Timothy

Allred, but there aren't as many of them as we'd expect in such an elaborate crime."

"Meaning what?"

"Meaning, usually—and nothing about this is usual—that other people might have been involved."

Ciccotelli occasionally comes up with a comment that sends my blood racing to my heart, and this is one of those.

I try to block out this insinuation, maybe pointing a finger at someone else in my former friend group, but my mind is constantly turning over the details.

Eventually, he shrugs. "I guess we'll never know."

"Guess not."

Mostly, though, he just runs through the facts, creating a timeline for himself so that he can understand the crime itself.

It makes perfect sense to me.

While Audrey certainly elicited the help of Timothy Allred to take me and the other Suicide Blondes down, to me it speaks much more fundamentally to her own deep-seated insecurities and sense of honor. For twenty years, she held this belief that Madeline St. Clair actually determined the trajectory of her life, and she never gave up that idea.

It led her to do the things she did, and she just reached a point where she could no longer live in a world with Madeline or the rest of us.

"She must have kept that plan in her back pocket for *years*," Ciccotelli says one night, after he's had a couple of drinks.

I think about that for a while. "Maybe," I reply, and he moves on, coming to some other personal revelation.

Though I don't think his assessment to be true. I'm a firm believer in fate, and somehow I believe I was bound to end up in this spot, no matter how long it took me to get back to Nashville. Even if I never stepped foot in the Music City again, I remain convinced things would have played out the exact same way.

But it's too crazy a thing to admit out loud, so I keep it to myself, even when the silences between myself and the detective get too long and uncomfortable for either of us to bear.

I get several requests from true crime podcasts to go on and discuss everything, but I decline their offers as meekly as possible. Some of them get angry, but what I don't think they realize is that I am the least qualified steward for this story. I have lived in the middle of it for so long that I would be such a bore to speak with. The people on the radio, the ones with all of the time and interest, they have the answers.

I've lived it, and that's enough.

My name has become synonymous with all sorts of tawdry events, so it is no surprise that the coverage surrounding me does not move the wheel in any way. A tracking poll on CBS or Fox or somewhere posits that sixty percent of people asked still believe that I had something to do with the death of Everett Coughlin.

But that's okay, I guess. I'll have to live with it, either way, so it might as well let people believe what they want.

And they are not wrong, not really. I *did* have something to do with the death of Everett Coughlin. I was there, on the computer, with all of the girls who orchestrated it and then pinned it on me. I said nasty things. I started disgusting rumors. I reveled in the misery of another human being. That I didn't clean out his file is of no importance. I might as well have, and that is enough to make me want to hang my head for the rest of my life.

Eventually, there is another big crime—a murder or a robbery or something—and the news drifts away from my case. I am brought in several times over the course of the next few weeks—and will spend a dozen hours or more on the phone with police officers—as they finish up the case so they can close it out. But just as fame is given, so it is taken away.

And I couldn't be happier. This latest set of circumstances has only convinced me my life will never quite be normal in the way that most people define it, but it's normal enough, I guess, and I just have to deal with the other stuff.

.   .   .

BUT ON TO AUDREY, the belle of this little ball.

She receives the very public exposure she so desired. Problem for her is, she's dead and can't defend herself. Not that anyone would probably buy it. As I told her in the garage, she's no Madeline St. Clair.

She is absolutely shredded in the press, and over time the local newspapers name her The Nashville Ripper, the Social Media Monster, the FaceBook Firing Squad, and anything else that seems topically appropriate.

The internet absolutely loses its *shit* over her...for about a day.

And yet, all the coverage is a blip in the media cycle. It's a super-nova of a story, white-hot for a few days and then nothing at all. Even in the wake of Audrey Winstead's master plan, it doesn't amount to much. The President somehow manages to wrestle attention away from it, and for that I'm glad.

Things begin to settle back into a normal ebb and flow.

After weeks of watching this horrifying story unfold, members of DDA's alumnae organization decide to hold a memorial service for everyone affected, even the husbands. It is a grand event on campus, featuring giant, photographs of Gillian and Madeline and the others, and though they include Audrey Winstead in the event, her photo is much smaller and is shunted to the side of the stage where the speakers and attendees are not forced to stare into the eyes of the killer in their midst.

Audrey's mother and father do not attend.

No one can really blame them. There is plenty of pity to go around, but this tragedy must weigh especially heavily on them, given that they have to think about how they created such a monster and then released her into the world. If I had an opportunity, I'd tell them it isn't their fault. We all decide who we're going to become, and even if we don't, many times it is despite our parents' best efforts and not because of them that we step out into the void.

It was us. The girls. The Blondes. We were always the impetus for all the sickness in this situation, and we have no one to blame but ourselves.

On the day of the event, I dress myself in muted colors and try to blend in as much as possible. It doesn't help. Somehow, I feel like I am part of this vigil, even though I am very much alive. The eyes of every attendee focus on me like I have risen miraculously from the grave.

Because of some insistent prodding from the organization's director—which began a few days before—I speak on stage about my experiences for a few brief minutes. I talk candidly about my relationship with the girls and where it came from and how, even though I was sometimes an oddity to them, a plaything for them to torment for their own enjoyment, that I still very much felt the kind of love for them only a sibling can experience.

Throughout the whole of my speech, I notice the faces of the people in the crowd, every single one of them a broken mask, revealing their true selves. For a brief time, my mask falls away, too. I allow myself to be the girl I was in high school, to relate how such a thing can happen to quote-unquote *good* people. All these years, I've resented the things I did and the person I was, but on this podium, there is only a need for catharsis.

The event's somber mood is buoyed only by the support I receive from people I didn't even realize knew me. People who endured the wrath of Madeline or managed to escape the pincers of Audrey Winstead. While sipping rosé in the banquet hall, our discussion turns into a kind of referendum on the horrors of high school. And though I know most of them are just being nice, just trying to connect in some way with the alien among them, it feels good to have something to bond over.

I exchange numbers with a few women who might have been friends with me in another universe, and we promise to keep in touch, but I know it's probably not going to happen. Still, there's hope.

After everyone is gone, I sit in the front pew and clasp my hands in my lap—and just cry. I glance from poster-sized image to poster-sized image and weep as openly as my whole body will allow. It isn't until the cleaning crew arrives and glances wide-eyed at me from the back entrance that I realize it's time for me to go.

WHEN I RETURN TO SEATTLE, the people at Morning Manatee greet me with a standing ovation, and the next few weeks are absolutely magical, in a way. I'd always enjoyed my work because it afforded me anonymity and silence, but for the first time, I begin to learn the names and interests of the people at the startup, and it is actually exhilarating.

There is still an awkwardness to it all, and so for long stretches during the day, I find myself staring out the window at the Seattle skyline. Ian told me when I returned that I could ease myself back into the work, to take it one day at a time, but everything is so fast-paced, I find it hard to do so.

"We can cover the work," he tells me. "We are a *family* here, and we will do whatever it takes to make sure you get what you need."

The is an in-house therapist, and Ian convinces me to go, but my first time on the couch I spend most of the hour just kind of spacing out, so the tidy woman in glasses tells me to prepare for next time to discuss some things about my past that aren't painful.

At first, I tell her there is nothing, that my whole life has been my fault and I shouldn't be allowed to mourn my own situation. However, eventually the veil separates, and I spend the next few days digging back into my life, and a memory appears in my mind. It is untarnished by time or by my relationship with my mother or the other girls from my high school clique, and it seems meaningful enough for me to explore.

In this memory, I am with my father, and he's carrying me through a playground. I'm too young to remember exact details, but I can feel the sunshine peeking through the trees in the distance. I slide the slides and glide up and down on the see-saw. I run freely through the grass, spongy and inviting beneath my feet. I can feel my father behind me, always in my presence but always just out of sight, the way that I used to think of God. He's watching over me, and occasionally he laughs or compliments my physicality. My head practically buzzes with my father's love.

In the end, the sun dips low in the sky and sends shadows streaming all over the park, and even though it's getting too late for us, my father lets me have a few more minutes, just a few more minutes, before we have to go back home and face the first day at school. I play and play, trying to escape the shadows overtaking my surroundings. No matter how hard I play, the darkness persists, and eventually I am led, hand-in-hand, back to the parking lot.

When I am placed in the car, I peer through the back window at the playground, and even though I recognize the space as my own, it is now more sinister than before. The shadows cause my heart to skip, and I begin to cry, and even though my father eventually manages to mollify me by talking about how bright and beautiful tomorrow will be, once the sun comes up, I can't help but dwell on a single thought.

The darkness is coming, and it's always getting closer.

THIS EMAIL LIST MAY RUIN THE EDGE OF YOUR SEAT

Get the first book in the Rolson McKane series, 'Crystal Queen,' absolutely FREE, when you join!

https://mailchi.mp/668a05145352/crystalqueen

Made in United States
Orlando, FL
06 June 2022

18549093R00162